LANCE & LEO

UNZIPPED

Published by Unzipped Books, an imprint of Lethe Press

ISBN: 978-1-59021-731-3

Cover artwork by Dandy Lyonne;
cover design by Frankie Dineen;
interior design by Steve Berman

This book is dedicated to the gay male porn performers of the early- and mid-Eighties, few of whom survived to see the 21st Century. AIDS took a staggering tool on them, but during their moment in the sun they brought intoxicating visions to life on films that continue to entertain and enchant. May they rest in peace.

SEXUS INTERMISIT

The motel was seedy and run down, in need of a paint job and some long-overdue maintenance. The type of place most people instinctively avoided. Graced by a huge, garish neon sign of a cowboy riding a bucking bronco, it was hard to miss. Although I knew it was the right place, I drove past it several times, carefully confirming the address and scoping it out. And yeah, summoning my courage to park my car and get out. The spookiness of the dark, moonless night and blustery spring wind weren't helping.

The vintage complex dated from the dawn of the era of automobile road trips when it was one of a myriad of single-story motels that lined Colfax Avenue west of Denver. The motel strip had attracted thousands of Midwesterners succumbing to the lure of Colorado's mountains, but time had taken its toll. Most of the motel's neighbors had met the wrecking ball, and the few that remained attracted itinerants and the homeless. Or couples renting by the hour.

Maverick picked the place. I'd volunteered my tiny, exorbitantly expensive apartment in Boulder instead, but he was insistent on a room at the 8 Seconds Motel. We'd never met, but if he was anything like his Grindr profile suggested, the night promised to be memorable. Well, an hour or two might be memorable—he made it clear he wasn't interested in an entire one-night stand. I just wanted to finally lose my virginity. Even an hour would require him not backing out after seeing me. He'd assured me he didn't mind skinny dorks, so I was hopeful, although I'd been optimistic about hookups in the past only to be left at the altar.

Hell, I'd never even been in the same time zone as the altar. I'd been using Grindr long enough to know most men didn't drop trou for guys like me. I wasn't looking for love—you don't do that by swiping right. I needed some passion. When Maverick unexpectedly surfaced on Grindr and hit me up, I jumped at the opportunity. I wanted to relinquish my crown as the oldest living gay virgin in the 303/720 area code. I was horny and lonely, so hyperbole seemed okay.

Maybe the motel's garish neon sign appealed to Maverick, who claimed to be a cowboy fresh off the ranch and in town for a couple of days of sex, partying, and…more sex. I hoped he'd soon be mimicking the neon sign, riding my ass and pounding me with the steely erection he'd posted on Grindr. I'd memorized what it looked like within minutes after we connected.

I parked my car, grabbed the six-pack of beer and two joints Maverick told me to bring, and found room 112. The motel was largely deserted, but the lights in 112 were on, and I heard the sounds of a loud television. I steeled myself for the possibility, even the likelihood, that the pictures Maverick posted on Grindr were from fifteen years ago, thirty pounds ago…maybe both. He might look nothing like his profile. But I'd resolved myself to go through with straddling the mattress regardless of what he looked like. My courage was born of being out for four years and failing to experience more than a few bouts of mutual masturbation and disappointing oral sex. I was ready to let whoever was behind the door of room 112 to inaugurate my ass.

Maverick opened the door wearing only boxers and boots. Cowboy boots. My eyes went wide. If anything, the dude's Grindr pictures didn't do him justice. He had a broad, pumped chest, a hard, ripped six-pack, and muscular, veiny arms. A swirl of elaborate tattoos decorated his torso. His square jaw was covered by a light scruff that looked precisely trimmed…did authentic cowboys manscape? His black hair was messy, greasy-looking, and on the long side.

He grinned. "Cody? Glad you came, babe." Taking my head into his hands, he planted a big kiss on my lips. I opened my mouth and in no time he was exploring it with his tongue, one of his hands holding the back of my head while the other drifted down to knead my ass. I was at a disadvantage because I was holding the beer and only had one free hand, but I ran it along his side and back. His flexing muscles and smooth, tight skin were erotic.

We stood in the doorway sucking face for a long time. I wondered if anyone could see us, but Maverick didn't seem to give a shit. Fuck whoever didn't like him kissing another man in plain view.

He broke the kiss and gave me a lecherous grin. "I'm fucking horny," he said, taking the six-pack from me. "Thanks for bringing this." He butchered the brand name; the tongue that worked wonders in my mouth fumbled over umlauts. "I'm not much on trendy shit. More of a Coors Light man." Pausing, he asked, "You bring the weed?" Horny or not, he was collecting the price of admission before letting me into the room.

I pulled two joints from my pocket. I was a lightweight when it came to marijuana, but I'd smoked a little during high school and kinda got into pot brownies during my last semester of college. But getting stoned alone depressed me, and I hadn't gotten high since graduating and starting a job almost a year ago.

I followed Maverick into the dimly lit room. The motel's management was apparently trying to save money by using nothing but forty-watt bulbs. The way they flittered, they might be twenty-five. Maverick flopped on the bed, still wearing his boots, which had mud on the heels. I took off my shoes and joined him, wondering if I should strip to my underwear too. Since he hadn't said anything, I left my clothes on. No reason to test whether he'd take one look at my emaciated body and call the whole thing off. He lit a joint, sucking in deeply before passing it to me, and opened a beer, guzzling half of it before opening a second one and handing it to me.

We smoked both joints and killed the six-pack. Actually, Maverick killed the six-pack and did most of the damage on the weed. I had to drive back to Boulder, so I limited myself to a beer along with a couple tokes. Even that gave me a major buzz.

Once stoned, Maverick became chatty. He claimed he was indeed a cowboy, growing up in Wyoming and still working on a ranch there. He told me he was twenty-eight, six years older than me, and ventured to Denver three or four times a year when he tired of fucking the same handful of dudes. Helped along by the booze and dope, my head was spinning, and I had visions of *Brokeback Mountain* as he went into considerable, mouthwatering detail about cowboy sex.

His talk apparently had gotten him ready. "Why don't you take your clothes off, kid?" I stripped down to my underwear, praying our hookup wouldn't end prematurely when he saw me naked. My homely, Alfred E. Newman face—big ears that stuck out too far, flushed red cheeks and a spray of freckles across my nose—hadn't changed his mind, but my gangly physique might.

Maverick lazily squeezed his cock through his boxers. "Don't get too many skinny dudes on the ranch. Not since the foreman's kid split three years ago. He had more muscles at thirteen than you do now. I like a cherry ass, and his was tight. Shame that he became a college boy." He tsked as if wounded that a twink would make the sorry choice of abandoning a stud for an education.

"Mine's gotta be tight, too."

He flashed the same lewd smile I'd seen in the doorway.

He pulled off his boxers, tossing them on the floor. Unlike my soft cock, his dick was semi hard. It was thick and meaty and looked delicious. A cock I never thought I'd get to play with. He cupped his hand around the base, causing it to thicken.

"Why don't you suck my tits and then give me some head, dude? Nothing better than having a buzz on, getting sucked, and letting your nut build." He stretched out, put his hands behind his head, and closed his eyes as I crawled on top of him, nuzzling into his chest.

One of his nipples was pierced with a silver barbell and I played with it while licking and sucking his other nipple. "Oh yeah, bite me. Use those teeth."

I was cautious, nipping at his tit a couple of times, gradually biting harder. He groaned happily before pressing my head toward his junk. I worked my way through his washboard abs, circling his belly button with my tongue. Taking his heavy tool into my hands, I started licking.

My cocksucking experience was modest to say the least, but I was determined to perform like I knew what I was doing. I got his shaft wet with spit, took the head into my mouth, gradually coaxed it into an erection and then worked it down my throat. I gagged involuntarily more than once. That only turned him on. "Yeah, knock yourself out on that cock," he growled. "Suck it!"

Maverick pulled my underwear down, tracing my ass crack with a long finger. It was good he wasn't interested in my cock. It was limp. Bizarre, because I'd gotten an erection while looking at his Grindr pictures yesterday and it had persisted for much of the day and night. I'd even gotten hard in the car driving to Denver. Yet my boner took an extended leave once I pulled into the parking lot. Maybe approaching the hookup as a check-the-box chore wasn't the way to get turned on.

He pulled me off his cock long enough to stick two fingers into my mouth and wet them, and then he shoved my head back on his dick and both fingers into my ass. With my mouth full of cock, I only gurgled. His fingers hurt, not a good sign when his cock was dramatically larger. Perhaps the idea of losing my cherry wasn't such a great one. I willed my ass to relax and after a while the cowboy's big fingers felt kinda good. *I can do this after all.*

"So, you like taking it in the ass?" He continued to poke my hole.

"Uh, huh." I'd never actually had a cock in my ass, but I wasn't admitting that embarrassing fact. Getting finger-fucked suggested it might hurt like hell. I resolved to suffer through it anyway, although I feared that resolve would be tested if the stud delivered a brutal fuck. He didn't have a huge cock, but it wasn't small either.

"Thought so. Your little boy pussy is super tight. It takes me a long time to cum when I'm drunk and stoned, but your sweet hole might get me off fast. Does it stay this tight even on the third or fourth fuck of the night?"

I had no idea. I was desperate to get to fuck number one. However, the talk about anal sex raised an issue I had to broach. As reluctant as I was, I had to ask Maverick to use a condom.

There was a reason. I was close to only one family member: my Uncle Ben. He'd always been around when I was growing up, buying me my first bicycle and later taking me on long bike trips. We'd gotten even closer after I came out and my parents died. He'd been single as long as I'd known him and when I asked why, he told me about his life mate, Lincoln. Lincoln was a few years older and died of AIDS several years after they met. My uncle had never gotten over losing him. He pleaded with me to always, always use a condom.

"Um, I want you to use a condom. I brought some."

Maverick frowned. "You'll like it raw. Nothing like skin-on-skin breeding. And it's a shame to waste a tight hole by using cheap latex. That's what dudes use when they're with whores."

Shit. I feared this might happen but didn't have a plan B.

Maybe the cowboy sensed my dilemma and decided to cut me a break. Still finger-fucking my hole, he said, "I could use one the first time. It's hot seeing a hungry slut slurp cum from a condom after I fill it up. You into eating jizz? You gonna suck every drop of my ball juice out of the rubber?"

I eagerly agreed. I was left to ponder whether Maverick's reference to the 'first time' meant he intended to fuck me more than once tonight or was proposing to hook up again sometime later. Either answer gave me a little thrill. Until he hit me up yesterday, I never thought I'd be in bed with a man as hot as he was. Now he was talking about fucking more than once. Perhaps there was hope for my forlorn love life after all.

What happened next was a blur. I heard the whirring of the room's electronic door lock, and a blast of cool air hit me as the door opened. Whoever entered had a full-on view of my bare ass hosting Maverick's fingers and my head buried in his crotch.

Two pairs of hands hauled me off the cowboy's erection. I glanced left and right to see two policemen. A third cop, a tall, muscular black man whose chest and arms threatened to bust out of his uniform, said to Maverick, "We can take if from here. Thanks for your help." He pulled a stack of bills from his pocket, and I stared in disbelief, trying to process what was happening.

Maverick wasn't bothered to be naked and sporting an erection in front of three cops. Or bothered to have been interrupted while getting blown. He got to his feet and took the money, his slick cock bobbing with each step. "Mind I if keep the room tonight? I have three, maybe four tricks lined up."

"Suit yourself. Hand me Cory's clothes. We'll be out of here in a minute."

None of this made sense. How did the black policemen know my name?

"Uh, you've got the wrong guy," I told him.

He clenched his jaws and glared at me. His long dreadlocks were tied into a ponytail that reached halfway down his back, and his hands were massive. Hell, his entire body was massive. "Cory Montrose, age twenty-two? Residence Boulder, Colorado? Recent University of Colorado graduate? We have exactly who we want."

"You've made a mistake! I haven't done anything wrong!" I struggled to free myself, but without success.

"We know."

"I don't have anything you want!"

"It's you we want. Inject him Anders. Let's get moving." I felt the sharp jab of a needle in the bag of bones that made up my upper arm.

Maverick grinned at me and shrugged. "Sorry, kid. A job's a job."

He'd been paid for the hookup. I should have known it was too good to be true. His payday appeared to be a fat one from the stack of twenties he held. That was the only reason a stud like him would be interested in a skinny dweeb like me. Even if he was into twinks like he claimed—which I now had reason to doubt—there were hundreds better than me. Thousands.

But why did the cops want me?

I was fading fast. Maverick's handsome face and awesome body swam in front of me. His cock was still rock hard. Mine had never gotten stiff and now had shriveled to be embarrassingly tiny.

"I enjoyed talking to you, Cody. I would have fucked you, too, if these dudes hadn't shown up early."

Great. I missed out on a mercy fuck.

MISSION IMPROBABLE

I woke to find myself in a small, windowless room. White walls, white ceilings, white floors, white bedding. Bright lights. Hooked up to fluids, I assumed I was in a hospital bed. I tried to move but couldn't, although I didn't see any restraints.

Moments later, a young, shirtless guy entered. His lean torso was covered with detailed tattoos more intricate and colorful than anything I'd seen before. I was mesmerized by the way his taut muscles moved beneath his smooth skin.

"Glad to see you're awake, Cody. How's the headache?"

"Um…not too bad." I lied; my head was pounding, threatening to explode. How did he know about my headache? Since when did hospital nurses walk around shirtless?

"Give it another couple of hours and it will be better. Drink some water. That should help." He lifted a cup with a glass straw to my lips.

It tasted cool and imported. "Uh, can you release the restraints?"

He frowned. "I'll check with Wells. She'll probably want to be here when we do that. Get some rest, and I'll be back in a couple of hours." He disappeared, leaving me frustrated, wishing I'd asked any of the thousand unanswered questions swirling in my mind and wishing I still had his body to stare at. I didn't last long before falling back asleep.

The next time I woke, the tatted man was smiling down at me, confirming my earlier sighting of him wasn't a dream. He introduced himself as Danny and asked if I was feeling better. The headache had receded, although I was still woozy.

"A shower will help. Do you feel up it?"

"Yeah." I was mostly interested in being freed from the restraints. Danny's fingers flew over a panel at the bottom of my bed, and I could move. It was as if whatever hidden bonds had held me had vanished into thin air.

Danny asked if I needed help in the shower and cheerfully offered to get in with me. I turned him down, then immediately regretted my too-quick decision. How awesome would it be to see the man naked and feel him soaping up my back? My cock stirred with residual horniness from my failed liaison with Maverick. It was just as well I'd be showering alone. I'd only embarrass myself by sprouting a boner.

I peppered Danny with questions, but he wasn't talking. *Had I been kidnapped?* The night with Maverick was crystal clear in my mind. The taste of the dude's dick was still in my mouth, and I could almost smell his masculine scent. Yet as I thought back, the kidnapping part was so outlandish, maybe I imagined it. Perhaps he slipped something into my beer, and I flipped out and was now in a recovery ward.

The shower turned out to be as bizarre as the bed's mysterious restraints. It wasn't running water but an intense spray that scrubbed off a layer of dead skin and instantly invigorated me, leaving me feeling like I'd had a full body massage. As good as water from a hot shower felt, this was better.

Danny left me alone to eat a quick meal that appeared while I was showering. It didn't look like much but tasted great, maybe because I was starved. He returned with some loose-fitting clothes like expensive, luxurious pajamas. At least he wasn't putting me in a hospital gown with my bare ass showing. Once I dressed, he walked me down a short hallway into a small conference room.

Inside were the three policemen who'd kidnapped me and a black woman. All four were dressed in the same pajamas. They rose and shook my hand. The woman introduced herself as Agent Wells. The black muscleman was Agent Kravitz. The middle-aged white man and the young Asian who had grabbed me at the motel were Agents Anders and Kato.

Kato looked fit. He could have been as young as me but probably wasn't. Anders was nondescript, looking like a fifty-something man used to sitting behind a desk, a little overweight, balding, and not imposing. The woman was younger, perhaps forty. She carried plenty of weight.

Kravitz's age was a mystery. His body and long dreadlocks were that of a man in his twenties, but his lined eyes made him look twice that. He was daunting—attractive in a harsh, masculine way. I couldn't shake the image of him dressed as a policeman, his body threatening to rip his too-tight clothes. It morphed into a bondage fantasy.

Crap, I gotta stop doing that. I wasn't even into BDSM. Maybe if I whacked off more, I'd have less sex on the brain. Perhaps if the three men had busted into Maverick's motel room twenty minutes later, I wouldn't have been so horny. Of course, that would have required my dick getting into the action, which it had shown no signs of doing.

Wells motioned for me to sit down. "First, Cody, let me apologize for the way we brought you here. Unfortunately, we were operating— are *still* operating—under an extremely tight timeline that required some, uh, unusual steps." She glanced at Anders. I assumed drugging and kidnapping me were the unusual steps, although maybe hiring Maverick fit into that category, too.

"Why am I here?"

She exhaled. "Put simply, we need your help, Cody. All of humanity needs your help."

Right. I get that all the time.

Even if someone needed my help, arranging a hustler to lure me to a seedy motel and then forcibly nabbing me was a strange way to ask. More importantly, why would anyone want my help? I had a joint engineering physics and computer engineering degree with a specialty in nanotechnology, but hundreds of people had that background, virtually all of them with more experience. I must have looked skeptical. Lord knows I was.

"Let me explain some background," Wells said.

Well, thank you.

"We work for a government agency called Tempus Peregrinatione Imperium. TPI for short. Do you know any Latin?"

I shook my head, although I recognized tempus as related to time and imperium sounded like imperial.

"Loosely translated, Tempus Peregrinatione Imperium is Time Travel Command. As its name suggests, TPI exists to regulate time travel."

Time travel. Sure. My skepticism was growing. I looked back and forth among the four agents, but they were stone faced. This wasn't a joke.

"Agents Kravitz, Anders and Kato traveled back in time to pick you up and bring you here, to the year 2060."

For some reason, all I thought of was their police uniforms. "Are you the police?"

Wells looked mystified. Anders responded instead. "Ah, the uniforms. Those were borrowed. We needed clothing that wouldn't look out of place in your era and guns in case anything went wrong. The police academy had different sizes for those of us who don't fit into normal clothes." He glared at Kravitz.

Kravitz snorted and returned the look. "Innocent spectators were also less likely to report a man driving erratically if they thought he was a policeman."

Anders waved his hands. "Hey, I hadn't driven an automobile for thirty years! At least I knew how to drive one."

The story was becoming more outlandish. Could the people around me be from the future? They looked normal. They weren't dressed in metallic spandex outfits, although the pajamas were a little weird. I didn't see any light sabers or phasers. Of course, my concept of the future might have been unduly influenced by watching too many science-fiction movies.

"Enough, gentlemen," Wells said. She turned to me. "I realize it is difficult to accept you've traveled to the future, and, unfortunately, TPI will not allow us to show you much of 2060. You may eventually return to the past, and any knowledge of the future you take with you could result in a disruption of the timeline, something TPI is charged with preventing. However, I can share with you some information that might help you get your arms around the situation."

She touched what I thought was a placemat on the table in front of her, but it came to life. The one in front of me did, too. They were tablets with incredibly high-resolution screens.

"When we picked you up, we changed the timeline. If we hadn't intervened, you would have done a long bicycle ride the following day from Boulder to Carter Lake and on to Horsetooth Reservoir west of Fort Collins. On your return late in the day, you were hit by a pickup truck. Your injuries initially weren't considered life-threatening but were severe enough to require a blood transfusion. Unfortunately, you have an extraordinarily rare blood type. In your time fewer than fifty people were known to have it. It's not clear why it wasn't detected before your accident, but it meant you could only receive transfusions from one of the handful of blood donors who shared your blood type. You went into hemorrhagic shock before any could reach you, and you died from exsanguination—blood loss—before the doctors could save you."

The tablet had pages of newspaper and website articles about the accident. They looked legitimate. Even more spooky, however, was Wells's description of my bike ride. It was precisely the ride I'd planned, yet I hadn't mentioned it to anyone. Nobody could have known about it and it wouldn't have been easy to guess because few people did the entire ride of over a hundred miles. If she'd fabricated the story and the news articles, she'd done a great job on a random hunch.

"Your death became a *cause célèbre* because witnesses suspected the driver hit you intentionally. The Confederate flag decal on his truck, splattered with your blood, didn't generate sympathy for him in Boulder. But none of that matters now because it never happened. Instead, you're here."

I flipped through the articles, and the story began to be real. I was stunned. Not many people live to hear a crisp description of their death. Was she telling the truth? How could I know? I vacillated between feeling grateful and manipulated.

Still, it didn't make sense. "If the timeline already changed and I'm alive, where did these news articles about my death come from?"

"Lois has volumes of data about old timelines before they change."

"*Lois?*" I'd been on the verge of accepting Wells's elaborate tale, but I was back to considering it preposterous. Who was Lois, a librarian with glasses on a chain?

"Lois is a nickname for the artificial intelligence regulating time travel. Their work is extremely restricted. We can't have people jumping back in time to make a fortune on stocks or pick the correct lottery number. If returning to the past was easy, tinkering with it would be far more appealing than dealing with the present. Interactions with the past have potentially serious repercussions, possibly altering the timeline in devastating ways. Lois was created after time travel was discovered. They ensure that travel to the past is rare and authorized only when justified by the most compelling reasons. Which, unfortunately, is what brings us here today."

Breathe. My mind was racing from my obituary to AI running things to questions about time travel.

"The problem we face today is a massive pandemic that has destroyed most of humanity. It could result in the complete elimination of our species. We're facing virtual extinction. We can only speculate, but the signs are not good."

First time travel, then my death and now a chilling pandemic. Could that happen? One of my college roommates, who'd moved on to medical school, had suggested something similar during an *après* ski celebration a year ago when we got wasted on Bourbon and nursed sunburns. He maintained humanity was dramatically more susceptible to a single, killing disease as travel linked distant parts of the globe and our gene pool became less unique. He believed the coronavirus scares—COVID-19, SARS, MERS, and the others—were merely mild cold snaps before the coming killing frost.

Anders and Kato had pensive expressions that didn't look good. Kravitz was impossible to read. Wells seemed tired. I liked her. She was warm and nurturing and reminded me of my aunt, my mother's older sister who'd unfortunately died when I was in high school.

Wells paused before continuing. "The origin of the epidemic was a previously benign virus. Earlier this year, the virus, carried by a large part of humanity, suddenly morphed and turned deadly. The virus's change was apparently a natural step, like the way a caterpillar becomes a butterfly or humans undergo puberty. After its transformation, the virus produced millions of airborne spores that took only hours to kill. Incredibly painful, but fast. We think a single virus wiped out much of the population of Johannesburg." She paused before shaking her head. "Nothing is quite as dreadful as the screams of a dying city."

The room was deadly quiet. I didn't hear anyone breathing. I wasn't.

"Within days, a countless number of other viruses morphed as well, almost as if they were acting in concert. In little more than a few weeks, much of humanity was wiped out. We're racing against time. Few of us remain, and we have no idea how long we have.

"Lois can't tell the future—at least we don't *think* they can—but they instantaneously project known trends. As soon as the outbreak in Johannesburg occurred, they summoned every TPI agent to this facility and sealed it. Oddly, we're not far from Boulder, under Cheyenne Mountain near Colorado Springs. A century ago it was a Cold War facility used by the North American Aerospace Defense Command, or NORAD. NORAD abandoned the place, and TPI moved in when time travel was discovered. The underground temperature stays a consistent twelve degrees Celsius, which creates a perfect heat sink to cool Lois's processors. No virus spores can enter, but we have no idea how long their seals will last, and our supplies may run out."

She sighed, glancing at the other three agents. I thought I detected a tear welling in Kravitz's eye.

"The virus itself is a mutation of the AIDS virus. For years, scientists believed two primary forms of the virus existed, HIV-1 and HIV-2, along with several variations. We now know there is a distinct, third AIDS virus—HIV-3, technically HIV-3J7—which is the virus that is threatening to wipe out humanity today. As best we can determine, HIV-3 mutated from HIV-1 in the relatively recent past. Lois has run countless simulations of its development and spread, and most point to the early Nineteen-eighties as the time when a single HIV-1 virus mutated and became HIV-3. HIV-3 then spread in the same way that HIV-1 and HIV-2 spread but was dormant for almost eighty years."

The picture was dismaying. Maybe not all that surprising. Over time, countless species had disappeared from Earth, from dinosaurs and wooly mammoths to animals hunted to extinction. Maybe it was simply nature's time to extract her revenge for the species humans destroyed.

Wells sighed. "TPI has been tasked with catching the HIV-3 virus in its infancy and rendering it harmless. That means going back to the early Eighties before the first HIV-3 virus appears and ensuring it never evolves to the deadly killer we know it to be today."

Perhaps Wells or one of the other agents could pop back to the past with a ray gun modified to kill the virus. Somehow, I knew it wouldn't be that easy. "What's your plan?"

Wells pursed her lips. I instinctively trusted her for some reason. She was like Oprah Winfrey and Whoopi Goldberg rolled into one. "We've developed a possible approach. I can't go into detail because of TPI limitations. However, we have a nanocell that, when introduced into the human bloodstream, attaches itself to an HIV virus—HIV-1, HIV-2 or HIV-3, it doesn't matter—and disarms it. The virus still exists but is isolated and imprisoned. Once encased by the nanocell, the virus is rendered incapable of compromising the human immune system and will be unable to transform into its deadly version. Think of the nanocell as a shell enclosing the virus, trapping it in a secure prison and keeping it in stasis."

This sounded promising. "You can travel back in time, so why not immunize everyone a few years ago, before the virus strikes?"

"Not feasible." Wells had obviously confronted these questions before. "The nanocell can't be delivered easily. Even if we solved the transmission problem, the task of getting to every single human, when millions are born each day, is simply unworkable. We must target HIV-3 in its infancy, the Eighties, when its numbers were minimal."

She rubbed her eyes and looked tired. "Delivering the nanocell is a challenge. It's temperamental. Outside a tightly regulated lab environment, the only place where it reliably survives is in the human bloodstream. Even there, until it's established it can be destroyed by a high fever or low body temperature. Our delivery method will be to use a stable host who carries the nanocell to the Eighties in that person's blood."

Blood. I had an extremely unusual blood type. What else would explain TPI kidnapping me and bringing me to 2060?

"My blood."

Wells nodded. "Exactly, Cody. It's why we desperately need your help and why you're the first person to ever travel into the future."

That was weird to think about. "What's the big deal about my blood, other than it being unusual?"

"Your blood is more than unusual, Cody. It's the rarest blood type on Earth, by far. It's technical designation is Rh-null. The null identifier means it contains no Rh antigens. It's considered a universal blood type, meaning anyone can receive a transfusion of it, even those with rare blood types within the Rh system.

"Normally, when the nanocell is introduced into a carrier's blood, it mimics the antigens in the host's red blood cells to ensure the host's white blood cells won't perceive it as a foreign infection, attack it and destroy it. However, once the nanocell copies a host's antigens, it will be attacked by the white blood cells of any person whose blood lacks those antigens.

"Because your blood has no antigens, your nanocells have nothing to mimic. Instead, they will be able to enter the bloodstream of virtually anyone. Your blood is a uniquely valuable resource. Rh-null blood's life-saving capability has been enormous in the past and now it may be tasked with saving the lives of every human on Earth."

So much for a ray gun killing the HIV-3 virus. More accurately, the ray gun was a living person. Me.

"You want me to carry the nanocell to the Eighties."

"Precisely."

"Why me? You said there are other people with the same blood type."

"None of them are as well positioned as you are. Most don't speak English. Of those who do, none are the correct age or can handle the cultural challenges of the mission to the past. You also have positive attributes that will be important. You're smart, capable of recalibrating in the field and thinking on your feet. We know you can be trusted with the extremely sensitive nature of everything I've told you. You're the right man for this mission, Cody."

I'd barely accepted the possibility I'd traveled forward in time, and now I was supposed to travel back in time. It actually sounded... great. How many people could say they had done that? Okay, I was talking to at least three, maybe four who had, but still.

"Cool," I replied, beginning to relish the assignment. "Once I'm there, what do I do?"

"In theory, you find the person who carries the first HIV-3 virus—the "Alpha Carrier,"—and transmit the nanocell to that person's blood. I say in theory because we don't know who the carrier is. The best information we have suggests a male living in California in the early to mid-Eighties. He was infected with the HIV-1 virus, which mutated at some point into the HIV-3 virus. From statistics for HIV infections during that period, the likelihood is that the Alpha Carrier was a sexually active gay man, relatively young. Not that older men—or straight men, women, whoever— weren't infected in the Eighties, but again, we're dealing with the odds."

"If you don't know who the Alpha Carrier was, how will I know once I'm back in the Eighties?"

Wells shook her head. "You won't. Even in the unlikely event that you succeed, we'll never identify the Alpha Carrier with any specificity. Unfortunately, this part of the mission has an element of searching for a needle in a haystack."

"The *unlikely* event that I'll succeed?"

"Yes, Cody," Kravitz interjected. "Though you are by far the best positioned to achieve the goals of this mission, we estimate your odds of success are only ten to fifteen percent. Those odds depend more than anything on a single variable: how well you do your job until we pull you out."

I was detecting some negatives. "Until you pull me out? How long will I be there?" This was not shaping up as a nine-to-five job with me commuting to the Eighties each morning and coming home at night and on weekends.

"That's not entirely clear," Wells said. "It depends mostly on your frame of reference with respect to time. At one extreme, it could be a matter of days. When we send you back, the timeline will alter, and here in 2060 we'll instantly know if you've been successful. After all, for us, whatever you do in the Eighties will be distant history. If the HIV-3 virus is still attacking humanity, we'll know your mission failed and you were unable to neutralize the Alpha Carrier. In that case, we'll pull you out as soon as possible. If your mission is successful, we'll leave you in the past long enough to reach the point of success. We'll triangulate to determine the window during which success was achieved and pull you out shortly afterward."

I chewed my lip. "What do you mean by triangulating?"

Kato launched into a complex description of time travel methods and how Lois would identify the minimum time I needed to be in the past. My head was in a fog. I didn't follow the details, but I got that I would bounce back and forth between 2060 and the Eighties several times as the window narrowed.

His explanation raised a red flag. "You've never tried what you're planning, have you?"

Wells glanced at the rest of the group, whose faces betrayed nothing. "No," she replied sympathetically. "Our previous jumps into the past have always had a scheduled return. What you might view as a short round trip. You're undertaking a potentially long trip with an open return. Contrast that with the trip Agents Kravitz, Anders and Kato took to pick you up. They were in your time for two days, only long enough to hire half a dozen people to solicit you and then collect you after your hookup and before your bike ride and death."

"Half a dozen? I only heard from the one dude."

Kravitz glared at me like I was dense. "We couldn't chance you not being interested in Maverick. We had an array of men with a wide range of ages, ethnicities, body types, and sexual kinks lined up to contact you on Grindr if you hadn't taken the bait with him. The fact that you eagerly pursued the first man who hit you up is promising for your trip to the Eighties."

I resented Kravitz characterizing me as desperate. Entirely accurate, but still...I also wondered why that bit of trivia was promising for my venture to the Eighties. I didn't press the point. Something else was bothering me.

"If I change the timeline, how much of the old timeline will I remember?" Wells shrugged. She looked tired, drained. I felt sorry for her, thrust into the role of pulling off an improbable rescue of humanity. Not humanity in the abstract, but likely her friends, family, and relatives. I wondered if she was married and had kids.

"Not entirely clear. If you make a single jump to the past and return after, say, three years, we believe you'll remember the old timeline up to the point you jumped as well as the three years you spent in the past. When you return, you'll enter a timeline you never experienced. You'll be the only person alive who experienced the original timeline. With limited time in the past and minimal changes, the difference will be so small as to be almost meaningless. However, your mission is designed to change the past in a significant way, so what you remember today may be quite at odds with what will happen in the new timeline."

I wouldn't be journeying to the past and returning to find everything the way it was. It could be like returning to a different planet. Strangely similar but disturbingly different. I'd remember things that never happened. There was a term for people like that.

"So, when I return from the past, I'll be a crackpot. Crazy. A guy who babbles about things that didn't occur."

Kravitz frowned, clearing his throat. "Please, Cody. In 2060, the terms 'crackpot' and 'crazy' are considered pejorative. We don't use them. We prefer 'mentally divergent.' It's less value laden. Who's to say your reality is any less legitimate than my reality or Wells's reality?"

Fake news notwithstanding, the several billion people who agree on what happened in the past, that's who. I sighed. *Mentally divergent. A great future to look forward to.* "What happens when you triangulate and the timelines multiply? What will I remember then?"

Wells sighed. "In theory, only the final timeline you experienced, because the earlier ones never happened. However, it is entirely possible you'll subconsciously recall other timelines. Humans have always had premonitions. Are those partial remnants of previous timelines? We don't know. Perhaps some see the future because they already lived through it in an earlier timeline."

I frowned. "I might remember living in the past for decades, because that was when you started triangulating, even though in the final timeline I would have only been there a year?"

"Possible, yes, probable, no. We haven't been able to study the stress of a long stay in the past and a repeated series of unpaired jumps. You're the guinea pig."

Guinea pig. A crazy—oops, mentally divergent—guinea pig. Great. Exactly what I'd always aspired to be. "You aren't sure any of this will work." I knew the answer but wanted it out front.

"No. We know little about time travel outside a narrow band. What you are doing is best thought of as experimental."

I had a sudden vision of the classic *Star Trek* episode where some poor soul gets lost in the transporter beam and Scotty can never put the fellow back together. Maybe I would find myself in the middle of World War II instead of the Eighties, and TPI would never find me because I'd been shot in the back by a Nazi. I wondered if I should read Mark Twain's *A Connecticut Yankee in King Arthur's Court* to pick up pointers in case I was stranded in the past.

Whatever. I didn't want to dwell on those prospects. "So, um, what do I do when I'm back there? I mean, to deliver the nanocell to the Alpha Carrier?"

Wells's body language set off alarms. She exchanged nervous glances with Anders, who looked at his feet and chewed his lip. Kato was a silent statue. Only Kravitz was on message. "Unfortunately the transmission technology we use today can't be taken into the past, and the facilities we'd need to recreate it in the Eighties don't exist. The only reliable delivery method is sexual. The highest odds of a successful transmission come with anal sex. Active and passive anal sex have roughly the same success rates, as high as ninety-eight or ninety-nine percent. Delivery rates for oral sex and exposing a cut to blood are low, but not insignificant, around ten percent. Even kissing works in rare, isolated instances. Nonsexual transmission such as sharing needles is modestly effective, but that isn't a viable option. Drugs would interfere with your abilities and might destroy the nanocell."

The group fell silent as they stared at me. I looked back and forth between them in shock.

Kravitz glared at me and exasperation sounded in his voice. "That detail shouldn't bother you, given your sexual orientation."

I'd heard plenty of strange things in a short while, but this was the most bizarre. TPI was sending me back in time to have sex. My job was to fuck and get fucked. Not figuratively, but literally. This had to be a joke. A test of some sort. "You're kidding, right?"

From Wells's serious look, I knew it wasn't a joke even before I asked the question. "No, Cody. I grant this makes our request for your help unusual, but outside this sealed mountain, ten billion corpses are rotting. It's the best plan to avoid that outcome."

"Think about it," Kravitz said with a smile. "You're a twenty-two-year-old gay man. Your job will be to sleep with every gay boy you can. What young gay man wouldn't think he had the best job in the universe?"

Me, for one. Obviously, stereotypes of sex-crazed gay men hadn't disappeared in 2060. Kravitz's words began to sink in. "What the fuck? Everyone I can?" I was still in shock, but none of the TPI agents reacted.

However, the plan had a major, glaringly obvious flaw. "So, there's one little tiny problem with this plan. Is *this* the body of a man who can lure gay men to sleep with him? We'd all be lucky if I found one man who wanted to have sex me, but more than that? You're crazy." Oops. I should have said mentally divergent.

"Don't sell yourself short, Cody," Kravitz said confidently.

Right. With his incredible body, he had no clue what life was like as a ninety-eight-pound weakling.

Wells rebounded from her reticence to talk about sex. "Your body won't be an impediment. When we send you to the Eighties, you'll look quite different than you do now. You'll have a body many gay men will be attracted to."

How would they accomplish that improbable feat? Lord knows I'd tried myself, starting with hours in the gym lifting weights. My body was allergic to muscles but regrettably not pimples.

"Let me explain. Lois analyzed hundreds of thousands of possible approaches to finding the Alpha Carrier and neutralizing HIV-3. Balancing TPI's obligation to minimize disruption of the timeline and the urgency of achieving success, they formulated a plan. You'll exchange places with a man in the Nineteen-eighties named David Alan Reis."

Wells's fingers flew over her placemat, and a low-resolution picture of a smiling young man appeared. He was a cute, sexy teenager, too young to have achieved the distinction of being handsome although that would come. He had a slender frame, shaggy blond hair, a friendly face, and a slightly goofy smile. "This is Mr. Reis."

"Why him?" I scrolled through a few more pictures, pausing on one showing Reis shirtless. He had a damn nice, smooth torso, with a defined chest, hard abs, and a narrow waist. His muscles weren't the product of long hours in the gym, but unlike me, he had muscles. Okay, he was hot. Sexy. A nine or a ten. *Fuck!* Maybe an eleven. Totally out of my league. Of course, virtually all gay men were out of my league. I looked up to find Kravitz giving me a knowing smirk. He'd read my mind.

"Only Lois knows the reasons why Reis is the right person. They have run vast numbers of simulations, and those suggest he's the best candidate. Some things are obvious. Because of his past activities and what you could call his career, he occupies a unique position that fits perfectly with your mission. He's your height, and his skeletal structure is remarkably like yours. Even the same shoe size. With surgery, we can make you look virtually identical to him, so close that his own mother couldn't tell the difference."

"I'll look like that?"

"Yes. We've already sent some of your stem cells to the lab to create the muscle mass, skin, and other elements we'll need. The process should take six to eight hours at most. You'll go to sleep looking like Cory Montrose and wake up looking like David Alan Reis. You'll have a few days of discomfort as your body settles in and you get used to it, but the process is largely pain free."

Damn. I'd be getting test tube muscles that would make my body hot and a remade face that would make me attractive. Even likely to be considered handsome in time. How many times had I wished I had a hunky body like the dude in the photos? Fuck! Who wouldn't want a better body? Billions spent on minimally effective plastic surgery, and I was being offered the gold standard version for free.

Wells made it sound like it was no big deal to rework my body. Say goodbye to my dopey-looking face and stick-figure body. This bizarre mission to the past promised an incredible side benefit. I was once again excited about the adventure and ready to sign up.

Kravitz spoke up. "Mr. Reis was an Eighties gay male adult film performer. His film credits were under the name Lance. He didn't use a last name, although he was billed as Lance Craner in one, and he did some still photos under the name Lance Kelly. He was born on November 25, 1962 in Oklahoma. Some sources say Arizona and some say Santa Barbara, but we think that was designed by adult film industry marketers to make Mr. Reis more of a California beach boy."

So, TPI planned for me to take the place of a porn star. Sure I'd watched my share of it, but filming it? I didn't voice my reservations, and Kravitz went on. "Reis attended to Capuchino High School in San Bruno, California. He caused trouble most of his teenage life, drifting in and out of foster homes until he was eighteen. He didn't clean up his act as an adult, abusing alcohol and drugs continuously from an early age until the end. He died of complications from AIDS in May of 1991, at twenty-eight.

"Lance—David—did his first professional photos when he was eighteen and his first movies at nineteen. Those were tame, solo jack-off scenes or oral sex scenes. In 1983, he hit the big time, shooting a film called *Leo & Lance* that became hugely popular. His scene with Leo Ford in that movie has been cited as one of the best scenes of that time period. The director was William Higgins, a top director of such films during the era.

"Lance did a handful of other films after *Leo & Lance*, but he was reported to be difficult to work with, skipped shoots, was drunk or high, and developed a bad reputation. He frequently engaged in prostitution, but that wasn't unusual for such performers. Higgins once labeled him the baddest of the bad boys. Directors steered away from him. His last film was in 1986."

The tall, imposing man barely paused before continuing. "After the surgery, you'll look like him, but you're smarter than he was. Off the charts smarter. You have an early 21st century education, a rudimentary understanding of early computing. You lack his upbringing, having never been in foster homes or been incarcerated. While your voice tones will be made virtually identical, nobody would confuse the two of you when you open your mouths. Remember this.

"To take Mr. Reis's place, you'll need to become intimately familiar with every bit of trivia we've been able to collect about him. You'll study these in detail later, but here are some more images to give you a better picture of the body you'll be stepping into." A smile played across his face.

My placemat exploded with grainy photos. More than a few were erotic porn images of Reis, featuring his incredibly prominent member. My eyes shot open again, and my mouth dropped. I looked up to see Kravitz grinning at me with a knowing smirk. "Twenty-four centimeters if you're counting. And all men count, even if they steadfastly claim otherwise. Penis enlargement was quack science in your time, but it's perfected now for those inclined toward a makeover. We'll even restore your foreskin to make your cut cock match Mr. Reis's uncut one precisely." Wells cleared her throat and gave Kravitz a disproving glare. Perhaps she wasn't a fan of his graphic descriptions of male anatomy.

I was, however. Handsome *and* hung. TPI had me, and Kravitz knew it.

Except I'd never fucked a guy or gotten fucked. I was supposed to take the place of an Eighties porn star and sleep with as many gay boys as possible. TPI might make me hot and give me a stud-luring cock, but that didn't mean I could mentally shift gears and become what Reis had been.

Kato chimed in. "Because we don't know who the Alpha Carrier is, the more times you have anal sex, the more likely you'll transmit the nanocell and be successful. This is one assignment when promiscuity will be a big plus."

"I've never even had the chance to be promiscuous. You know that, don't you?"

"Of course. It would be better if it came to you naturally, but it can be easily learned."

TPI was disappointed I wasn't a slut but thought I'd easily jump into the role.

I must have looked skeptical, because Kato gave me an exasperated look. "Physically, this mission won't be an issue for you. Mentally, getting over any hesitation you feel is merely a matter of putting your mind to it and disciplining yourself."

Wonderful. I was being asked to be everyone's stereotype of an irresponsible, young gay man—promiscuous, hedonistic, living only to fuck. Ready to sleep with every willing man. Rather than using a gun or a secretive high-tech weapon, TPI expected me to use my dick and my ass. And they wouldn't even be mine.

It then dawned on me what would happen from having bareback sex in the pre-condom Eighties. "I'll get AIDS, won't I?"

Wells nodded. "You'll almost certainly be infected with the HIV-1 virus, if that's what you mean. But the nanocell will immunize you. You'll be safe."

Yeah, safe so long as TPI's high-tech gizmo works. "You're sure the nanocell works? I mean, what happens if it shuts off after fifteen or twenty years?"

"We've studied that possibility and a thousand others. The nanocell is an inert hybrid biological and mechanical device. It doesn't age, doesn't change over time. We believe it won't fail you. We're depending on that nanocell to protect humanity from the HIV-3 virus in 2060, a much deadlier threat than HIV-1 or HIV-2."

Wells was back to pacing. "We're planning to locate you in 1983, which our simulations target as a year or two before the most likely time when HIV-3 emerged. In 1983, the HIV-1 virus was being passed to more and more people. The more people who carry the nanocell attached to HIV-1 viruses in their bloodstream, the more likely it is that the nanocell will trap the mutant strain, ready to seal it away forever the moment it mutates."

"This is a solo mission, isn't it?"

"Yes," Anders said. "You'll be a modern Johnny Appleseed, single-handedly spreading the nanocell instead of *Malus domestica* seeds." He didn't catch the irony of his seeding analogy.

"Even if we had a hundred people who fit the requirements as closely as you do," Wells said, "we don't have permission from Lois for an intervention on that scale. Sending even a single person back in time for a mission of this scope is unheard of, given the likelihood that you'll cause significant disruptions in the timeline. A hundred people flooding back to the Eighties would never be approved." She sighed. "Although if you don't succeed, that may well be the next frontier in this fight."

If I failed, TPI would try again. Maybe they had already sent someone else, or maybe I'd done this before. Maybe I'd failed a hundred times and this would be attempt one hundred one, tweaking slightly what had happened in the previous efforts.

"What sort of timeline disruptions will I cause?"

"Think of the timeline as a river. Everything you do in the Eighties that differs from what happened originally is like throwing a rock into the stream. You buy a magazine that was never sold in the original timeline. Highly unlikely to affect anything, like the impact of a single rock. But thousands of rocks? The flow of the stream invariably becomes disturbed. Just try not to flood the banks."

"As Agent Wells said, the nanocell immunizes the human body against AIDS. The longer your mission takes, the more men you'll inoculate; to defeat HIV-3, your nanocells will imprison all known HIV virus in your sex partners. You'll be saving lives. Perhaps a great number of them. If you pass the nanocells to someone with the right blood type and immunization structure, they'll pass the nanocells to others. The effects will snowball—tossing more and more rocks into the timestream. It's both unavoidable and desirable to a point."

"So all the people who died during the Plague Years...I'll be saving them?"

Wells looked uncomfortable. "Mathematically, complete eradication of all viral strains is nigh-impossible. Cody, you must understand that when someone travels back in time and saves another person from dying, the timeline changes. Forever. An avoided death is a delayed death that has a ripple effect. The restoration of bright futures from people cut down in their prime will have unforeseen influences on the new future. To put it bluntly, for every Keith Haring or Clark Tippet you save, you will also be saving a Roy Cohn. And so, we need you to focus on the Alpha Carrier."

My head was spinning from the ramifications of time travel. The room felt hot. "I think I need a break."

"Quite right, we all do," Anders said. He rose and suggested a walk down the hallway to get a drink.

"This is a little confusing," I said to him.

"Welcome to TPI. Every time I think I have a good grasp on time travel and its implications, something turns things upside down."

"How much have you travelled back in time?"

"Very little and only recently. Ironically, because of your mission. I've gone back on several occasions to prepare."

"What preparations?" Anders was warmer than Kravitz and someone I wanted to trust, although Kravitz was the muscle you wanted to protect your back.

"Since you'll be exchanging places with Mr. Reis, we've gathered intelligence on him. Much of what we know is sketchy, but Lois doesn't want us in 1983 any more than absolutely necessary. We've pinpointed a day in his life when his disappearance and your appearance will raise the fewest questions. It is shortly after he moved to L.A.; he had few close friends or acquaintances there. That will reduce the risk someone will suspect something when you take his place. Still, you'll need to be careful."

I began to see the challenge of stepping into someone else's life. I might look like Reis, but anyone who knew him would instantly know something was wrong when they met me.

We collected what tasted like iced tea from a machine. Apparently vending machines were still a thing in 2060. A thought occurred to me. "If I'm in the Eighties for a long time, won't Reis be here a long time, too?"

"We'll have the pleasure of hosting Mr. Reis only long enough to let him recover from the time travel, which won't be easy for him given his fondness for drugs. If you thought you had a major headache when you arrived, his will be epic."

ENTER THE SEX MACHINE

Anders walked me back to the conference room and excused himself, leaving me alone with Wells. She smiled. "I want to show you something, Cody." She pulled me aside and whispered, "Lois won't be happy about this, but I haven't done anything to upset them for at least a day or two."

I liked her attitude.

We wound our way through a series of hallways that all looked alike before coming upon an enormous glass window. Behind it was a massive indoor greenhouse. Every inch of space was used, with vertical lighting and tall columns of plants. It was a high-tech jungle that took my breath away.

"Advanced hydroponics," Wells said. "We're able to feed everyone in the facility, and the plants produce oxygen. We're self-sustaining, at least for a few years and assuming we don't have any accidents." She pointed out several shrubs with fat, purplish berries. "*Leea indica*. Those aren't for food, though they are edible. It's a highly medicinal plant and the source of one element we used to create the nanocell."

"How long were you working on the nanocell?"

"We started four weeks ago, the moment the pandemic struck." She chuckled. "By the look on your face, you seem impressed. Do keep in mind we have an asset that makes research and development incredibly fast: time travel. In linear fashion, it took a decade or more to perfect the nanocell. Within a few hours of the crisis, Lois sent a team of TPI agents into the past to enlist the scientists we needed. Since that first venture, dozens of teams have gone back, each time inching us closer and closer to perfecting the nanocell. The first goal was to immunize the TPI agents inside this facility so that the HIV-3 virus in one of us didn't kill everyone here."

We ended in a small, comfortably furnished room. It looked like someone's apartment, down to the bed in the next room. At the end of the room was a massive screen where a painting might have hung. It displayed a city sitting on a broad plain next to a range of mountains. It was early evening, and a layer of clouds to the west was producing a spectacular sunset.

"Wonderful, isn't it? That's a live shot of Denver, taken from a camera on the side of the mountain we're beneath. Until two months ago, the sky above the city would have been filled with vehicles of all types—airplanes, delivery drones, personal transport pods. Today, only a few birds. It's beautiful from this distance, but if you zoomed in, you'd see an appalling scene of disaster. Decaying bodies strewn everywhere. People died walking their dogs, jogging in the park, driving to visit loved ones, or watching the news, asking themselves if the pandemic could actually be happening."

She turned to me with an expression I couldn't decipher. "We desperately need your help, Cody. You understand that. But I won't force you into this mission."

I didn't have much of a choice. What person rejects a desperate plea for help from the entire species?

"I'll do it."

She smiled, a tear forming in her eye. "Thank you, Cody." She looked at video screen and sighed. "My wife lives—well, lived—in Denver with our two small children. I miss her and the kids so much."

I swallowed, blinking a couple of times to keep my eyes from getting too wet. "I'll do my best."

"I know you will. All our research suggested you would be remarkably loyal, determined, and committed. I was skeptical about what you would be like in person, but I'm now convinced."

I was far from confident about pulling off the mission in front of me. Lois gave me long odds of success, and they probably weren't even factoring in how inept I'd likely be at job one: sex.

Wells continued to stare at the video screen. "If you're successful in this mission, I won't remember meeting you today. No one in 2060 will. In the new timeline you'll create, the nanocell will keep HIV-3 harmless and at bay, and we'll have no reason to look for a savior."

Another baffling aspect of multiple timelines. "Will I remember any of it?"

She nodded. "You will. But *only* you. Time travel seems always to demand a certain irony." She turned to me with a pensive look. "There's another aspect of your mission that we should discuss. Not only will nobody here remember you, nobody in your time will either."

"What?"

"After surgery, you'll no longer resemble yourself, which means you can't step back into your old life. Your reappearance would only cause uncertainty, raise the sort of questions we need to avoid. Then there's Lois. They hate timeline changes. They insisted we abduct you the night before your death, and they have already had us stage it. We found a homeless teenager who unfortunately died on the day you were killed. His body stood in for yours in the accident. Given the normal injuries from a bike accident, the physical resemblance was enough.

"When you return, we'll give you a new identity. A bit like a witness protection program."

The new information didn't change my mind. I was committed to the mission. It wasn't like I had much of a life to lose. The handful of friends I had in high school and college had scattered across the country, and I wasn't all that close to any of them. My parents were dead and I didn't have a family except for my Uncle Ben. I didn't want to lose him, and if I made it back, I'd track him down. I'd be a stranger to him, but I'd know things only Cody Montrose knew, so maybe he'd believe my improbable tale of having my body remade and journeying to the future and the past. Lois wouldn't want me telling him about time travel but fuck them.

"Sorry to drop that on you. Some TPI agents didn't want me to reveal your staged death and new identity for fear you wouldn't agree to undertake the mission. I ruled that out; I wouldn't feel right not telling you. We may be facing a dire situation, but we can't compromise our principles."

"I appreciate that. It will be a clean start. Plenty of people would love to have that."

She smiled. "You're not convinced that's best, but I appreciate you looking on the bright side." She took a deep breath. "We should confirm you can host the nanocell. The tests suggest it's a virtual certainty, but if there's a problem, we'll have to abort the mission. Any questions before we start?"

I had a thousand, but for each one answered I'd have two more. I shook my head.

Wells escorted me back to the room where I first woke. Danny, still shirtless, greeted us. I assumed he would inject me with some swirling, bio-luminous liquid. He hooked me up to an apparatus that would monitor the nanocell and did exactly that. He had to poke me in the ass because my arm was too thin, but most of the people I'd met in 2060 had already seen my bare butt, so modesty wasn't the order of the day.

Danny studied a screen for a few minutes. "Success! The nanocell is already replicating."

Wells smiled. "Good. Do you feel up to getting a new body, Cody? Not completely new. None of your internal organs will change, only your muscles, skin, hair, and some other miscellaneous parts. You'll have to make do with the same old brain."

Things were happening fast, but I was curious to see what I'd look like. "Sure, if you're ready."

Wells grinned. "While you were recovering from the jump, Kato took your stem cells and tissue back to the past—nine months ago— and started the development process in a locked, restricted part of this complex. The new you is ready to go. We can complete the process overnight if you'd like. As you can imagine, we're eager to move quickly."

I ate another meal that was short on looks and long on taste while Danny busied himself with the arrangements.

"Are you a TPI agent too?"

"Heavens, no. Only a lowly medical technician. But one who was fortunate enough to be married to a TPI agent. When Lois put the call out summoning agents here, my husband had the presence of mind to ask if, given the crisis, a medical technician might come in handy. So here I am."

I suspected he was gay, but you never know if gaydar works around men from the future.

"Who's your husband?"

"You spent all day with him. I hope he wasn't too much of a jerk. He's not a guy who shows a ton of sympathy."

There were three possibilities. I picked the one I considered most obvious. "Kato?"

Danny laughed. "No. Cute boy, though, and I'd do him in a minute if he weren't monogamous. You'd think that would be extinct by now, but his boyfriend is the jealous type. No, my beau is Kravitz. Dreadlocks, incredible body, surprisingly gentle in bed." He winked. "Well, sometimes."

Danny, Kravitz, Kato, and Wells were all gay; that left Anders, who might have been the token straight man. I wondered if Lois took sexual orientation into account when staffing my mission. I wanted to ask about gay life in the future, but I figured Danny wasn't permitted to talk about 2060. I asked about his tats instead. The intricate lines of ink on his skin were spectacular.

"Each has a detailed meaning. I'm an open book." He began pointing out portions of his body. "This is a simple one. It says I'm three-eighths Caucasian, two-eights Latin, and two-eights Asian—Japanese to be precise. The last eighth is half African and half a mélange of races. This has my medical job credentials, and this has my medical history." He pointed at a large, colorful tattoo on his right pec. "This one has all the important data. It announces my sexual orientation, preferences, and availability. *Very* available. Technically married but in an open relationship. Anyone interested can scan my ink and instantly get a full profile, including explicit images and details about the variety of kink I'm into."

I blinked, trying to digest it all, and resisting the urge to ask exactly what flavor of kink. The tech wizards of the future had rendered the hook-up apps of the early 21st Century so redundant that they now seemed silly. Imagine just scanning a guy to find out he's gay? It really was gaydar. "So if you have your shirt off, anyone can read that and tell you're gay?"

"Yes, but I never wear a shirt, as you call it. Generational thing. Anyone under thirty wears tops only for formal ceremonies. Advances in plastic surgery mean that if you're embarrassed by your body, you fix it immediately."

He grinned at me. "You're probably not supposed to know this much about 2060. I'd better shut up before Lois zaps me and kicks me outside to fend for myself."

I couldn't stay awake any longer and, as I drifted off, I envied the men of the future. And yet, they needed someone like me.

For a second time, I woke up to Danny's cheerful face. "How are you feeling, Tiger? You look amazing."

For a second time, I lied. "Um, okay." Unlike yesterday, my head wasn't pounding. Instead, a dull pain throbbed in every part of my body. Even my ears hurt.

"I need to make sure we got everything attached correctly. You were easy to work on. Hardly any fat to remove. Can you sit up and walk a few steps? I have you on a regulator that will keep you from movements that might prematurely stress the grafts. Can you walk over to that mirror?"

I was so eager to see my new body, I would have crawled on the ground to the mirror. I got to my feet unsteadily, but Danny's regulator was like a dozen hands keeping me upright and stable.

Damn. The ugly duckling had turned into a swan. I had Reis's body. Shaggy, surfer blond hair and a slender, buff body. I didn't recognize myself, but I recognized him. I also recognized his prodigious uncut cock, now dangling between my legs. I looked down to confirm it was really there. It was. It felt heavy.

I wanted badly to touch it. To see it at full mast. To… well, to find out what it felt like when I climaxed.

But I couldn't bring myself to do it with Danny staring over my shoulder. "Don't tell anyone, but for artistic reasons and because of the nature of your mission, I took the liberty of making a few improvements. Often big penises don't get that hard, but I engineered better blood flow to ensure rock hard erections. I enhanced the musculature of your sphincter, so you will have the tightest ass in California. And while I wasn't supposed to tinker with your internal organs, I couldn't resist juicing your prostate. Getting dicked is gonna feel better than it ever has."

I bit my tongue, unwilling to confess that I had no baseline of what having a cock in my ass was like.

"That's the internal stuff that isn't visible. As for what you can see, I was restricted in what I could do, but I made a few slight fixes. I was unable to resist molding your ass a bit. Well, more than a bit. Reis frankly didn't have much of one. Too flat and nondescript, but with his oversized penis, it's doubtful anyone paid attention to his glutes. I'm particularly proud of how they came out. Well-developed, noticeably rounder and much more prominent. You've got a damn nice shelf of muscle below your back. I'm sorta a connoisseur of bubble butts, but you've probably already detected that from my choice of a husband. If your cock and balls don't attract men, your ass certainly will. They're a lethal combination. If you're asked about why your ass is so much better, you'll have to claim you did weeks of squats to beef it up."

I glanced at the tattoo that now prominently graced my new, muscly left bicep. It looked like the snarling head of a big cat, maybe a cougar or tiger, and was mostly black and dark blue with red accents in the sharp-toothed mouth. Reis's tat, now mine.

Danny must have seen me looking. "Sorry about such a pathetic tattoo. Lois insisted it mimic Lance's—frankly his was atrocious. I deviated somewhat to improve it. If the changes are too noticeable, tell people you got it touched up. I incorporated some modern thermal features in the ink. In case somebody wants to fuck outdoors when it's cold, the weather won't impact you."

Danny was giving me a hungry look. No man had ever looked at me like that. "You're now a sex machine." He slapped my buttocks, and I groaned as pain radiated through my ass. "Oh, I'm so sorry! I didn't mean to do that. I got carried away. Are you okay?"

The pain was receding, and I nodded. I couldn't help but fixate on Danny's words. *I was a sex machine.* I was having trouble digesting that fact.

PREP FOR THE EIGHTIES

After almost two days of recovery, I asked Anders about the next step. He said dryly, "We need time, pun intended. Time to get you trained. Time to immerse you in the Eighties. Time to turn you into Lance. We have little given the emergency, and while we allotted two weeks, your healing from surgery took a little longer than anticipated."

Wells arranged an intense Eighties immersion mixed with physical therapy to get me used to my new body. It took a while before I saw my reflection in a mirror and didn't wonder who was looking at me.

I watched old movies and television shows to pick up slang. I had mini-history lessons and was reminded at every step I had to forget anything after the spring of 1983. At night, I listened to music of the era so I'd recognize and learn lyrics. It was like being in the studio where the performers recorded; earbuds had come a long, long way. However, my crash course on the Eighties cutoff abruptly with the spring of 1983; knowing what happened beyond that would only complicate my assignment.

The one exception to the 1983 cutoff was anything on Lance, particularly video footage, because I needed to be him. I watched his porn films repeatedly. They weren't great. They weren't even good. They were laughable. The videos were far from digital quality, the acting and dialogue made me roll my eyes, and the plots were mind numbingly boring. Not that porn in my era was all that great. High resolution but the same forgettable plots and lines. I doubted if it was better in 2060.

Of course, despite all that, I watched with a mixture of interest, intrigue and intoxication. The eye candy never got boring. The anticipation of the bottom getting boned never grew old. The money shots never ceased to grab my attention. People watching gay porn don't demand Oscar-worthy performances, memorable plots and stunning cinematography. They demand one thing, and I was all over it. I was excited to step into that world, something I never thought possible.

I had to force myself to stop being entertained by the films and instead study each frame in slow motion. I ran through a scene watching only facial expressions, then again watching only hand movements, and so on. Anything I could copy. Anders and Wells occasionally slipped into the screening room to remind me I had to become Lance, had to know him so well I'd act out his part perfectly.

Kato, who was TPI's expert on impersonations, give me pointers, flagging Lance's mannerisms and tendencies, most of which I wouldn't have noticed even if I had watched his videos a hundred times. He remained upbeat. "You'll be the best adult performer in the world. Admittedly that's like being the world's fastest snail, but inside of a couple of weeks, you'll have more training than any gay adult film star in history."

Despite Lance's high-profile porn career, he was only in fourteen scenes in ten films spread out over six years. He topped but never bottomed on screen. Stills existed showing him bottoming when he was young, maybe not even eighteen, but no film evidence existed.

I was to take Lance's place early in his career, after the third of his fourteen scenes, a mutual suck-off that was his first non-solo shoot. It would be me and not Reis who would perform in Lance's celebrated porn videos. Assuming they all got made. I was nervous about screwing up. What if I was so bad I completely changed the timeline and nobody hired me?

Kato and Anders assured me I would be fine. "No real acting happens in the adult film industry," Kato said. "Look at your assets. Big dick. Check. Hot body. Check. Handsome face. Check. Add to that not being late, not being drunk and not being a jerk, and you will be a director's dream come true."

I spent as much time as possible surreptitiously working on a personal project. Thinking about my Uncle Ben one night, it came to me that the timing might be such that I could save his lover Lincoln from AIDS. I wished I had more details about him, but from Lois's data banks, I ferreted out that he'd been in the Marines in the early Eighties and was stationed in Southern California from 1983 to 1985. It left me hopeful.

Danny was tasked with checking me out one final time before I left. He relished examining my newly buff body, which was a highly unusual experience for me. Dudes did not get off on my body. They went out their way to avoid looking at it, not to mention feeling it up.

He insisted on a prostate massage to ensure "all the plumbing worked well." I could have told him that it did, as I'd been jerking off every day since the post-surgery soreness left my body. I justified using my right hand so much on the grounds that I needed to get used to my newly acquired dick and familiar with its foreskin.

Danny began inserting a slender, flexible rod into my ass while his other hand slowly slid up and down my new shaft. He nodded in time with the rhythm and I kept seeing his face get closer and closer—I didn't know if his scientific curiosity might lend itself to blowing me. The physical stimulation, the thought of Danny's lips around my dick, the sight of his amazing body; it was too much. I gasped and thick ropes of cum erupted from my cock. I blinked in surprise. Hell, if I'd realized what my prostate did now, I'd have been fingering it every time I jacked myself.

Danny smiled as he loosened his grip. He scooped up a dollop of semen and transferred it to some odd-looking device set in a crevice. A happy chime sounded.

He then surprised me with a sudden kiss. Soon our tongues were intertwined. I felt him push a small disk into my mouth. I hesitated, not knowing what he was doing.

"Swallow," he whispered in my ear. "I love saying that to a hot man."

I did as instructed. Whatever it was had little or no taste.

When we broke for air, he grinned at me and said, "That was a final precaution for your mission. The affectionate delivery method was, well, unauthorized and unorthodox. I apologize, but I couldn't resist. That tab you swallowed immunizes you from every STD to be found in the Eighties along with a few that didn't emerge until years later. For your mission you need to be the biggest slut gay boy to walk the streets in 1983, and we all know the risks of that."

"Don't apologize. The delivery method was delightful."

Danny chuckled and held me tight. "You have no idea how honored I am to have met you and played a small role in your mission."

It was sweet. And sad because if I succeeded, Danny would have no memory I even existed. I wondered if I should proposition him. He had an open relationship and frankly I needed some sexual experiences involving something beyond my right hand. However, Wells came into the room at that moment and Danny quickly threw a blanket over my sticky crotch. "He's ready."

We gathered in the conference room for a final briefing and logistics discussion. As usual, Wells took the floor.

"We've timed your jump to correspond to one of Mr. Reis's drinking and drug binges, which will make it easy to enter his apartment and remove him. You'll still feel the effects of the jump, so you may not remember much, if anything, about those first few hours. Anders, Kravitz, and Kato will go with you. They'll leave some cash and the specifics of a special bank account that will be funded regularly."

I didn't use cash. Who did? "Um, what about some credit cards? That's what I use."

Kravitz shook his head. Over the course of my training, he'd played the role of my perpetually annoyed big brother. "Too much of a paper trail, and too many places in 1983 won't take them. Try to use a credit card to buy a drink in a bar, and the bartender will laugh at you. It would also be out of character for the role you're assuming. With his poor credit history, Mr. Reis would never qualify for credit. We'll leave you an ATM card you can use to withdraw cash."

Fuck. How was I supposed to know how much cash I'd need in advance? Counting change would be a pain, to say nothing of lugging around a pocketful of coins. It was a tiny reminder of the challenges I'd be facing to fit into 1983.

Wells pursed her lips. "Cody, we know you're the right man for this project. I have no doubts. But you'll be on your own. You'll be the only person who knows who you are, and invariably you'll begin to question the mission. Keep focused, keep balanced. Two things to bear in mind. The first is that you'll be tempted to observe or interact with your parents or family members. Not a good idea. Even if you think you can do that from afar, don't chance it. Any interaction with a relative or someone close to them is strictly forbidden. So don't be tempted."

My parents were teenagers in 1983. They met ten years later while serving in the Peace Corps, and I'd come along four years after that. Curiosity and the thought of seeing them again aside, the idea that they'd be gangly teens, younger than me, was creepy. "Understood."

Wells exhaled. "Last, remember the old Spider-Man comics, where Spider-Man can never forgive himself for not saving his Uncle Ben? There's a clinical term for that—the superhero complex. It occurs when you know how much good you can do but can't put boundaries on it. You'll experience that. Every man you have sex with will be a man you may save from AIDS. You'll be tempted to save everyone. You can't endanger the overall mission to help every man you meet. Having the power to help people but not using it will be terribly hard. But it's what you must do."

The conundrum Wells outlined hadn't occurred to me, but I wondered if her choice of Spider-Man and his Uncle Ben was coincidental. She was warning me off my planned project to save Lincoln, but her talk about Spider-Man only strengthened my resolve. I couldn't save everyone, but maybe I could save one man.

Anders interrupted my train of thought by clapping me on the shoulder. "You'll work it out, Cody. You're the right man for the job."

I wasn't so certain.

I didn't have more time to contemplate Lincoln and Uncle Ben before Kato escorted me into a bare, small room. "Are you as bothered by time travel as I was the first time?" I said to him.

"No. For whatever reason, Anders Kravitz, and I tolerate it well. That's part of the reason we're assigned to this project. We've also adjusted over time. We've each made enough jumps to acclimate somewhat."

Kravitz overheard us and snorted scornfully. "Tough it out."

Okay, I was a wimp, at least compared to the mountain of muscle.

We waited a few seconds, and a bluish light flashed. In the blink of any eye, we were in a dark apartment. My head threatened to explode.

Fighting the pain, I was only vague aware of what happened next. Anders guided me to an unmade bed and checked the apartment while Kravitz and Kato eased a dazed, confused, and belligerent Reis off his couch. Another flash of light, and the four men disappeared, leaving me alone in the darkness.

I was nauseous and afraid to move, concentrating on breathing deeply. I was seeing flashing lights, although maybe they were only my eyes betraying my brain's complaints about time travel. I fought panic when they got worse. I kept my eyes closed, not wanting to hallucinate. The lights reached a crescendo, like fireworks going off in my brain, before they slowly subsided. My headache expanded to the rest of my body and I ached, feeling like every bit of bone and muscle had been abused. The sheets were damp from my sweat.

After several hours, the aches and pains receded. I cautiously opened my eyes and surveyed the nondescript bedroom, getting to my feet slowly and unsteadily. The bedside clock read 4:24. Probably 4:24 a.m., because it was dark outside. I took a step before another wave of nausea washed over me. I collapsed back into bed.

I woke again in a couple of hours and hauled myself out of bed. A faint light filtered through the cheap curtains. Ignoring how awful I felt, I stumbled to a window. A narrow, hilly street was surrounded by big trees and populated by two rows of ancient cars in mute silence. The boxy Oldsmobiles, Pontiacs, and Plymouths confirmed I was in Reis's apartment in the spring of 1983.

WEST HOLLYWOOD, CIRCA 1983

I explored Reis's place, feeling guilty as I rifled through his closet and belongings. I turned up an address book, a checkbook, and some scribbled notes that were meaningless to me. The checkbook for the TPI account was there too, along with a short note of encouragement from Wells. I wondered if she'd broken TPI protocols by sending a message to the past, but I appreciated the gesture and carefully folded it and put it away. Who knew if I'd need it to reassure myself my memories of my first twenty-two years and the time I'd spent in 2060 weren't evidence I was crazy?

Uh, mentally divergent.

Spotting a record player and a rack of vinyl albums, I couldn't resist playing one. Uncle Ben had a stack of them that we played on an old turntable he showed me how to use, and he swore they were better than digital tracks. Between the albums, a land line, an answering machine, and a Sony Walkman cassette player, I had all the tangible reminders I needed to confirm wasn't in Kansas anymore. Reis was apparently a Journey and Foreigner fan. Could have been worse.

I hesitated to go through his wallet, feeling it was somehow improper, but it was my wallet now. I tested his keys to find one that fit the apartment locks and ferreted out his car, although it took a long time despite the description Anders left for me.

Most of his clothes were in a pile of dirty laundry, so I washed them. They fit reasonably well. His jeans and shorts were big in the waist but tight in the ass, a consequence of Danny's sculpting of my newly rounded butt cheeks. I'd never had the body to wear my pants low and ironically, now that I did, all the pants rode high and tight. Go figure.

Reis's shirts were tight across my chest and arms, but the worst was his profoundly embarrassing collection of underwear, a combination of stodgy tighty-whiteys and skimpy, multicolored briefs. I wasn't relishing the prospect of wearing them but resigned myself to making the best of it.

I found what I assumed were drugs and got rid of them, spreading them among several dumpsters. Perhaps TPI could get me out of legal trouble, but I had no desire to take chances, and Wells had said drugs might harm the nanocell. I kept some marijuana in case it might help in a sexual tryst. If I wasn't doing it solo, getting high might be fun. The nanocell wasn't bothered by marijuana or alcohol, so I had *carte blanche* to party as long as it didn't hinder sex.

I took a walk after West Hollywood stirred to life. I bought the *Los Angeles Times*, more to confirm the date than anything else. If that weren't concrete enough evidence I'd traveled through time, I had conclusive proof from the hulking cars on Santa Monica Boulevard—vintage and strangely new at the same time—along with the clothing styles of the men and women on the sidewalk. I witnessed fashion mistake history as dudes paraded by in bulky white tube socks and short shorts. However, after being cooped up in a cave for almost a month—albeit a high tech 2060 cave—it was good to be outdoors. I explored the city with the fascination of a tourist seeing mundane things for the first time.

My second purchase in 1983 was a map of L.A. I didn't have Google Maps and had to function in a city I didn't know. I missed the little dot on my phone screen that showed where I was. Hell, I missed my phone.

I wandered into All American Boy and International Male, clothing stores on Santa Monica that served predominately gay male clientele. The clothes were ridiculously inexpensive, although if I reversed decades of inflation maybe they weren't that cheap. The styles looked odd, and buying clothes didn't make sense given I didn't know how long I'd be in 1983. My tour of Reis's closet suggested he wasn't a regular shopper at either store, so he'd find it odd if he returned and discovered a strange new wardrobe.

As I headed back to the apartment, the bars on Santa Monica were growing crowded for Sunday afternoon tea dances. Looking at the young men dancing, chatting with their friends, and hunting for sex, I had the odd feeling I was witnessing happy hour on the Titanic. Within a decade, many would be dead and the rest would have their lives changed dramatically.

I could save some of them. Maybe many of them, but only if I didn't locate the Alpha Carrier quickly. I recalled Wells's caution about having the power to help people but not using it. The thought made me melancholy. I'd undertaken a mission to save humanity, not save individual lives, but I'd do a little of that along the way.

Wells had suggested I take my time adjusting before fully embracing my mission. Truthfully, I was relieved about a slow start and happy to have an excuse to delay the inevitable. The thought of having sex with every man I could lure into bed was daunting.

Hell, having sex with a single man was daunting. Too bad I couldn't summon Maverick with Grindr. A web app would have been damn handy for my mission.

I spent time reading newspapers and watching television. Studying 1983 from 2060 only got me so far in understanding the era, so I did a crash course in current events. Listening to Ronald Reagan and Margaret Thatcher on TV made me feel like I was watching old documentaries rather than real people. Reading about Phillips and Sony introducing the compact disc made me chuckle. Virtually its entire life history would occur during the years I'd skipped over.

Watching sports was fun at first. It was cool to see Magic Johnson and Wayne Gretzky and Martina Naratilova in their prime. Still, I couldn't shake the feeling I was watching the history channel. It didn't help that flat screen TVs didn't exist, and I was peering at Reis's ancient cathode ray set. I'd never memorized things like who won the 1983 NBA or NHL titles, let alone who won particular games or tennis matches, so I didn't know the outcome in advance, but I couldn't shake the sense that the outcome was pre-determined.

Movies were a little better. I'd seen *Return of the Jedi* several times, but who didn't like seeing it on the big screen? I liked Johnny Carson and *The Tonight Show*, but I had a hard time getting into other TV shows. It was the era of *Dallas* and *Dynasty*, but I had little patience for either, particularly after the producers of *Dynasty* backed away from Steven being openly gay. Not that gay characters on TV were all that prevalent in my era, but in 1983 they were essentially non-existent. It wasn't much better in the movies.

Getting news through a newspaper or TV was a big adjustment. I missed the ready availability of the internet. I missed my cell phone. I felt naked without it and jumped whenever Reis's landline rang. It was usually a telemarketer, never anyone who knew him well. TPI was correct about him having few friends in L.A.

My first mistake was an effort to buy a six pack of beer in a small liquor store. I'd settled on something mundane after my search for a good microbrew came up empty; apparently, microbreweries were still to come. Without thinking, I showed the clerk Reis's driver's license, which documented he wasn't twenty-one. The clerk chuckled at my flustered reaction and then let me buy the beer anyway. Being hot had advantages outside of hooking up.

I later found three credible-looking fake IDs. I had to use my head more in the future.

Before arriving, my image of what I would find in 1983 was influenced heavily by the hours I spent watching Lance's films. I had the vague sense that pre-AIDS gay ghettos like West Hollywood were all about sex. It didn't turn out to be quite as free and open as I envisioned. Rent boys strutted their stuff at all hours on Santa Monica Boulevard, and the closing of the bars set off a sexual feeding frenzy, particularly on weekends, but for the most part, life was surprisingly normal.

Except for the cruising. I got stares from dudes walking down the street, from customers and salesclerks in stores, from waiters in restaurants, even from guys using urinals next to me. I'd never experienced anything like it. Two weeks passed before I stopped looking behind me to see who the men might be staring at.

If I thought the streets were cruisy, I was in for a shock in West Hollywood's gay bars. In the era of web apps and online hookups, picking up a guy at a bar was quaint if not accidental. But in 1983, gay bars were ground zero for men looking to meet other men. They had a hedonistic, meat market atmosphere, with gay boys reveling in free and easy sex. I had to adjust to the clothes and hairstyles, to say nothing of the perpetual haze of cigarette smoke in the air.

While the attention I received did wonders for my ego and I gradually relinquished my ugly duckling self-image, I didn't pursue any offers. I told myself I needed to get comfortable and focus on Lance's budding porn career to make sure I didn't screw up the timeline. In reality I was nervous as hell. Being a gay slut boy would take some work.

I told myself I had time to adjust. But did I? As my stay approached two weeks and TPI hadn't pulled me out, I figured I'd ultimately succeed, but when? If it took twenty years, I'd be returning to my time in a forty-year-old body. The initial excitement of living in a different era waned, and the reality of the job ahead of me sunk in. I began to feel lonesome and isolated. I would have enjoyed seeing Wells. Hell, even Kravitz.

My quiet introduction to 1983 came to a screeching halt after hitting a gay bar on Santa Monica one night. As I left, a young, tough-looking guy stopped me and grabbed me by the arm. "Hey, David! Long time no see!" With a big smile, he hugged me.

Fuck! I didn't know the guy. He was apparently a friend of Reis's or at least an acquaintance or sex partner. Not, however, someone TPI told me about. "Hey, what's happening?" I said, my heart beating rapidly.

My question was met by a sneer. The dude leaned close. "What's happening? I'll tell you what's happening, faggot! You still owe me for those ludes I sold you last month, that's what's happening. When you gonna pay?"

"I, uh, forgot about that," I said, trying to buy time to think.

"Oh, big surprise! You have problems remembering things you like to forget. Have ever since high school. Good news. I'm here to remind you. I'll tell you when you're gonna pay up. Now. This instant."

I debated whether to stay on the sidewalk in plain view, which might be safer if he turned violent, or to suggest we duck into an alley and discuss things off the street, which might be safer if one of the passersby turned us in for dealing drugs. "Uh, man, I'm really sorry about that. How much is it?"

"You fucking asshole! Like you don't know. Ten ludes, two hundred bucks, my friend. Interest and my late charge are another hundred, so it's three. You used to make that much money in a couple of nights whoring your donkey dick. Bet you still do."

I wasn't getting off the hook with a polite reminder. Three hundred dollars was real money in 1983, and I wasn't carrying anything close to that amount. I had it at Reis's apartment but feared inviting the dealer there.

"I'll get it for you."

The dude laughed at me scornfully and shoved me against a wall. "How stupid do you think I am, fuck boy? I let you sneak away last time, but not now." Before I had time to react, he pulled Reis's wallet from my jeans and rifled through it, removing the cash.

"This will do for a down payment," he said with a self-satisfied grin, pocketing sixty bucks. "Now, what about the rest, porn boy? You want me to whore your ass out until I get the money? You whined and complained the last time. You were easy to sell, pretty boy. There's a market for blond boys with oversized cocks, but I gotta tell you the deal will be different now. For my trouble in finding faggots interested in buying you, I pocket all but ten bucks. At ten bucks a pop, you're gonna be working some long, long nights to pay off three hundred bucks. This time that freak dong you're so proud of won't be the only thing that's for sale. Nope! I'll peddle your ass to men who get off on roughing up the trade. They pay more, but guess what? You're still only getting ten bucks out of it. Whaddya say?"

What he was proposing would dovetail nicely with my mission, but only if the guys fit the Alpha Carrier's demographics, which seemed unlikely. I wasn't ready to jump into having sex yet, and I had little doubt getting pimped out by a drug dealer would be dangerous. "I told you I'd get the rest of the money. Tonight. Wait here and I'll come back. I have it."

The man laughed again. "Not on your life. You and I will get the money together. If you're making this up, you're gonna regret it."

With no good alternative, I headed toward Reis's place, trying to make out exactly what weapons the guy might be carrying. Gun, knife? Probably both. I was on my own and had to defend myself if it came to that, although the presence of two of the dealer's goons left little doubt about the outcome.

We marched down Santa Monica Boulevard, the dealer keeping one of my arms twisted behind me to keep me from bolting. His men trailed us. Before we reached the apartment, however, it occurred to me I could withdraw the money using an ATM. The only question was whether the withdrawal limit was less than I needed. My heart was beating like a drum, and I practically held my breath the entire way to the bank.

Paying off the dealer was a non-event. I inserted my card and the machine allowed three hundred a day. I started to punch in two-fifty, but the dealer grabbed my hand with a gloating grin and hit three hundred instead. "Sixty bucks was my tip, faggot."

The machine spewed out the cash and the dealer grabbed it all. He smiled, happy over his payday. "Nice doing business with you, David. I won't hold this against you when you need something else. I got some really good stuff right now. Since I know you're good for the money, I'll restore your credit line. I'll even have José, my Mexican runner, deliver it and let you use his ass. I know how much you like cute brown boys. He wasn't happy about the last time, but he does what I tell him to do. Whaddya say?"

Buying drugs was the last thing on my mind. I politely declined, claiming I was staying away from them. Reis's dealer gave me a sarcastic laugh, but the look in his eyes turned harsh and he glared.

Too late, I realized my mistake. Reis would have eagerly taken the drugs. The dealer sensed something amiss. With a sudden, cat-like movement, he shoved me into the alley next to the ATM machine and pushed me against a wall. He closed a strong grip around my neck while producing a knife, confirming my earlier speculation about at least one of the weapons he carried. He held the blade against my cheek and laughed.

"José does what I tell him to do and guess what? You're gonna too. Putting up with you has been a fucking pain in the neck. We're not done, not by a long shot. If you think I'd ever let you buy from someone else, you've got another one coming. This blade could make you less pretty. Real quick. You wouldn't like that, would you? Your looks are important to you. Always were. Important to your ability to whore your prick, too. Be a shame to lose all that."

"Don't cut me," I pleaded.

The dealer's eyes glinted. He slowly slid the blunt side of the knife across my cheek, seeming to debate whether he wanted to see the shiny blade in action. "I'm not gonna cut you. At least not tonight. But don't test your luck with me." He pulled a plastic baggie of dope from his pocket and pressed it into my hand.

"It's good stuff, David. You'll like it. Guaranteed to take the edge off the next time a rich old faggot uses your ass as a convenient hole for his shriveled pecker. You don't need to pay me back for two weeks. Plenty of time to raise the money."

I exhaled. I'd learned a quick lesson. Saying no wasn't an option.

The dealer laughed, still holding the side of the blade against my cheek. He gazed at the knife fondly, as if transfixed by it, then looked back at me. "We have a deal then, fag boy." I began to relax, but the dealer had a parting shot to deliver as he slowly put his knife away.

I think he sensed deep down I wasn't Reis. I looked exactly like his old buddy, and he couldn't put his finger on the difference. That disconnect made him angry. "Get on your knees, faggot," he growled, clenching his jaws, "and tell me how thankful you are that I didn't cut your pretty face to shreds. Kiss my feet to show your gratitude."

Having learned my lesson, I complied quickly, dropping to the ground and pressing my lips to his boots. Gazing up at his sneer, I knew he'd never have asked Reis to do it, and Reis would never have done it, either. In a matter of minutes, I'd permanently altered the relationship between the two.

"I didn't hear you say thanks, fag boy."

"Thank you. You'll have your money in two weeks, I promise."

"Damn right I will, loser. José hasn't forgiven me for letting you destroy his ass, and if you don't do exactly what I say and when I say it, I'll let him extract some revenge. You might like it, though. Getting gang raped by pendejo thugs your thing? He'll bleed you after his boys are done, though, so you better be a good little faggot from now on."

A passing siren caught his attention. He reacted instinctively and stalked away, snarling, "Two weeks, cocksucker!"

I breathed a sigh of relief, glumly accepted he'd be back regularly, and forced myself to relax. I hadn't gotten killed or beat up, and I gained some valuable insight into Reis and his lifestyle. Impersonating him would be more dangerous and challenging than I'd anticipated.

THE FILM: LEO & LANCE

After two weeks of knocking around Reis's dark, depressing apartment and missing the conveniences I'd grown accustomed to, I was lonely and feeling guilty I hadn't started on the key part of my mission: having sex. I kept putting it off, rationalizing it was more important to assimilate as much of 1983 as possible before hopping from bed to bed. In truth, I was nervous about the prospect of losing my cherry.

When the call came about *Leo & Lance*, I'd been expecting it and was ready. My jump to 1983 happened after Reis was hired for the film but before his scene was shot. Wells told me the original filming caused some issues because Reis was supposedly under an exclusive contract with someone other than William Higgins, the director of *Leo & Lance*. To avoid problems in my remake, Lois took the precaution of solving the exclusivity problem. I didn't ask how.

Initially, Higgins only planned to star Leo Ford in the film and had a different title in mind. He added the scene with Lance after much of the shooting was done. One of his cameramen shot Lance in *Good Times Coming* the year before, and Higgins liked his looks and equipment. He'd been enough of a pain in the neck that the cameraman never wanted to work with him again, but Higgins took the chance and the rest was history.

History I was now rewriting. Thanks to TPI, Higgins was taking a chance on me rather than Reis. His scene with Leo in *Leo & Lance* was the stuff of porn legend, propelling him onto the cover and into the title of the video. It vaulted him into the big time and catapulted Leo's career into stardom. But what would happen if I fucked up? I'd totally screw up the timeline. Maybe my scene wouldn't even make the cut, and I'd never work in porn again. Maybe my failure would cost Leo his stardom. A filming disaster might not kill my mission, but it might cripple it.

I wore the same tight polo shirt Reis wore in the video, along with his jeans and gold choker. The shirt was tight on him, but ridiculously tight on me due to my newly sculpted and more muscular shoulders and biceps. It looked like something I'd worn in high school and outgrown. The sleeves were far too short, hitting the middle of my deltoids, and I was constantly tugging them down, only to have them slip back whenever I moved my arm. The shirt wasn't long enough to stay tucked in for any length of time, not that there was room for a shirttail in the tight jeans anyway. For years kids around me had the waistline of their jeans in the middle of their asses, but now I was in pants that might as well have been molded around my ass cheeks.

Reis's gold chain looked expensive, and I wondered if he bought it with money from his porn movies. More likely, it was from hustling; porn didn't pay as much. Maybe a man had given it to him. I didn't like the idea of wearing it but was determined to stay in character.

Without a GPS device, I worried about finding the filming location in Big Bear. I also faced the challenge of maneuvering Reis's big boat in L.A.'s traffic. I left early to be safe and arrived even earlier than I planned when I didn't run into traffic.

I spotted Higgins and introduced myself. He was gruff and seemed annoyed that I arrived so early. Taking the hint I should stay out of the way, I stood off to the side and watched the crew set up, trying to calm my nerves.

A car pulled up and Leo Ford got out, his blond hair shining in the sun. *Damn.* He was strikingly handsome in person, much better in the flesh than in the grainy photos and poor-quality videos I'd studied. I was in awe of having sex with the man, even if it was only happening because I was in a remade body, and he was getting paid.

Leo wasn't as quite as muscular as I was, and his hair was darker than the brilliant, almost-white blond in some later pornos. He made the rounds with the crew, smiling and laughing. I felt like I knew him even though I'd never met him. He recognized me and crossed to where I stood, waiting nervously.

He didn't shake my hand and was wary, less friendly than he'd been with the crew. Either his jaws were clenched or that was the way his chiseled features made him look.

"Well, well, well, David, we meet again."

Crap. Someone else Reis knew. My excitement turned to dread, and my stomach knotted. I'd managed to avoid disaster with Reis's dealer, but faking it with Leo posed a bigger challenge. How did they meet? How well did they know each other? TPI hadn't warned me.

I took a deep breath and exhaled. "Um," I said, trying to buy time to think.

Leo smirked. "You don't remember, do you?"

He'd read me in an instant, but not for the reason he thought. "Well, uh, not really."

"I'm not surprised. It was that party down at Black's Beach in San Diego last year. You were drunk and wasted. Strung out. You weren't so out of it that your big dick wasn't working, though. You chased a Brazilian boy and nailed him, and the two of you put on quite a show until he had enough after the third fuck. You single handedly turned that party into a full-on gay orgy, not that it wouldn't have happened anyway. Your boyfriend was pissed, though. Cute blond boy with a nice body. What was his name, Thor? The guy you filmed *Good Times Coming* with?"

I grimaced. "Sorry about that." Reis's past continued to pose challenges, but I'd apparently dodged another bullet from someone who'd met him.

"No reason to apologize. At least not to me. Save it for Thor."

"We're not, uh, together anymore."

"Why am I not surprised? That man had to be a saint to put up with you as long as he did."

Not wanting to take risks by provoking more conversation about a past I hadn't experienced, I shrugged and didn't respond.

"When Higgins asked me about using you, I told him you had the goods, but the challenge would be tolerating your attitude... and you staying off drugs long enough to get through filming."

"I've cleaned up my act."

He cocked an eyebrow, giving me an apprising look as if seeing me in a fresh light. "Whatever you're doing appears to be working. You look good. A helluva lot better than that night at Black's." He reached out and felt my shoulder, smiling faintly. His touch sent a little thrill through me.

Leo's smile faded. "Don't fuck this up."

"I won't." I hoped I'd fulfill my promise. If I fucked up, it wouldn't be because of drugs or attitude or anything Leo suspected.

He nodded and walked away. I watched him, feeling a twinge of excitement that I'd escaped another near disaster. At least so far. I felt another sort of excitement too, because the dude had a sweet ass.

The crew trooped to a field nearby to film an outdoor jack-off scene starring Leo. It was late spring, and pockets of snow remained although most of the ground was clear. I think Higgins wanted to juxtapose the snow against Leo's bare skin, his blond hair shining in the sunlight. In the original video, Leo beats off and then Lance walks through the field, spots him and starts throwing snowballs. I rolled my eyes the first time I saw it. As if throwing a snowball would be what a gay guy would think to do when he spotted a hot, naked dude with a big erection. Still, the opening scene, which started with Leo running through the forest shirtless, his letter jacket slung over his shoulder, had a fresh and authentic air. It was barely four minutes long.

Leo was a natural, putting everyone—including me—at ease with his easy banter and calm demeanor. He wasn't doing the porn shoot reluctantly; he wasn't resentful; he was in his element. He kept his cock hard despite the chilly weather while the crew shot different angles. He not only didn't mind being naked in front of cameras and a crew of fully clothed men, he seemed to enjoy it. Kravitz said you had to be an exhibitionist to be in porn, and Leo was. He joked with the cameramen and never complained when Higgins asked him to change a pose or reshoot footage. I worried how I would handle being in front of the cameras.

Leo shot his load, and Higgins was happy with the scene. I expected him to turn to the snowball fight next, but to my surprise, he told Leo to get dressed and the crew began packing up the camera equipment.

This isn't right. Filming the snowball scene later made no sense. In a panic, I wondered if Reis had instigated the snowball fight but wasn't here to do it.

On the spur of the moment, I flung a snowball at Leo. He looked stunned as it hit him square in the chest. Laughing, I aimed another one at him. He blocked it, but snow splattered over his bare chest and legs. In the sunlight, ice crystals glittered in his hair and glistened on his chest, little drops of water running down his abs as they melted on his hot skin. Leo let out a curse and grabbed a handful of snow to retaliate. I always thought he threw like a girl in the original video, and this was no different. His snowball fell harmlessly at my feet.

"Wait, wait!" Higgins yelled. Leo already had another snowball in his hand. "This is good. Leo, stay where you are. David, get over to that snowbank. No, go back down the field and walk this way. I want to film the two of you in a snowball fight."

I breathed a sigh of relief. Maybe the snowball scene was trivial and wouldn't have mattered if it had never been filmed. Who knew? Maybe the snowball scene was important to the success of *Leo & Lance*. It was unexpected in a porn video and was a lighthearted introduction to the movie. Leo was completely naked, which gave him a certain erotic vulnerability because Reis was fully clothed. From my view, the less interruption in the timeline the better.

Still, the episode forced me to confront what I was up against. I wasn't Reis and didn't have his impulses. Physically, we could have been twins, but the similarity stopped there. It was absurd to think I'd do the same things he'd done. With every action—or inaction—I'd alter the timeline, perhaps in significant ways. All I had was memories of a few Eighties video clips, and the snowball scene made it clear those wouldn't take me far.

Did it matter? I was here to alter the timeline in a major way. It wouldn't change significantly if Reis ordered pizza when I ordered pasta. I remembered Wells's comment about altering the timeline being like throwing stones into the water. I'd throw plenty of stones, but perhaps little would come of them.

Higgins got enough footage of the snowball fight to fill an hour-long documentary. Leo was freezing, naked in the chilly air while my snowballs spattered on him periodically, but he endured it with a dry sense of humor.

The crew filmed us walking back to the house where our sex scene would be filmed. "That was inspired," Leo whispered. "Costly for you but inspired. You'll pay later." He grinned and grabbed my butt, leaving little doubt about how he intended to extract his revenge. "Nice ass, by the way. If I'd noticed it at Black's, maybe that night would have turned out differently." His comment gave me a little thrill.

Higgins shot a bunch of stills, one of which ended up on the cover of the video—Leo in a letter jacket that made him look like a preppy college man and me with my chin on his shoulder like I was his goofy little brother, still in high school. He'd used Reis's version of the photo in the original video. My version was worse.

Higgins filmed in a vintage A-frame that looked dated even in 1983. Leo and I started making out on the floor in front of a fireplace, still in our clothes. For me it was a good introduction to being in front of Higgins and his cameramen without being naked. I also got used to Leo, pressing my body against him and letting him explore my mouth with his tongue. I was totally into him, feeling playful but loving every moment of kissing. I thought he was into the action, too, although maybe it was only acting. Some of the chemistry between us had to end up on film.

Between the fire and the camera lights, it got hotter than hell. I was about to beg for a breath of fresh air when Higgins called a break. In the original video, the action in front of the fireplace occupies barely a minute, but it seemed like we'd been sucking face for an hour. Not that I was complaining, except for the heat.

Leo and I went to the deck of the A-frame and chatted while cooling off. I found him charming, friendly, and damn sexy. Maybe I'd been programmed to think about him as sexy because of his career. But damn, I was ready to get it on with him. I wanted him. I might have a different body, but I was still the kid who had never been able to lure a man into bed. The anticipation of having sex was overwhelming.

When we returned Higgins directed us upstairs, and we quickly got into tugging off our clothes and a little playful wresting before some oral sex. The original video was unusual as porn goes because Leo and Lance were in their underwear for much of the footage. My least favorite, tighty-whiteys. Yet they looked hot on Leo. Somehow the underwear lent authenticity to the action, like we were so excited and into each other we couldn't be bothered to undress. As far as I was concerned, that wasn't far from the truth.

Leo used his mouth on my rod like an expert. Hell, he was an expert. I struggled with his dick at the beginning and found swallowing nine inches of hard cock was a challenge; it was by far the biggest of the handful of dicks I'd sucked. Once I got it all the way down my throat and relaxed, I did better. I was determined not to have Higgins interrupt us and complain about my inept cocksucking skills.

The A-frame was far from the best place to film a porno. The upstairs bedroom was tiny, with little room for anything other than the bed, and the ceiling sloped so that the cameramen couldn't stand up straight. They had a hell of a time crawling here and there to get shots.

I distinctly remembered the original film had a clumsy scene where Lance grabbed Leo's underwear to rip it off, tugged and pulled at it, but all it did was stretch. He eventually tore the leg open, but Higgins skipped to the ripped underwear being tossed to the floor. I wondered why he didn't reshoot the scene. Maybe nobody had an extra pair of briefs. Or maybe Higgins liked the natural way the action unfolded.

Knowing what I was up against, when we got to that point, I popped up, grabbed Leo's underwear and jerked as hard as possible.

The briefs tore quickly. Feeling triumphant and a little cocky, I shoved Leo to the bed roughly and crawled on top of him, pinning him down, grabbing his throat. His eyes betrayed surprise, his mouth open.

This isn't supposed to happen. Higgins hadn't said anything about me roughing up Leo. Maybe Reis did the same thing, and the footage never made it into *Leo & Lance*, but given his struggle with the briefs I suspected not. Recalling that Leo and Lance went back to sixty-nining each other, I quickly turned around and shoved my cock down Leo's throat, but in haste, I did it too hard, maybe even a little viciously. He gagged and gurgled as he fought to get his breath.

I'm fucking up! I've got to stick to the script. I was back to being nervous as we filmed.

The action went back to what it was supposed to be, but Higgins called for a break. That bummed me out because I was totally into the sex. Leo and I went outside to get some air and stood naked on the front porch, silent, breathing in the cool spring air. I tried, with only partial success, to avoid blatantly staring at his hot body, which did nothing to help my dick go down. Between making out and rolling around with Leo, standing next to him as he looked incredibly sexy, and knowing we'd be back at it shortly, I was sky high.

Leo turned to me with the same serious look he gave me when we first met. I worried that he was angry about the underwear fiasco. "You're into this, aren't you?"

I couldn't deny the obvious. "Yeah."

"It shows. I like that. Keep it up. It comes through in the film." He walked back into the house, leaving me feeling like a lovesick girl. Hell yeah, I was into it. Even if we were only getting it on for the camera, I was into sex with him.

When filming resumed, we exchanged some rimming and were ready to fuck. Remembering Reis's line from the original video, I asked, "Is it all right if I whip this in your ass and fuck you?"

"As long as you fuck me good," Leo replied, exactly from the original. Great dialogue it was not.

He got to his feet, standing over me on the bed, flicking his hard cock and making it bounce against his tight abs. He crouched down and grabbed my dick, pumping it a couple of times, and then lowered himself on it.

In the original, Leo sat down too quickly. He looked up in shock with his mouth wide open as Lance moaned, "Oh, yeah!" Leo was a trooper, blinking, swallowing, and hesitating for a couple of seconds before starting to move up and down on Lance's dick. On screen, he was flying up and down on Lance in no time, his mouth open in ecstasy, although who knows how long it took for him to get to that point.

I fucked the scene up. Between the reality that I would get my cock into an ass for the first time and the ass would be Leo's, I was so turned on that I grabbed his hips and thrust my cock upward as he lowered himself. He grimaced in pain and yelled. "Fuck!" He pulled off, his eyes shooting daggers at me.

Higgins called, "Cut," and asked Leo if he was okay.

Leo paused a couple of seconds, clenching his jaws and gasping for breath. "I'll be okay. It's this fucker who won't be okay when I finish with him." He gingerly sat back down on my dick, and Higgins resumed filming.

Anal sex occupied less than three minutes in the original video, less than a quarter of the action in the A-frame. For most of it, Leo rode Lance, his smooth skin glistening with sweat. We filmed a ton more than that. Doggy, missionary, on our sides, you name it. It took a supreme effort on my part to avoid climaxing inside him, which I knew was a colossal mistake even a rookie porn actor wouldn't make. Whenever I got close, I distracted myself by recalling the original video, wondering if I'd left anything out and debating if I needed to perform differently.

"We have enough," Higgins finally announced. That was the cue to let the cum fly. In the original, Leo's first couple of shots flew over Lance's shoulder like geysers, then splattered on his face, leaving a big blob on his upper lip. This time, however, Leo got a wicked look and aimed his dick directly at my face. The first blast caught me squarely, stinging my eyes. The second and third eruptions coated my face. One of the cameramen zoomed in and got closeups of his thick cum covering my forehead, cheeks, and lips. I remember wondering how he could shoot so much after already blowing a load in the forest. Squinting through the jizz curtain, I watched him drain himself, spunk dripping over his fingers as he sat on my cock, a contented look on his face. After Higgins called "Cut," Leo snickered, "Gotcha, sucker."

The last scene was anticlimactic. I stood next to the bed and jerked off, shooting on Leo's face as well as the cameraman filming the action from below. Higgins's original film doesn't show Lance blasting a big load. My weeks-long cum build-up, however, meant my climax was different. My first spurt shot at least two feet straight into the air before spattering into Leo's hair. By the time the rest of my load fired, his face looked worse than mine had after he coated it. Cum was dripping everywhere. Leo took my softening cock into his mouth, licking out the last drop, and left me weak, almost trembling.

Higgins announced, "Cut. Final."

I was still in the glow of having fucked Leo Ford and pumped out a long overdue load, but he bounced up, grabbed a towel from one of the crew and wiped his face. "You need to milk that damn fire hydrant more often."

"What about you? Were you trying to drown me?"

Leo gave me a sly grin. "You deserved it after that little move you pulled when you rammed that donkey dong into my ass like you were trying to rip me a new hole, not to mention tearing my underwear off. You fucking owe me a new pair." He sounded pissed, but I didn't think he was.

Leo collected his clothes and pulled on his jeans, intentionally claiming my underwear and leaving me to go commando. I stuffed my dick, still half-hard, into Reis's tight jeans. My bulge was clearly visible.

I thought Higgins was pleased with the shoot, but I had no frame of reference. He paid us in cash, and it was late afternoon as we got ready to head back to L.A. I stalled, watching Leo as he talked to the crew. Eventually he walked by my car, smiling. "I wish all my shoots were like this one, hot stuff."

I almost melted and couldn't help but break into a big smile. "Me, too." *How lame.* To partially salvage my comment, I added, "Went by fast."

"It was quick, particularly for a Higgins film. It may have been a record short porn shoot. A lotta guys get soft and everybody has to wait for someone to fluff them up, but you were rock hard the entire time. Impressive. Higgins usually wants to film over and over, but this time he liked our first effort. Almost like we read his mind about what he wanted."

Not exactly. I had perfect insight on Higgins's artistic vision.

I stared as Leo slid into his car, my heart beating rapidly. He put his keys into the ignition, but rather than starting the car, he got out and approached me again. "You're a keeper," he laughed, "and I'm hanging on to you. You up for filming more porn?"

"Sure!"

"Higgins is shooting a final scene in a couple of days. If you're up for it, I'll talk to him about us doing another one at the same time. I have an idea I think might be hot."

"Yeah, I'd like that." *Hell, yes, I wanted to have another round of sex with Leo Ford.*

"Okay, it'll be Saturday if it works out. Higgins's office will call you. Save it up. Gotta have a big cum shot."

"Great. It sounds really good."

Leo gave me a cocky smile. "Higgins hasn't focused on your amazing bubble butt. I have. Remember that. Be prepared."

I watched him drive away, belatedly realizing what I'd signed up for. He planned to fuck me on film. I was still a virgin, and I worried if I'd be able to take it. I recalled Danny saying I could handle it physically. What had he mentioned, my sphincter muscle tone? Still, Leo's big dick was hardly the best way to introduce my asshole to bottoming. That plus he was the last guy I wanted around if I embarrassed myself.

Why the hell did I care so much?

I hadn't admitted to anyone at TPI that I was an anal virgin, but nobody asked. I'd been too embarrassed to bring my virginity up on my own. I halfway assumed the organization had a detailed history of each of my sexual activities. A thin file of course. Maybe they didn't, and instead assumed as a twenty-two-year-old gay man, surely I'd fucked and been fucked repeatedly. If they knew anything about how appearance mattered in the gay world, they'd have known better.

Okay, stop worrying and get on with it. I was destined to lose my cherry on my mission, and I'd found the man who I wanted to take it. I wanted him to fuck my ass long and hard. I'd been ready to give it up to Maverick, but with Leo it was different. I *was* ready.

Three days of anticipation later, I showed up early once again but Leo was already at Big Bear. He met me as I climbed out of Reis's car and, to my surprise, gave me a peck on the lips. "Ready for some action, Tiger? Let's go."

He tossed me two white blankets from the trunk of his car and grabbed a backpack. We hiked into the woods along with a lone cameraman. Apparently, I'd lose my virginity outdoors.

We ended at a large snowfield. Leo told me to arrange the blankets in the snow. "We'll film surrounded by snow. The light reflecting off the snow and the blankets will reduce the shadow effect and because everything around us will be so bright, our bodies will look dark. Higgins thinks this is crazy, but I want to see how it turns out."

"Doug, we're gonna do cum shots first," Leo told the cameraman. He turned back to me. "Takes the pressure off and makes it easier to film for a long period without getting too close. Can you get it up after climaxing?" He wrapped his arms around my waist. "Yeah, you can. I wouldn't risk it with most actors, but after the show you put on, I have a feeling your big cock won't have a problem staying hard."

What he didn't know was I'd been so horny thinking about giving it up to him that my dick had been constantly hard for three days running. I was worried about cumming prematurely.

We stripped. My cock was already rigid. Eyeing it, Leo said, "Looks like you don't need any help, but let me suck you anyway." He dropped to his knees and swallowed my manhood. His warm, wet mouth sent an electric shock through me. He bobbed back and forth for three or four minutes, and I had to pull him off to avoid shooting my load down his throat. "That was fast," he said.

Leo got on his back. "Sit on me like I'm fucking your ass." I crawled on top of him, feeling his semi-hard prick pressing against my crack. He grabbed my shaft and began to pump. "Lean back. That way the camera gets a good shot of your abs and chest. And lift and flex your butt, like I'm fucking you in the ass."

He didn't have to work my uncut rod for long before I was at the finish line. "I'm cumming!" I moaned.

"Yeah, give it to me."

I did. Two volleys of cum rocketed over Leo's shoulder before the next one spattered on his face, chest, and abs. Jizz was everywhere by the time my dick stopped shooting.

"Damn, Tiger, you really did save it up. Now lick it off and feed it to me. Play to the camera." Eating my own jizz was another new experience, but I wasn't about to complain to Leo, so I dutifully set to work and licked virtually every inch of his chest and face before the cameraman cut. Not as gross as I feared.

For Leo's money shot, I was on my back with his big prong hovering over me. I sucked on him for a long spell, concentrating on getting his big shaft all the way down my throat. When he came, he pointed his dick at my face and fired cum rockets. I swear I had cum in my mouth, my nose, and my ears, not to mention the ribbons decorating my face. Leo licked me clean and pointedly fed me blobs of ball juice.

We took a break, enjoying the sun and not bothering to get dressed. Leo and I talked, but when he probed into my background, I intentionally said little. "Trying to forget most of that." Not that I had memories of it in the first place. However, Leo was open about his life. He was twenty-five and would be twenty-six in July. He'd grown up in Ohio, dropped out of college to spend time in India, started a business in Florida and then moved to San Francisco before L.A. He got into porn in 1981 with a scene for J. Brian, a pioneering gay producer. He flip flopped fucked with Jamie Wingo, his lover, in what may have been the only time the camera captured him when his chest wasn't smooth. Both soon were doing other films and Leo had found his calling.

I knew all of that from my crash course in 1983 history, but TPI had been careful not to reveal anything beyond 1983 except for David's story, so I was curious about where Leo was headed and asked what he wanted to do. He was ambitious. He was interested in producing and directing, stage acts and setting up his own company to peddle his porn videos. He said he'd been reluctant at first but now was all in on adult entertainment. The scene we were about to shoot would be his first effort at directing.

Leo got dressed before we resumed shooting but told me to stay naked, lie on my stomach on the blankets as if I was asleep, and not move until he kissed me. "Push that ass up. I want it to be so enticing no man could resist it. Which it pretty much is already." Despite the blankets, my chest was cold, although the bright sun made my back hot an odd, but not uncomfortable combination. The anticipation was causing my cock to get hard again.

Keeping with the theme of *Leo & Lance*, Leo walked shirtless through the woods, his letter jacket slung over his shoulder. I heard him approach and after spotting me, whistle and strip. I didn't move, even after he got on top of me, sliding his stiff boner into my ass crack. My own cock was like a steel rod pressed into the cold snow.

Leo finally kissed me, then spread my legs apart and ate my ass as I moaned happily. He rimmed me for a long time before slipping a finger inside me. I flinched at the intrusion. Fuck. His finger hurt, which did not bode well for what my ass would feel like with nine inches of stiff porn cock inside it.

Leo muttered, "Damn, I've never seen an ass so tight. I'm gonna have to open you up before we fuck."

He rummaged in his backpack for some lube and liberally coated my ass before sticking his finger back inside me. "You gotta relax. Push out like you're taking a shit." My hole began to feel better, at least until he inserted a second finger. I grimaced and was back to start. I hoped Danny was right about the muscle tone of my sphincter, whatever the hell that was, but the early returns were not promising.

I don't recall how long Leo worked to loosen my virgin hole. He finally said, "This is gonna hurt, Tiger, but you're gonna take it because this ass is mine. You owe me after ramming your tool into me the way you did while we were filming. I'll enjoy this!"

Doug resumed shooting, capturing Leo crawling on me, grabbing my shoulders with his hands and prodding my ass with his hard dick. With a thrust, the head of his cock breached my sphincter and invaded my hole. I gasped.

For several long minutes, it was excruciatingly painful as he slowly pressed inside. I grabbed the blanket like I was hanging on for dear life and focused on breathing. *Relax!* He pulled out and started over and for some reason his prick didn't hurt. Recalling our lines from a couple of days ago, I moaned and hissed, "Whip that cock in my ass and fuck it good. Fuck that ass. Fuck it!"

"I plan to. Your hole will never be the same." Leo had no idea how right he was. I was getting fucked. *My first time.*

Leo forced himself all the way inside, taking complete possession of my ass as I whimpered. He began pounding me, pulling all the way out before plunging back in. *Damn.* I couldn't rule out the possibility that the cock inside me felt so good because it was Leo's, but my TPI assignment to get cornholed by every gay man in L.A. was looking better than ever. It might be fabulous.

Leo worked my prostate, getting me close even though I wasn't touching my dick. Danny's alterations were a marvel. We rolled around and tried position after position. Doggy, missionary, side-by-side, standing. I loved them all. Leo liked them, too, growling about how tight my ass was. We didn't take breaks, and I ended the marathon fuck session riding him, but with my back to him. I would have preferred facing him so I could bend down, kiss him and ogle his tight body as I lowered myself onto his rod, but he explained the other way was better because the camera could get both his dick sliding into my hole and my big prong flopping up and down, slapping against my hard abs.

I'd been on the verge of a second climax since Leo popped my cherry and started pumping away. "I'm close," I hissed, thinking he'd want to stop and cool off before fucking some more.

Instead, he panted, "Blow for the camera, hot stuff. Let it fire!" I bounced up and down a couple more times, feeling my climax build, but before I nutted, he clamped his hands on my hips, holding me down as he thrust upward. I leaned back to support myself and his jizz rocketed into my hole. I was stunned. My cock fired moments later. Thick white ribbons of spunk arched upward and fell gracefully onto my abs.

I'd lost my virginity to Leo Ford, and in the course of that he'd fucked the cum out of me, hands-free.

Doug was ecstatic, giving us lots of thumbs up. He'd filmed me backlit by the sun against a dark tree when I shot, and my cum glimmered on film. He caught it turning into a small river and running through my abs. Higgins would have two cum shots to choose from. Maybe he'd use both.

We rolled on our sides and Leo stayed inside me as we snuggled while the cameraman packed up. I was high on sex. Having his cock in me and his arms wrapped around me was heaven.

Back at the parking lot, Leo said casually, "So, uh, some of the guys are getting together at my place later tonight. To celebrate the end of the filming. If you want to drop by, that would be fine."

"Hey, yeah, it sounds great." I was all over the thought of spending more time with him. There was even a reason related to my TPI assignment. Wells mentioned Leo and Reis hustled together, and while Reis knew hustling, I didn't. Leo was the key to opening that world for me.

He gave me a little smirk. "You have an amazing ass. Might as well take advantage of all the work I had do to loosen it up."

The results of the last three days—performing on film successfully, fucking my first ass, taking my first cock, and hearing Leo Ford suggest he wanted an encore—put me on cloud nine. My biggest fears about carrying out my mission had dissipated. In an answer that would define my relationship with Leo, I smiled and quickly replied, "Whatever you say." He raised an eyebrow but grinned back and handed me a scrap of paper with his phone number and address. Another reminder that neither texting nor Google Maps existed yet. "Around nine or so," he said. "Hell, any time before dawn."

I was thrilled, ready to let loose and party.

LIFE'S A (VENICE) BEACH

The late Seventies and early Eighties cars cruising Santa Monica Boulevard were fascinating. Vehicles I thought of as vintage were practically new. I wondered how long it would be before they no longer looked odd to me. SUVs wouldn't come along for another decade, and pickup trucks were small and scarce; California in 1983 was the land of the big, boxy sedan, mixed with the requisite dosage of fancy sports cars.

It was still before sunset and the dinnertime crowds at the gay bars in West Hollywood were sparse. A handful of bored hustlers loitered along the street. They'd be thicker and doing a brisk business later in the evening.

Killing time before Leo's party, I wandered west, through Beverly Hills and up Wilshire Boulevard to the UCLA campus. It was Saturday evening, and I watched students come and go, headed to parties rather than the library. A group of boisterous frat boys walked past, drunk and intent on partying, and one guy gave me a long, hungry stare. I was still getting used to dudes checking me out; in college, it would never have happened. That seemed like ages ago, but it was a year in the past and decades in the future. With a new body, a new cock, and plenty of time on my hands, maybe I'd play with some college men.

A clock tower chimed, jolting me back to reality. *Shit.* I'd lost track of time and ventured way too far west. I had to hustle back to West Hollywood. It wasn't like I could hail a taxicab—I was in L.A., after all. I didn't understand the bus system, and buses didn't run often on Saturday nights. Even jogging part way, I didn't reach Leo's house until the party was well underway.

The house was smallish, and I heard music from halfway down the block. Leo met me at the door. "Nice of you to drop by," he said. "I said by dawn, but I wasn't expecting you to take me at my word."

"Um, sorry, I was, uh, doing something and lost track of time."

Leo gave me a knowing smile. "Ahhh. You look flushed and sweaty. How much did you pocket from the trick?"

I became flustered. Apparently either it was taken for granted guys doing porn hustled on the side or Reis's reputation preceded me. "Uh, the usual," I said. Confirming Leo's assumption was less embarrassing than admitting I got lost on a walk. *Who the hell walks in L.A.?*

"I'm impressed. Most boys wouldn't consider hustling after a porn payday until they were broke again. You must be desperate for money or still horny, but if you're horny after I fucked your ass all afternoon, I'm kinda upset."

"Maybe I'm still horny *because* you fucked my ass all afternoon and I didn't get enough." I added a sly grin for emphasis.

Leo laughed. "I'm glad you're here. It's time to party!" We went inside, and someone handed me a drink. Leo surveyed the room and introduced me to several of the partiers. The crowd was thick with young guys who took their clothes off and fucked in front of the cameras. I recognized three dudes from the final *Leo & Lance* scene filmed at Big Bear earlier in the day while Leo and I were rolling around in the snow.

The partiers looked as out-of-date as the big sedans cruising Santa Monica Boulevard. Way too young, clothes that were "vintage" to my eyes, hair covering their ears, smooth faces. The scruffy three-day-old beard was decades away from being in vogue. There weren't many muscular guys. The young men were slender and somewhat toned, but not what I considered buff or ripped. It apparently wasn't yet trendy for gay boys to hit the gym.

Many guys were smoking—sometimes joints but mostly cigarettes. Getting used to smoke filled rooms might have been the hardest task I faced in the Eighties. The crowd was ready to party. Marijuana and alcohol weren't the only drugs in evidence. Needles and pills weren't hard to find. Getting high was on the menu and getting sex on the agenda. A couple of guys were making out in a corner chair, and I heard two guys balling in a bedroom off the main living room. Either that or a very realistic porn video was playing.

Leo led me through the tiny house into the backyard where a keg rested under an old tree. Away from the pounding dance music, he leaned against the side of the house and handed me a joint. I took a drag and returned it; he sucked it in and passed it back. "You surprised everyone this week."

"How so?"

"Your reputation around town isn't pristine. Missing shoots. Crappy attitude. Drugs. Jail. Telling cameramen to fuck off. Directors too. Trouble with a capital T."

"Oh." I should have left it at that, but I felt compelled to offer an explanation. "Like I told you, I'm trying to clean my act up."

"Whatever you're doing worked. You don't know Higgins, but he was really, really happy with the scene in the A-frame. Your big dick stayed hard as a rock the entire time. Lotta hung guys have a helluva time keeping it stiff. But damn, your leaky tool was like a steel rod. The shoot took half the time it normally would, and Higgins went into it worried you wouldn't even show, or if you did you'd be drunk, strung out, or too much of a jerk to work with."

"Good, I'm pleased." It didn't hurt I knew exactly what Higgins wanted in the final cut. It didn't hurt I was so into Leo.

Leo took a drag. "Today was awesome, too. I'm looking forward to seeing how the film turned out. Your ass was frigging tight, and your cock was rock-hard the entire time I balled you. One in a hundred guys would keep an erection like you did. Damn, your prick was stiff and leaking constantly. I totally loved fucking the cum out of you."

"I loved it too. First time." *First time taking a dick in my ass, too.*

He grinned and groped himself. "So you were into this cock?"

He wanted more than an ego boost; he wanted me to confess that I was hungry for him. I was ready to surrender. "Totally." Leo smiled, and my heart pounded a little harder.

We smoked the rest of the joint. My head was spinning.

"You've got what it takes. Body, cock, looks. Bring the right attitude and a little self-control, and you could be in line for gobs of work if you're interested. They're shooting a ton more stuff this year."

"I'm interested. Can't complain about getting paid to fuck."

"You'd be surprised by how many guys do." He moved closer. "Enough about that. I know you like being paid, but what about fucking for free?"

I smelled alcohol on his breath but didn't think he was drunk. He was putting the move on me, and I was ready. "I'm open to the right offer." I took a gulp of my drink. It was strong.

The gap between closed until his face inches away. Time seemed to stop, and after a moment, he pulled me into a kiss, his tongue exploring my eager mouth. We'd kissed during both porn shoots, but for the camera. Now it was because he wanted to. I enjoyed every second and could have sucked face forever, but he broke away, staring into my eyes. "And what might the right offer look like?"

"Hot guy, big dick's a plus."

"You just described every guy here." He laughed, adding a little sneer.

Hell, I knew where this was headed. We'd end up in bed together, and I'd get my ass fucked again. Leo was hinting, but I'd already put my cards on the table and saw no reason not to go for it. Fuck, I wanted him. "Okay, six feet tall, nine-inch cock, blond hair, smooth chest, nice tan, and a little cleft in the middle of his chin, right here." I touched the cleft in his chin. "A guy who's been around, a little older than me. A guy who's done plenty of porn. A guy who knows how to fuck. A guy who thinks I have a mighty fine ass. A guy who will fuck my brains out." Looking at him defiantly, I downed my drink.

"Darn," Leo deadpanned, shaking his head and stepping back. "Those specs fit only one guy and he's taken. Boyfriend's the jealous type, too."

Fuck! Leo had a boyfriend! I'd forgotten about Jamie. What game was he playing?

He smirked at my crestfallen look. "Jamie and I both hustle and do porn, but he frowns on me playing around unless I'm getting paid. I guess you'll have to be content with a different dick tonight. Or dicks."

I was stunned by the about face. *He'd played me.* But what was I thinking, anyway? I wasn't in the Eighties to sleep with one man. I shrugged. "If you can't have the best, you still can play the game. There's something to be said for quantity along with quality."

Where did that come from? I sounded like a slut.

Leo blinked a couple of times. He wasn't expecting my response. His chuckle almost sounded forced. "I worked a long time to get your tight ass loosened up. No reason all that effort should go to waste."

He hauled me into the house. I was dazed as he called for quiet. The assembled porn stars and hustlers stopped talking and someone turned down the music. The crowd looked at Leo in anticipation.

"Guys! I want you to meet one of L.A.'s newest porn stars. He's gonna be big. Actually he *is* big, but I digress." The crowd snickered. Everyone's eyes were on me. "He's gonna be a great porn star. Everybody, this is David. Onscreen he's Lance. No last name, just Lance. In case you're wondering, he's got the killer combination of nine plus inches that doesn't get soft, and the tightest bubble butt in California. A boy made for sex." He bent to kiss me.

The crowd murmured and someone proposed a toast. A guy handed me a new drink, and I downed it. Leo continued. "Since David is a newbie, he's gonna go through a little initiation. One night only, anybody who wants his sweet ass can enjoy it. He's tonight's party favor. Get him into the sling! The party's just getting started!"

The crowd roared its appreciation. I watched stupidly as a couple of guys pulled off my shirt and jeans. They were reaching for my underwear when Leo stopped them. "Wait, those are mine." He ripped my briefs off as the guys around him hooted and hollered. He sneered as they strapped me into a sling in the corner of the room.

The group milled around, making suggestive comments and feeling me up, but nobody made the first move. Several guys mentioned the size of my dick and others talked about my ass. I felt like a piece of meat.

It didn't take long for the bait to attract a hungry shark. A slender dude I recognized as one of the actors in Leo & Lance stepped up, fisted his tool into an erection and lubed it along with my ass. Someone handed me a joint, which I sucked in greedily. Not one but two bottles of poppers appeared, one under each nostril. I breathed in, my head spinning. He rammed his stiff cock inside me, and I felt some pain but not as bad as I feared. In no time, he was ripping into my ass, moaning about how tight it was.

The dude juiced me, and his cock gave way to another and then another. Periodically someone poured a drink down my throat, stuck a joint in my mouth or shoved poppers under my nose. My ass didn't hurt after the first cock, and I wondered if the combination of booze, poppers, and dope was masking the pain and eventually reality would make an unwelcome appearance and I'd be in anguish. Until that happened, I was in awe of how great it felt, particularly with poppers shoved under my nose.

Every forty minutes or so, the mix blaring from a stereo repeated a Culture Club song that was popular at the time, "Do You Really Want to Hurt Me?" I wondered about Leo. I wondered about the dudes pounding my butt. Man after man stepped up to the sling, slapped my ass and plunged a stiff cock into my sloppy hole, using me as a cum dump.

Leo's party turned into a porn star orgy that in time became legendary. Everywhere guys sucked face, mouthed dick, pounded ass, and got plowed. A steady stream of cheap booze and fat joints flowed, and at some point I passed out. I vaguely remember being unstrapped from the sling and aimed at a bed. I instantly fell asleep.

I woke sometime during the night. I was stuffed between Leo and Jamie, with Jamie's arm in the middle of my back, and Leo's leg on top of me. I was miserable but too tired to move. I faded, drifting back to sleep.

The next time I woke, I was alone. Sunlight streamed through the bedroom window. I found the restroom, took a piss and gulped down a big glass of water. Still dizzy but somewhat revived, I stumbled into the living room. Dirty glasses, empty beer cans, dry popper bottles, and spent cigarette butts were everywhere. Two guys were still asleep, one in the corner under the sling and the other sprawled on the couch. I heard voices in the kitchen.

Leo and Jamie were drinking coffee at a small table. Both were naked, which made me less self-conscious about my own lack of clothes. Leo greeted me with a big smile while Jamie grinned and said, "He's alive." He spanked my bare and, I discovered, very sore ass.

I had a hard time believing what Leo put me through. I halfway wanted to lunge forward, wrap my hands around his throat and ask, "Why the fuck did you do that to me?" I halfway wanted to kiss him, despite his boyfriend sitting next to him. In the end I did neither, merely accepting a cup of coffee and swallowing it, desperate for anything that might make things less fuzzy and reduce the pounding in my head.

"Ready for the beach?" Leo said. His cheerful demeanor suggested he'd recovered far quicker than me. "That's the only way to recover from a big party. Surf and sand. You bring a swimsuit?"

I shook my head, causing the pounding in it to worsen and make me instantly regret the sudden movement. Why Leo would think I'd brought a swimsuit? I didn't even know where the clothes I'd worn the night before were, although I recalled my underwear meeting an untimely end.

"Not to worry, I have an extra that will fit you." Leo reached over and cupped my limp dick. "Might be a little tight around this big boy, though. Let's get rolling."

I would have preferred to nurse myself back to life in a dark, quiet room, but the three of us showered in thirty minutes, and Leo kicked the last two partiers out of the house while collecting the most obvious piles of trash. We crammed into Jamie's convertible. It was a two-seater whose passenger seat was not made to accommodate two nearly-six-foot guys, but Leo and I endured it long enough to reach Venice Beach.

I sat on his lap, and he kept playing with my junk. I wanted to die when we pulled next to a pickup truck at a light and Leo yanked my swimsuit down with both hands, my boner flopping against my stomach. The young woman driving the truck grinned and honked.

"Meet us at the beach!" Leo shouted. I scrambled to stuff myself back inside the swimsuit as Leo's erection pressed against my butt.

It was afternoon by the time we wandered onto the beach. I regretted the sunglasses I'd borrowed weren't darker. I also regretted the swimsuit Leo loaned me was a Speedo. It might as well have been a G-string compared to the knee-length swimsuits I was used to. Leo and Jamie were also wearing them, so I didn't stand out. If anything, Jamie's was skimpier and showed a good chunk of his ass.

We joined a big group prepared with all sorts of food and booze. I was famished, and the food made me feel better. So did the booze, which I turned to reluctantly after discovering the only drinks were alcoholic. I knew I was only postponing the inevitable crash but dozing in the sand with the sun warming my chest, I didn't care.

The yoke of my virginity was behind me, and I relished being around Leo, happy he already considered me a friend and eager to spend more time with him, even if he had offered me up as a party favor the night before. I rationalized that the fuck fest was perfect for my mission. I wished I'd learned more about him during my TPI briefing, but Lois had avoided giving me information after 1983 for fear I'd say something that revealed I knew the future. Of course, whatever future I would have recalled might already have been wiped out and changed forever.

Leo and Jamie knew every gay boy on the beach. Leo introduced me to a bunch of guys, and I gave up trying to remember names. Several acted like they'd fucked me at the party the night before, raving about how tight my ass was but joking that it was too sloppy. I didn't remember them; not surprising. Leo made it sound like we were best buds going way back. The beach boys were hot, and I got plenty of subtle and not-so-subtle offers for sex. Exactly what my mission required. Stoned and drunk, the thought of sleeping with the guys around me was intriguing. As Cody, I would have been an outsider, knowing I wasn't into the scene. As Cody, I wouldn't have seen myself in the same league as the nearly naked boys surrounding me. As Reis, I needed to pretend I was one of them.

I gave out Reis's number half a dozen times and collected scribbled numbers. Dudes made no secret about being interested in my body and getting into my pants, but I couldn't complain. I had the same goal. I was looking for one-night stands, but only if one-hour stands or quickies weren't an option.

Between the night in the sling and the day at the beach, I couldn't have asked for a better jump-start to my TPI mission. I'd covered weeks of ground in one night and had enough leads for easy sex to keep me occupied for weeks. TPI probably owed Leo a finder's fee.

Much later, we left Venice Beach and drove back to West Hollywood, tired, drunk and sunburned. On the spur of the moment, Leo asked Jamie to let us out a few blocks from their house, saying he needed to move after being a slug all day long. I was happy to be alone with him without Jamie around. Jamie wasn't happy, squealing his tires as he pulled away.

"You and me, we're gonna do great things together," Leo said as we strolled up the narrow street, the setting sun throwing long shadows against the apartment buildings and single-family houses. Wearing only Speedos, we were completely out of place. "The last several days were the start of a great relationship." He paused with a slight smile on his face and his back against a big tree. I wanted to lean in and kiss him. He beat me to it, pulling me into an embrace, running his hands slowly down my back until they rested on my glutes and slipping his tongue into my mouth. We kissed passionately, Leo's hands drifting inside my Speedo and kneading my ass cheeks. After the previous night, there was no way I could take his cock, but I wanted him again.

I pulled myself back, breaking the kiss. "We shouldn't be doing this."

I don't know what I expected him to say. I wanted him to laugh and tell me, "Sure we should." I would have melted and let him do whatever he wanted.

"You're right," he said, withdrawing his hands from my Speedo. I felt miserable. His eyes betrayed a little sadness. As we stared at each other, whatever moment that might have existed for us to fall in love vanished.

Leo gave me his trademark grin. "Six blocks back to my place. You better hope I don't pick up a trick, or you'll be walking around in that Speedo all night long. I doubt Jamie will let you in to collect your clothes and keys. I don't think he likes you." He swatted my ass and took off up the street.

DANGERS OF HUSTLING

The lazy afternoon at the beach was the first of many informal, impromptu beach parties. Leo's friends happily accepted me, and I often hung out with them even when Leo wasn't around. I found their free-and-easy approach to sex awkward, but I soon fell into the routine because it was exactly the formula needed to fulfil my mission. I fit in with the crowd: plenty of spare time to hang at the beach, money to spend despite no visible means of support, a willingness to party nonstop and, most importantly, an easy hookup. The crowd thought I had the perfect, idyllic lifestyle. I didn't share their view. I didn't go to the beach to relax. I went to do my job. Still, I counted myself lucky that, unlike many of the beach boys, I wasn't whoring my ass to survive while worrying about starving.

The group's fondness for me was partially due to my role as a reliable source of free marijuana. I had an ample supply due to Reis's dealer, Nico, who forced a fat baggie on me every two weeks. Whenever I thought I'd escaped him, he'd appear with his goons, somehow having tracked me down at a bar or a grocery store or the library. They'd cheerfully escort me to the ATM machine, where he knew a quick three hundred bucks in unmarked bills awaited him, courtesy of the mysterious bank account TPI established and funded several times a week.

He'd take the cash with a big smile and shove some weed and occasionally other drugs at me. I smoked little of Nico's marijuana, instead giving it away. I cheerfully passed out joints but drew the line at anything harder. Whenever he foisted the hard stuff on me, I dispatched it to various trash dumpsters. I was vastly overpaying for dope, but he'd pegged me as an easy mark who couldn't or wouldn't complain. I was convinced he subconsciously sensed I wasn't his old high school buddy, but rather a look-alike faggot who could be easily manipulated.

The beach group was an informal, ever-changing clique of gay boys and hustlers. It was also a recruiting device for porn directors. New kids showed up in L.A. daily, and the first place they inevitably went was to the beaches lining the Pacific. They'd spot the beach group or someone in the group would spot them. The beach regulars were handsome and friendly, and one of them would soon take the newbie under his wing. And, of course, into his bed. Most of the fresh-faced kids were thrilled to sleep with a dude who knew his way around and had been in porn, and some were all over the prospect of shooting porn. Others had reservations, but took the porn path anyway, succumbing to peer group pressure and the lure of easy money.

I did my share of picking off newbies, finding it refreshing to bed a handsome stud before he'd become jaded by tinsel town. I also tried to dissuade some of the kids who didn't have the face, body, or cock to shoot porn and had no business hustling. I was one of the few of the beach boys who was friendly to them, and they were excited a porn star who'd performed with Leo Ford paid attention to them. We'd end up in bed. I wanted to pass the nanocell to them, and they were only too happy to get it on, at least until they contemplated what my huge prick might feel like inside their ass. I was fine bottoming; the odds of successfully transmitting the nanocell were equal either way. I tried to use our newfound intimacy to talk them out of the path they were on. With luck, I'd help them find a legitimate job and point them toward something better with some memories and boasting rights about bedding a porn star, along with a few of TPI's bucks in their pockets, and a shield against AIDS in their blood. I failed more often than I succeeded. Some kids couldn't be dissuaded, accusing me of lecturing and being preachy. Others thought they were in love and would show up at my apartment door again. I took plenty of heat from the beach regulars for my attempts, which mystified them.

Sex was never far from the surface at any gathering of the beach group. Guys talked about their latest porn films, comparing notes on directors, describing on camera fucks, and gossiping about big cocks and slutty whores. Members of the group hooked up regularly. It was taken for granted that sooner or later you'd sleep with everyone.

Most of the boys accepted veiled or blatant offers to fuck for money, no questions asked. A good offer warranted a spur-of-the-moment schedule change, disappearing for an hour or maybe the rest of the day. Johns who were young and handsome might not pay at all. Others paid richly. Money talked.

The boys believed they were selling their youth, looks, and innocence for a pittance on the street and in films. Yet when the pantry was empty, they easily succumbed to the ease with which the cash spigot could be opened in exchange for a few hours on their back. Their bitterness and resentment built in direct proportion to their dependence on sex money.

Sex was the glue that held the group together. Guys who hustled, did porn, slept around, and fucked whoever in the group made a pass were popular, but considered sluts. Those who didn't sleep around were shunned and considered arrogant jerks. Having started with a bang at Leo's party, I was firmly established as a slut, presumed to be an easy lay. I quickly fulfilled that expectation and continually reinforced it. I was an easy fuck, but the more I played the part of a slutty whore, the closer I was to fulfilling the mission's goal.

I got a reputation as a guy who was up for almost any sexual adventure but also as one-and-done. Sleeping with a man a second time wouldn't advance my mission. I overheard two guys talking about me one afternoon at the beach. One guy said, "Don't kid yourself. He's not relationship material. Who knows what he's looking for, but he's looking damn hard. It's weird. He'll hop in bed with a stranger in seconds, but if you've slept with him—and everybody around here has—he's not interested in a repeat engagement. Odd fellow. Lotta guys would love to get into a relationship with him, or even be fuck buddies, but he won't bite."

Without considering it, I'd essentially put my personal life on hold for the duration of my stay in the Eighties. If I were still here years down the road, maybe I'd take it off the back burner, but not before. I was envious of guys in relationships. Jamie and Leo's relationship was by no means a model, but at least they had someone they loved in the house at night. I didn't.

I hung out with Leo whenever the opportunity presented itself. He'd call and tell me he and Jamie were going to the beach, dinner, a movie, or the bars. Sometimes shopping or even to a museum. Occasionally it would be the three of us, but more often two or three other guys Leo or Jamie knew would join us. Frequently we were a group of half a dozen hot, sexy young guys who turned heads wherever we went. We were the in-crowd in West Hollywood, minor celebrities. Not guys you'd bring home to meet your parents, mind you, but guys you'd fuck in a heartbeat if you got the chance.

What I liked about those excursions was being around Leo. I found myself staring at him and watching him while we were out on the town. I'm sure Jamie noticed. He usually wasn't rude to me but was never warm. Leo was intelligent and quite sensitive, and we got lost in discussions about philosophy or sports or politics, you name it. I sometimes wondered if he found me interesting because he viewed me as having an uncanny knack for anticipating the future.

His smarts, charm, and magnetic personality stood out from most of his crowd. We were an odd pair. Leo, loving the limelight and comfortable with his fame, and me, hating the cameras and wanting to get my visit to the Eighties over as soon as possible.

With no day job and plenty of time to kill, I joined a gym on Santa Monica called the Athletic Club. It was cruisy, and the source of an occasional quickie, sometimes in the gym, sometimes in the showers, sometimes in a stairwell, sometimes in an isolated corner of the outdoor pool, often in private tanning rooms. I made regular post-workout trips to guys' beds. After a few months, the gym ceased being a reliable source for new sex partners because I'd had most of the patrons. Still, I enjoyed working out and having something to occupy my day.

Sex in the hedonistic period between Stonewall and the onset of AIDS wasn't hard to find if you made it a priority. I did. I could get picked up in any one of several gay bars in West Hollywood, but that typically involved investing an entire night for a single fuck. Rather than one-night stands, I was interested in something shorter. Half hour hookups readily accepted.

For quick, anonymous sex there was always the alley and parking lot behind a dive bar on Santa Monica called the Gold Coast. Guys called it Vaseline Alley, and by midnight it was turned over to cruising for sex. The crowd tended toward older, rougher-looking men than typical for West Hollywood. For guys drawn to anonymous public sex, Vaseline Alley had an exciting, raw appeal. The men in the bar understood what it meant to be asked if they wanted to get some air.

Another solution was any of several cruisy porn theaters. The routine was simple. Stand in back checking out the patrons until your eyes adjusted. Locate a dude who was hot or at least looked promising. Sit one seat away. If he didn't move, slide into the empty chair so your legs touched. It was decision time for the target. Change seats or it was game on. I didn't refuse overtures and seldom had guys refuse mine. After a while, the men running the theaters recognized me and admitted me for free. I was good for business.

The best option for a night of multiple fucks was one of numerous gay bathhouses—Leo's friends called them the tubs. I hit one or two every month, trying out different areas of L.A. The crowd was younger than you would have thought and included hot guys who could score with ease. For them, the baths were a means to get their rocks off with no commitments and the option of walking away at a moment's notice. Quicker and more efficient than wasting time at the bars. Foreplay and kissing were optional; short circuiting the preliminaries and going directly to a fuck was accepted.

Occasionally groups of friends would go together, but usually the tubs attracted single men hunting on their own. Like the theaters, I got comped after a couple of visits—customers sometimes asked what the crowd looked like before paying to enter. As a young porn star, I was a gold mine. It wasn't every day customers got a chance to fuck with a hot blond boy who'd filmed porn, particularly one who'd take anyone and wouldn't disappear for the night with a hot guy. I made more than a few men's fantasies come true while clocking time for TPI.

Hustling held promise because it permitted several tricks during a night. I casually put out the word I was interested in paying jobs, mentioning my rent boy activities during conversations with the beach boys. Most of the group reacted like I'd revealed the Pope was Catholic. Few shared good prospects. Once again, Leo was my entry. He suggested several of his regular tricks hire me, and whenever a man expressed interest in buying more than one guy, he always called me. He also advertised as an escort in gay magazines in L.A.—escort or masseuse being code for gay male prostitute—and set me up, helping me plan and organize my ads.

Leo charged four hundred dollars an hour, a huge amount in 1983. Supply and demand, he explained. He encouraged me to set a high rate, but money wasn't my object. My goal was to fuck frequently, so I set my rate lower. My ads probably could have read: "Under thirty? Will top or bottom for free." Ironically that would have either turned off potential tricks or been a big warning sign.

The prominent tattoo on my left bicep helped my hustling. Tats weren't that common in the early Eighties, and it gave me a boy-from-the-other-side-of-the-tracks look. Without the tatt, I would have been too pretty, but men took it for granted an inked boy was always on the edge of poverty and needed to fuck for money.

I'd been warned about the perils of hustling during training at TPI, but the risks seemed remote and theoretical until I was taught a painful lesson: always be cautious of who you hook up with. I was killing time on Santa Monica one night, planning to head to a bar later, when a car pulled up and stopped. A man rolled down the passenger window and motioned me over. Three young guys were inside, which should have been my first warning. Picking up a hustler is seldom a group activity.

The dudes didn't inquire about sex and how much it cost in the normal, roundabout way, instead asking if I sucked cock. That should have been my second warning. I answered jauntily, "Yeah, if the money is right." They asked if I took it up the ass. I smirked, "Anything you see is for sale at the right price." I mistakenly chalked up their direct approach to their youth and inexperience.

What should have been my third and final warning was their interest in taking me to a motel room they claimed to have rented. Lulled into complacency by the relative ease with which I'd dropped into West Hollywood's world of free-and-easy gay sex, I figured I'd get in three quick fucks and still make it to the bar by the time boys paired off for the night.

The next thing I knew, I was in the back seat of their car, hurtling into the hills above Hollywood with a switchblade at my neck. Stupid, stupid, stupid.

I pleaded with them to let me go. No dice. I told them I'd suck them off for free. That didn't sway them. I offered three joints I had, which they happily accepted, although they didn't cut me any slack. I offered them my money, which they pocketed along with my wallet and keys. My cash financed a bottle of tequila, which fueled them more.

The threesome found a deserted pull off in the hills and tied my hands behind me so tight I had to wriggle my fingers to keep the blood flowing. Guzzling the tequila and sucking down the joints, they taunted me, calling me a faggot and worse, and generally made it clear that they viewed any guy who sucked cock—or worse, took a dick in the ass—as the lowest form of human life.

Out of desperation, I begged. "I'll get you a big bag of that dynamite dope for free. Let me go, and I won't tell the cops."

"Faggot, what makes you think you're gonna tell anything to anybody after we're done with you?" snarled the driver. He brandished a nasty looking blade, bigger than the switchblade the dude in the backseat had already used to nick my neck and cause blood to trickle down my chest.

Think, Cody, think. I made up a story, hoping it sounded plausible. "If anything happens to me, the cops will be on to you."

"Fucking pigs don't care about shit-eating faggots."

"They don't, normally. But a string of hustlers disappeared recently under mysterious circumstances, and one happened to have a rich daddy. People are saying the cops are clueless and can't solve crimes, and the pigs aren't happy about that. They're paying attention for a change."

Switchblade dude laughed. "Lying sack of shit! You're only trying to save your neck, cocksucker. You're missing one detail. Nobody knows who picked you up."

"Oh, they do. You see, a buddy of mine writes down the license number of every car I get into. I do the same for him. Faggots look out for each other. If I disappear, the cops will come looking for your car. You should have used a stolen one." I hoped they hadn't, or the tale I was concocting would fall apart.

Switchblade gave me a skeptical look, but the driver frowned at the thought of his car being targeted. The third guy, who'd been less aggressive than his buddies, said, "Let him go. Why risk getting into trouble over a worthless cocksucker?"

Switchblade had a ready answer. "'Cuz faggots don't deserve to live."

I doubled down. "They'll trace your car. Word is that the cops want to nail some suspects and pin the whole string of disappearances on them so they can claim they've solved all the crimes. They'll be only too happy to take you off the street. I hear life inside San Quentin isn't pleasant." I was nervous as hell, my heart beating rapidly. My ruse was merely that and might backfire.

The driver glared and bristled when I mentioned the cops framing they for other crimes, confirming he didn't trust the police, an attitude I understood full well after spending time in the gay community in West Hollywood. I pressed whatever advantage that might give me. "Killing me won't do anything except paint a target on you. Let me go. It's not like I'd ever turn you in, not when the cops would rather bust me for hustling than let me file a complaint on another crime they can't solve."

They paused. Maybe my logic was convincing, but more likely they were mellowing out after smoking three joints. It was great stuff.

"Whaddya say you suck my cock?" Switchblade asked, changing the subject and taking a big gulp of tequila. "Then we'll decide what happens to you." He passed the bottle to the others. "Give me some good head, faggot, and *swallow*. Maybe I won't slice your neck."

With my hands tied behind me, I had to walk on my knees to get to the picnic table where Switchblade was sprawled. He pulled his cock from his jeans and I held my breath; he didn't understand the concept of hygiene and the funk of smegma made me gag before I bent forward to lick.

I never got my mouth on his dick. He kneed me in my jaw, catching my tongue in between my teeth, and when my head jerked up, he punched me in the face. I quickly had a mouthful of blood and the gay bashing was on.

The three punks kicked and beat me as I rolled into a ball and tried to protect myself. They got off on pounding me to a pulp so much that they forgot about their knives. I prayed they wouldn't remember them.

Ironically, my blood, which was why TPI targeted me to begin with, saved me. Blood was gushing from my busted tongue and when the driver jerked my head up so switchblade could punch me in the face, it shot out of my mouth.

"Fuck! Get the hell out of here!" They dropped me and within moments were inside the car, peeling out and pelting me with a spray of gravel.

I was panting and in pain. My wrists were still tied, but I struggled to my feet and staggered into the woods nearby, hiding in case the thugs returned to finish the job. When they didn't, I crept down the road to a residential area. I worried about the reception I'd get if I knocked on a door and begged for help, but fortunately a passing motorist alerted the cops. They took me to the emergency room.

I was lucky, if you consider a couple of fractured ribs, an array of colorful bruises, and a face full of stitches lucky. I didn't lose enough blood to require a transfusion, which would have been fatal given my rare blood. I was sidelined for well over a week. Even if I'd been up for it, nobody wanted to have sex with a dude who had a black eye and a body covered with ugly bruises and stiches.

The episode taught me caution. I also realized hustling wasn't the most efficient path for my mission. It made more sense to hire hustlers rather than sell myself; the math was convincing. Better to pass the nanocell to a man who'd have sex with countless other men. Less than fifty percent of men could retransmit the nanocell, but the more promiscuous the men carrying the nanocell were, the better the odds of neutralizing the Alpha Carrier. I spent plenty of TPI's money on boys shopping their wares on Santa Monica or advertising as escorts in the gay rags. They inevitably looked surprised when I opened the door. Men like me didn't normally need them. I was sorely tempted to tell them, "The world needs your help," as I dropped my pants.

CALIFORNIA STUDENT BODIES

Despite gorging on sex, I had way too much time on my hands. Outside occasional quickies at the gym or random pickups on the streets, sex was a nighttime sport and my schedule shifted. I seldom went to sleep before four a.m. or got up before noon. Even with a daily trip to the gym, I was bored. I wasn't into Eighties daytime television, and I didn't have video games or the Internet to entertain me.

I started reading in the West Hollywood library, which had the benefit of a modestly cruisy men's room. I got subscriptions to the *Los Angeles Times* and *The New York Times* and read them daily. Stuffed with advertisements and classifieds, they were fatter and far different than newspapers I knew. I also regularly bought books. Some of my favorite authors weren't writing yet, but I read classics I'd never gotten around to, starting with James Baldwin's *Giovanni's Room* and some Christopher Isherwood. I wondered how Reis would react when he discovered a library he didn't remember filled with books he never read.

I devoted time to trying to track down Lincoln, Uncle Ben's lover. When I hatched the plot to locate him, I didn't appreciate the challenges of finding someone in pre-internet days. Even if I found him, I didn't have a plausible way of seducing him. Convincing myself that I had time—and without any good ideas on how to proceed, short of hiring a private investigator—I worked on the project only sporadically.

Searching for porn jobs was slow going. Although *Leo & Lance* had finished filming, postproduction took a while and marketing and advertising ate up more time, so I wasn't getting offers because of the film. Reis's bad boy reputation preceded me as well. Leo admonished me not to take anything other than good quality projects, stressing I ran the risk of losing out on good films if I did crappy ones. But good opportunities began to appear before long.

My second porn role came courtesy of Aaron Gage, an actor in *Leo & Lance* who was a beach boy regular in Leo's group. He called and told me he'd given my name to the director of a porn video he'd been cast in. Aaron had curly brown hair and an awesome body, maybe on the slender side. He hassled me about getting star billing with Leo in *Leo & Lance*, given I was only in one sex scene while he'd done five guys in three different scenes, but was good natured about it and got over it. We became friends.

Aaron also suggested Rob Montessa to the director. Rob's real name was Gavin Burke, and he'd also been in *Leo & Lance*. Rob was shorter than me and had long, blow-dried brown hair, full lips, and a nice body. Aaron said, "You owe me one if you get this gig, because Rob is one hot little fuck. You'll enjoy his ass. I have every time I've done him."

The director of the new film was Jay Moran, who hadn't done much gay porn and apparently didn't have good leads for porn actors, although even I knew you could get as many porn star wannabes as you wanted during an afternoon at Venice Beach or a night at one of Santa Monica Boulevard's gay bars. Of course, being a good porn actor required more than a handsome face and a big dick. It helped if you could stay hard and not fumble lines with cameras shoved up your ass.

Moran's film was *California Student Bodies*. Reis had been in, and since doing it was consistent with the timeline, I told Moran I wanted in. He was skeptical, but I tried to sound cooperative and eager. He asked about my dick size, and this time I didn't pull any punches, asserting I was long, thick, and uncut. Nine and a half inches of hard meat made for the camera. Moran got more interested. He asked if I knew Rob. Knowing the kid bottomed for Lance in the original *California Student Bodies*, I assured Moran we'd make a great pair onscreen. Aaron's endorsement of Rob's talents made me think fucking him might be hot, which would be a plus because I was still worried how I would perform in front of the cameras if I wasn't paired with Leo.

Rob and I met Moran at his apartment. I wore the same tight polo shirt and jeans Reis wore in the film. I tucked the polo shirt in, which looked strange and felt stranger, but that was the way he dressed, and early on I told myself to get used to it.

Moran knew Rob and I had filmed for Higgins, so he didn't want a screen test. He told us he'd pay us right then to film a scene. The money wasn't great, but Rob eagerly agreed, and I was committed the moment I set foot in 1983. I was surprised by the suddenness of it all, although maybe it was best if I didn't have time to get apprehensive about filming.

The plot centered on Lance inviting Rob over to watch some straight porn. We'd get horny watching, strip, and fuck. I'd top and Rob would bottom, a given due to our porn personas. Memorable plot it was not, but I wasn't there to script doctor.

The set up and the dialogue were bad, too. Both of us were supposedly straight, and I was charged with complaining that my girlfriend wouldn't give me head the way the woman on the video was. After watching for a minute or two, we started feeling each other up, as if that were a perfectly normal thing for two straight boys to do.

Throughout much of our fuck, the dialogue from the straight porn video could be heard in the background. It was even worse than the dialogue Moran gave us. When I watched the original version of *Student Bodies* at TPI, I wondered why the director thought it would be erotic for gay men to see occasional screen shots from a straight porn video, but I didn't risk tinkering with the timeline for artistic purposes. Later, I heard Moran used the straight porn because he thought Reis was straight and it would help him get an erection. Go figure. He ruined a perfectly good scene because of false information.

Rob was a hot piece of ass, and I had no trouble keeping it up. I was relieved and comfortable I was pulling off the porn actor thing after all. Afterward, Moran wanted footage of our faces, me as I supposedly climaxed and Rob as I supposedly fucked him. I remembered the outtakes from the original film. Reis looked intent, like he was cumming, but then cracked up laughing and collapsed on the floor, making it clear he wasn't even having sex. I followed the script, doing the same.

As we left Moran's, Rob punched me on the arm. "That was great. Your dick is fucking amazing."

"Thanks. Your ass is damn hot, too."

Rob stopped and grabbed my arm, licking his lips suggestively. "It's yours anytime you want it. Having your fuck tool inside me made me hungry to get my ass pounded when we won't have to stop for the cameras, and you won't have to pull out for the money shot."

The kid was hot and I liked him. I didn't want to turn him down. However, fucking him again would be a diversion from my mission and wouldn't significantly improve the odds of transmitting the nanoprobe. I made up a flimsy excuse. "That sounds too good of an offer to pass up. But off screen I'm into something different in my sex life, if you know what I mean."

Rob frowned, contemplating the possibilities. "You're into chicks? You're gay-for-pay!?"

I laughed. "No, not that. Only guys do it for me. The thing is, on screen I only top while off screen I'm kinda the opposite."

"You bottom?"

"Yeah. Nothing like a hard cock up your ass."

"You **bottom**?"

"Well, yeah, you said yourself how great it is to have a stiff piece drilling you. Having a big dick doesn't mean I don't like getting it."

Disappointment was evident on his face. "Great," he said. "I meet the guy with the hottest cock in the business, and he's a bottom." I suppressed a laugh that would only have made the rejection sting more.

A week later, Moran asked us to meet the other actors on the UCLA campus to film the backstory. He asked us to wear the same clothes we'd worn for the scene in his apartment and shot a bunch of short takes, mostly guys walking or conversing. Every real college student in 1983 carried a backpack, but none of the actors brought one, so we carried books and clipboards in our hands. It looked more like the Fifties or Sixties.

After UCLA, Moran shot three scenes at a spectacular house in the hills above L.A. It had an amazing pool with a panoramic view and was owned by a man who liked watching live porn and had agreed Moran could use his place to film. Our host invited the actors to stay and enjoy the pool after the shoot and offered free beer and burgers. Half the cast high fived. Amazing how happy twentysomething dudes got over the prospect of a free beer. I suppose a paycheck for fucking didn't hurt their mood either.

The filming took most of the day because Moran shot over and over. He'd take a break from one scene to start on another and then go back to the first one. It made for a mystifying video because guys would disappear from the action only to reappear later. One moment an actor would climb from the pool dripping wet, and in the next frame he'd be completely dry. We had to get hard repeatedly as Moran took breaks, and the film was low budget enough not to have fluffers.

I filmed a three-way in and around the pool with a young black man, Cory Jacobson, and an older blond dude, Mike Skrzypcak, who used the stage name Erik Stryker although he'd been Mike Kelly and Noel Kemp in other skin flicks. He was almost thirty and was muscular and handsome, with stark tan lines. In contrast, Cory was skinny but had the requisite big dick. He and I hit it off and joked around when we weren't filming. By the time Moran called it quits, all three of us were drenched in sweat from fucking in the sun.

After the filming was complete, the cast hit the pool. Some hadn't brought swimsuits, but that was merely an excuse to skinny dip. Soon, we were all naked.

The owner was older but tall and quite attractive. He looked familiar, but I couldn't place him. The rest of the guys had no difficulty.

"That's fucking Rock Hudson!" Aaron said excitedly. I recognized the name but wouldn't have identified him. I vaguely recalled Wells saying Reis might have been involved with him. A full history lesson on Hudson would have to wait until I got to the library—the internet would have been damn convenient—but I gathered enough information from the other guys to fill in the basics. The man was a Hollywood icon.

The food and beer arrived, and the assembled porn stars climbed from the pool, toweling off but remaining naked. Hudson came down and talked to several guys. He announced the party didn't have an end time and everyone was free to invite friends. "As long as they're hot and horny," he laughed. I noticed he talked to Mike for a long spell but didn't think too much about it at the time.

We wolfed down burgers, and beer started flowing freely. Cory came over to me and gave me a hug. "I'm taking off."

"Why not stay? Might be a fun night."

Cory looked around and shrugged. "You're the only guy who wants me here. You're color-blind. Which is a good thing. The rest of them aren't. Besides, a white boys' party isn't my style." He grinned. "In this neighborhood, if they find a black man after dark who isn't cleaning or cooking, they beat him senseless, lock him up and throw away the keys."

I liked Cory better than any of the other actors and tried to talk him into staying. He didn't budge.

"Why not split with me? You owe me a go at your white ass after you nailed me today. I'd love to collect. Plus, a couple of my bros been asking me to introduce them to a hot, white porn star."

I was sorely tempted; the alternative was hanging by the pool and playing with the porn stars and other boys who were already arriving, ready to party. The sex agenda at the pool was perfect for my TPI mission, but hanging with Cory would be fun, and there was another appeal. During one of the breaks in filming, he mentioned a buddy in the Marines. I hadn't made progress in my search for Lincoln, and Cory's friend might be a lead.

Before I found my clothes, a tall, muscular man interrupted us. He was dressed in white uniform consisting of a pair of creased shorts and a crisp, collared shirt with epaulets that made his broad shoulders look massive. "Mr. Hudson would like a word with you, Mr. Reis. If you don't mind. No need to put on your swimsuit." The man didn't like me, for whatever reason.

Cory understood, before me, that you didn't say no to Rock Hudson. "Later man," he said, heading out.

The man who summoned me was in his late twenties, with striking blue eyes and blond hair cropped short rather than over his ears like most guys. His biceps stretched his shirt sleeves, and his thickly veined forearms were huge. He was starkly handsome in a rugged, don't-cross-me sort of way, far different from the beach boys around the pool. I followed him through the house to an outside deck with a great view of the action where Hudson waited. Even at close to sixty he was incredibly handsome. He towered over me, and I felt awkward shaking his hand while stark naked.

"Sit down, son," he said. He had a deep, commanding voice and continued to stand after I sat. "I'll get right to the point so you can go back to the party. I'm a fan of your work. Bill Higgins brought by a copy of *Leo & Lance* before it was released, and I was impressed. From the looks of things today, Moran has some great footage of you. Whether any of it gets into the movie is the question. Most of the good stuff will probably end on the cutting room floor, but that's a different issue.

"I'd like you to spend the night. Not tonight, too much going on. Next Friday." Hudson gestured toward the young man who had summoned me. "Dmitri will pick you up at seven. We'll have dinner, and after that...well, you weren't born yesterday. You'll find it lucrative."

Hudson wasn't asking if I was free and wanted to sleep with him on Friday, he was telling me I was booked. Understandable. Who wouldn't jump at an evening with Rock Hudson? He assumed I'd go to bed with him. Perhaps he knew I hustled or simply took it for granted no porn boy would forego a payday for hooking up with a big movie star.

I wasn't certain where things would lead, but I had to find out. I nodded. "Yes, sir. I'd be delighted." My voice sounded higher than normal.

Hudson took my answer for granted. It had been a long time since he'd been turned down, if ever. "Depending on how Friday goes, I may have other opportunities for you. We'll see. Now, go back to the party. Have fun." I'd been dismissed.

Walking back through the house, I was lost in thought when Dmitri grabbed my arm, spun me around, and pushed me against a wall. He clamped a massive hand around my throat. I was overmatched. Instead of chancing it, I quickly concluded not resisting was the best approach.

"Listen, pretty boy, I've got a good gig here. Incredibly good. I don't intend for a blond airhead with a tattoo and a big dick to screw it up. You're hired as the entertainment next week but don't get any ideas about *anything* more."

Wow. Dmitri was threatened by me and worried about his job. What I did next was solely instinct, based on little more than the man's appearance and the haughty way he carried himself when Hudson wasn't around. In one motion, I dropped to my knees, slid his shorts and underwear to his ankles, and swallowed his cock.

He was not sized to be a porn star. I looked up to find a shocked look on his face as I began sucking. "What the fuck are you doing?"

In between mouthfuls of cock, I mumbled, "Men like you take what they want. A boy like me knows better than to fight it."

Dmitri's dick was responding. "Fuck," he gasped. Either he was horny and liked getting head or was turned on by a blond boy submitting to him. I suspected both. He didn't take long to climax. He slammed my head against the wall, face-fucking me and growling. "Fucking cocksucking motherfucker, swallow my cum!"

Dmitri's cock may not have been big but his load was. He flooded my mouth and shuddered as I gulped jizz. I licked the last bit of cum from his dick but stayed on my knees, his spent cock dangling above my face.

He slapped his dick against my cheeks and I said, "I'm a born cocksucker, and I'm not looking for a promotion."

"Good. We understand each other." A look of satisfaction crossed his face, but there was something else, too. I'd confessed I was a cocksucker and demonstrated I was docile. In his world, cocksuckers weren't threats. By going down on him, I made him more of a man and that was important to his ego. Hudson probably topped him all the time, and the young tough endured it with buried rage.

In a short span, I'd gone from a possible threat to a non-threat he could control and manipulate. He *could* be an ally, albeit not a friend. I took a stab at it. I reached for his spent cock, gazing at him like I was still hungry for it, and kissed it. "Giving certain men what they want is smart, because they'll take it anyway. Take whatever you want from me."

He gave me a satisfied smirk and pulled me to my feet. Staring into my eyes, he laughed. "Get the fuck out of here and back to your party." Blinking in the bright sunlight after Hudson's dark house, I was shell-shocked, although I wasn't sure whether Hudson or Dmitri had affected me more.

I grabbed a beer and a joint and slowly relaxed. New faces appeared and joined the mostly naked party, beer disappeared rapidly, and the smell of marijuana drifted through the heavy night air. A few pills were shared. I didn't see needles, but guys would have sought privacy for those.

I sought out Mike. "I saw you talking to Hudson."

He smiled. "Let's just say the man of the house had a business proposition I accepted on the spot."

"You're kidding," I replied, feigning surprise. "What happened?"

"Gave up my ass, again." Mike smirked, downing his beer and grabbing another one. "Consider yourself honored. You were the warm-up act for Rock Hudson. He threw me on the bed and rode my sorry ass for what must have been an hour. Between taking you, Cory and him, my hole is so fucking sore I'm not gonna bottom for a week!"

"Sounds hotter than hell."

"Old guys don't do it for me, but if you're gonna do one, Hudson is as good as it gets. Paid well, too. He has a thing for beefy blonds with smooth chests. You better watch out."

"Hell, bring it on!"

Mike shook his head and frowned. "I'm in this for the money. I'm not a horny teenager any longer. You act like you love this stuff. Like you'd do it for free. That'll change."

At least the image I wanted to project was coming through. Still, Mike's comment raised the specter that my assignment would get old fast. It already was, despite having only been in the Eighties for a few months.

I surveyed the pool scene, which was rapidly devolving into a gay orgy. With luck, I'd pass the nanocell to the Alpha Carrier, although I halfway hoped I wouldn't finish my mission immediately. If I did, TPI would pull me out, and I'd miss sleeping with Hollywood royalty.

HOLLYWOOD ROYALTY

On Friday Dmitri picked me up as scheduled. He knocked on my apartment door, took one look at my clothes and shook his head, exhaling, "We need better than this, boy."

He surveyed my closet but predictably was not impressed. Reis was not a clothes hound. Dmitri ferreted out the only dress clothes in the apartment—a navy sports jacket and a pair of charcoal gray pants along with a passable white dress shirt. He paused, however, when he spotted a pair of baby blue shorts on a shelf in the closet. "Are these the shorts you wore in the jack-off porno in the dunes?"

It took me a moment to grasp what he was talking about. Reis filmed the scene in *Good Times Coming* before he and I exchanged places. I'd watched it at TPI so many times that I knew they were the same shorts. I nodded.

"They still fit?"

"Um, I think so."

"Try 'em on."

Embarrassed, I pulled my pants off and started to slither into the shorts. Dmitri stopped me. "No underwear." It felt oddly awkward stripping in front of him even though I'd been stark naked the first time we met.

The shorts were so tiny that my junk slipped through the leg hole. "Perfect," he said dryly. "Put your pants on over these. After dinner, excuse yourself, go to the restroom and come back to the table wearing only these. No shirt, no shoes, only these."

So much for no shirts, no shoes, no service. "You sure?"

In an instant, he slapped my face hard, making it sting. His round, Slavic face was dark as he scowled and clenched his jaws. "Of course, asshole!" I made a mental note not to question him again. In the future, I'd blindly do whatever the tall, tightly wound box of muscles wanted.

His angry glare faded. "Hudson loves that scene. Plays it over and over. Had me put it on last night. He'll go crazy when he sees you in these."

I pulled the dress pants on over shorts, skeptical about Dmitri's plan but resigned to follow it. Happily, he became friendlier after his outburst, as if we were long time buds. He gave me pointers on things Hudson liked, including pointing to a choker made of white shells that he spotted on Reis's dresser and instructing me to wear it. Perhaps the blowjob I'd given him was paying dividends.

As he walked me through Hudson's house, Dmitri stopped, frowned slightly, and unbuttoned the top four buttons on my dress shirt, exposing my bare chest. He nodded with satisfaction. "That's the right look for the old man."

Hustlers often complained about sex with old guys, but I found Hudson intriguing. Dinner, served by the pool, was elegant. He talked about Hollywood but seemed genuinely interested in me. I dutifully recited the sparse details I had about Reis's life, sensing Hudson had heard similar tales of woe on countless occasions. I wasn't the first young street boy to grace his bed. Not wanting to spend more time than necessary discussing an assumed identity I knew little about, I directed the conversation to Hollywood whenever possible. Rock happily talked about old icons, from James Dean to Marlon Brando to Liz Taylor. Dead legends for me, personal friends for him.

I got around to asking about Dmitri. He only stayed at the house when Hudson had overnight guests. It probably made sense as a security precaution. He was married to the daughter of Hudson's long-time housekeeper, although it was a marriage of convenience. It allowed him to live in the U.S. after escaping Russia under mysterious circumstances. He was either a KGB agent or a KGB target, although I suspected every Russian fit into one of those categories.

The Russian muscle man had changed from the uniform he wore when picking me up into his white shorts and collared shirt, and he looked damn hot in it. As he brought after-dinner drinks, he cleared his throat. "If the gentleman needs to excuse himself, there's a restroom inside the cabana." He gave me a scowl. I'd forgotten to change clothes.

I was apprehensive about disrobing, but Dmitri left no doubt about what I was to do, following me into the restroom and ordering me out of my clothes. "You're sure about this?" I asked again, immediately kicking myself mentally for breaking my rule about not questioning him.

At least this time I avoided a stinging slap. "I know the old man. Trust me. Don't worry if your dong slips out of the leg hole. Act like it's totally natural." He paused, inspecting me. "Actually, make sure it slips out. Apologize that it keeps doing it."

Nervous as hell, I returned to the table. Hudson greeted me with a big smile, which put me at ease. "Well, well, well. I was talking to Dmitri about these blue shorts last night." Before I sat down, he cupped my cock and balls, which predictably found the leg hole. He stared at my body with a mixture of lust and excitement. Dmitri's plan had been spot-on.

We never finished the after-dinner drinks, although I'd downed enough already that I didn't need mine. Hudson fondled my junk through the leg hole of the shorts, then went down on me, quickly bringing my tool to full mast. He pulled the shorts off and suggested I *might* enjoy a skinny dip in his pool. I dove in, fisted my cock to make sure it stayed erect, and stepped out the pool dripping wet and with my big uncut tool pointing to the stars. He was damn happy, directing me toward the bedroom without bothering with a towel.

Once there, he let me strip him and was delighted that I stayed erect. I suspected his other tricks didn't always pull that off, but the boner Hudson gave me at the table after dinner never disappeared.

Hudson told me he didn't bottom but was making an exception for my big ten-incher because it wasn't often he got an opportunity to ride on a cock that big. I didn't correct him on my size. It rounded up to ten.

For a guy who didn't bottom, the Hollywood legend gave every indication of loving it, blowing his load on his stomach. Lounging in bed afterward, I wondered if I was spending the night, but Hudson was in no hurry to dispatch me. He ran his hands over my body, and predictably I popped a boner. He told me he loved how I was perpetually hard and stroked me until I sprayed another load on my chest and abs. He played with it, smearing it over my skin and sticking his cum-coated fingers into my mouth. It wasn't long before he stuck a cummy finger into my butt and asked me if I liked it. Only an idiot would have said no. I rolled on my stomach, thrust my ass upward and begged him to fuck me.

It took him a while to get hard enough to enter me, but once he was inside, he punished my ass. "This is what Bill Higgins should film," he growled in my ear. "A stud like you with your big cock flopping around while his Daddy fucks his brains out."

Hudson enjoyed himself but was only good for the two rounds. That was probably one more than normal for him, but then, he was close to sixty.

Late in the night, I was awakened by the sound of someone entering the bedroom. Hudson was sound asleep on his back, and I was flat on my stomach. I'd barely turned my head to investigate when I felt Dmitri on top of me. He smelled of alcohol and was drunk, slurring his words.

"Yeah, pretty boy," he snarled. "I've had my eye on your incredible ass since the pool party. I shudda fucked it when you blew me that night. I shudda fucked it when you wriggled into those shorts in your apartment. You wanted it then and you want it now. When you sucked me, you said a man like me takes what he wants. You're right. Your ass is what I want and what I'm taking."

He put his full weight on top of me and kept my head pressed into the pillow with a hard forearm pressed across the back of my neck. He pulled his sweats down to free his hard cock, sliding it into my ass crack.

"Shouldn't we go someplace else?" I whispered. "What happens if he wakes up?"

"Notta chance. The drug cocktail he takes every night means he's dead to the world. You kept him up a helluva lot longer than usual. Kept me waiting, too. You're not going anyplace. You're right where I want you." He spread my legs and began to probe for my hole with his hard tool, keeping me pinned to the bed.

I didn't have a problem letting him fuck me. If anything, I owed him for his tips about Hudson and besides, maybe he was the Alpha Carrier. But he wanted more than merely the use of my hole. He wanted to dominate me, and I needed to the play the part. "Don't hurt me," I whined. "I'll do whatever you want."

He laughed harshly. "Play nice and you won't get hurt. Except your asshole. Rock tear your pussy up with his dick? Ha! You think that was bad, I'm about to fuck you so hard, you won't be able to walk for a week." He jammed his dick into me with a brutal thrust.

With my ass lubed and stretched from the lengthy fuck I'd taken from Hudson, Dmitri's prick didn't hurt at all, so I faked it, crying out. He laughed and started pounding me. "Take it, you slut. Take my big dick. You know something? You're never telling a soul I raped your faggot ass. If you breathe a word of this, you'll pay over and over."

Dmitri apparently had rape fantasies, but this wasn't rape. I was a willing victim and it never crossed my mind to say no. However, forcing, controlling and dominating me was part of the allure for him, so I gave him what he wanted. "I won't say anything. I know you'd make it worse for me."

"Damn right I will. I'm glad we understand each other. I'll do this anytime I want and you'll never say a word. I own your faggot ass." I moaned in a high-pitched whine.

The guy shot quickly when I sucked him off, but not this time. He was drunk and probably high, so it wasn't a quick fuck. When he climaxed, he was panting and sweaty. He collapsed on my back and was out a few moments later.

Feeling crushed by the weight of the muscle stud's body, I eased out from under him and tugged him down the hallway. Fortunately, his bedroom was close, and I didn't have to deal with stairs. I rolled him into his bed, took off his shoes, and returned to Hudson's bed. The tall actor hadn't stirred.

The next morning, Hudson was cheery while Dmitri was sullen. I suspected the Russian stud had enjoyed too much vodka before using my ass as a chaser. Hudson and I ate a leisurely breakfast by the pool. I did another skinny dip before we ate and never got dressed. He sucked me off again and handed me an envelope with a wad of bills before summoning Dmitri to haul me home. He told me he'd like to keep the blue shorts and had included an extra $100 to pay for them. I would have given them to him for nothing. David?— maybe not.

My tryout with Hudson was a success. While he only invited me to share his bed irregularly after that, he started taking me to big parties populated with Hollywood movie stars and moguls. The first time, Dmitri arrived to pick me up with a shopping bag of expensive new clothes. He afforded me no privacy as I dressed, watching the entire time like a fox. He carefully checked the fit on the clothes and ordered me to take off my underwear. When I protested that the outline of my junk would show underneath the tight pants, he deadpanned, "Surely you understand that's the point." When I pulled the pants back on, he grabbed my junk in a painful squeeze and announced the clothes were perfect.

He didn't suggest a repeat of our liaison in Hudson's bed. I wondered if he even remembered it. He showed none of the signs of the aggressive man who'd been intent on dominating me. Go figure.

Dmitri dropped us off at a spectacular mansion. Two tall, handsome waiters met us at the door. They could have been, and likely were, models. They were dressed as Roman soldiers, in gold helmets with big red plumes. Besides the helmets, they wore only sandals strapped up to their knees and a broad leather belt adorned with dangling leather bands that did an intentionally poor job of concealing their junk. Their torsos were bare, and they were painted from head to toe in metallic gold. I stared as Hudson took drinks from one of the soldiers he either knew or wanted to know and handed one to me.

Rock knew all of the guests. We slowly walked through the house to a broad terrace overlooking a spectacular pool and yard decorated for the occasion with Roman banners. We descended a wide, circular staircase and every eye was fixed on us. I guess that was the point of a grand entrance.

I hadn't been certain whether I was Hudson's date or merely eye candy. However, it soon became clear I was part of the entertainment. Once in the yard, Hudson whispered to me. "I'll pay my respects and show the flag. Mingle and enjoy yourself, David. Dmitri will find you when I'm ready to leave. Be careful and don't drink too much or accept drugs other than marijuana."

He paused and unbuttoned the top two buttons on my shirt, exposing my bare chest. He studied his work and undid two more buttons. Exactly the look Dmitri had given me before I had dinner with him. He smiled contentedly. "A boy like you should always show skin. Plenty. Enough to be unexpectedly and blatantly sexy. Enough so everyone knows you'll expose more for the asking. Enough to reveal you're a package that can be unwrapped with minimal effort and enjoyed all night long."

He gazed at me as if he were seeing me for the first time. "You won't stay wrapped long tonight. Everyone knows you've been bought and paid for. You're available to any man who wants you. Keep your head on your shoulders. If you perform the way I know you can, you'll get other opportunities to make a dime. Remember, 'no' is a bad word with this crowd. In fact, you'd best forget that word for tonight. You're bright enough to understand that." He gave me a peck on the cheek and disappeared into the crowd.

I stood by myself, drink in hand, not quite believing either Hudson's speech or the extravagant scene. At least twenty gorgeous Roman soldiers were milling around, serving drinks and hors d'oeuvres with bare asses and dangling dicks, shielded only by a few straps of leather. I took a second drink from a tall, muscular soldier, who gave me a devious smile and a long, lingering look. I would have gotten it on with him in an instant, but he wasn't on the menu.

The party was all about free-and-easy-fucking. Sex on demand. That aspect was ideal for my mission, and I didn't wait long for the first taker to appear. A curly-haired young man with a British accent came up behind me and wrapped his arms around my chest, sliding his hands inside my unbuttoned shirt and tweaking my nipples. He nuzzled my neck as he slipped a hand into my pants and closed it around my cock. "Mate, when I saw this inside your pants, I didn't think it could be real. Now that I know it is, I'm going to see how much damage it can do to my arse."

The dude was a figure skater who'd won gold at the 1976 Olympics. He was thirty-three but still had a tight, slender body and awesome thighs and glutes. I assumed most of the men hunting for sex would be Hudson's age, so I was moderately surprised by the turn of events. He liked it rough, but I was there to please.

Spending the night between the skater's wonderful legs would have been great, but that wasn't the agenda. By the time Dmitri located me, I was face down and ass up in one of the mansion's bedrooms. A movie mogul who'd done me was watching several of his boy toys take turns with me. I'd spent much of the night hard at work on my mission.

The crowd had thinned significantly as Dmitri steered me to the front door, where Hudson was saying goodbye to a middle-aged man I took to be our host. Once in the back seat of the car, Hudson patted my leg. "You did fine, David. It's refreshing you're so eager and excited. I like a boy who doesn't have hang ups about sex. I like that about you a lot."

"Thanks, sir. I really appreciate that."

"I must say, a boy who stays rock hard for hours, even after he's blown several loads and gotten fucked over and over, is a true find." His hand crept up the inside of my thigh and fondled my junk. Predictably, my tool responded with a happy lurch.

But rather than pulling my dick out of my pants, he wanted to talk. "I saw you speaking with Vladimir Pavlov. Did he propose anything?"

A tall, harsh looking man had introduced himself as Vlad but didn't give his full name. "He said he's planning an expensive porn movie and he wants to cast me in it." He'd suggested it would be a hugely lucrative payday for me. Unlike every other porn actor, I wasn't in it for the money, but the offer was flattering and given my assignment, not something I would turn down.

"You agreed to do it?"

"Yes." It seemed like a no-brainer.

"You'll politely and respectfully decline. I know I told you at the beginning of the night that saying 'no' shouldn't be an option, but there's an exception to every rule. Vladimir Pavlov is the exception to this one. While I like your unbridled embrace of sex, he's dangerous. Extremely dangerous. His taste in sex runs to the sadistic, and I'm putting it mildly. You'll stay away from him." I had no desire to get into serious BDSM so it was easy enough to agree. The episode was a reminder that hustling and filming porn was on the fringe and potentially risky.

I was still hard when we arrived at Hudson's mansion, which everyone called the Castle even though it was a sprawling Mediterranean and didn't much resemble a castle. I expected to accompany him to bed, but all he did was kiss me. "Dmitri will take you home. Enjoy the evening." It was close to dawn, so there wasn't much to enjoy. I was somewhat disappointed, although Hudson seemed happy with me. Maybe he was tired, or he'd played with some of the other entertainment while I was spreading nanocells far and wide.

On the way to Reis's apartment, Dmitri administered the final fuck of my night. He stopped the car in a deserted pull out in the hills, climbed into the back seat and shoved my head into his crotch. "You didn't think you'd get away without taking care of my cock, did you boy?"

"No, sir." It didn't take much mouth work to get him hard; he was pre-cumming like crazy. I wondered whether he wanted a blow job or my ass, but when he grabbed my butt with his big hands, kneading my glutes, and I knew the answer. It wasn't long before he was inside me, and as he pounded me he hissed "I own you, bitch. Don't ever forget that."

I grunted an affirmative answer, not realizing at the time his statement was a forecast of the future.

LIVE ON STAGE

A month after the Roman soldier party, Dmitri left a message on Reis's ancient answering machine instructing me to meet him for a late lunch at a popular, expensive place off Santa Monica Boulevard that boasted a big outdoor patio. It was breakfast for me; I seldom got up before noon. Dmitri ordered vodka martinis for both of us. A martini wasn't my normal breakfast beverage and my head was spinning even before he ordered refills.

Dmitri handed me a package wrapped in brown paper. "That's a porn video, *Roommates*. Mr. Hudson is fond of it. He's staging a private reenactment of the main scene. You'll be working with Kip Noll because the other actor in the original, Lee Marlin, hasn't done porn for a year and nobody knows where he is. Mr. Hudson decided you'd be good in his role. Study the video and be prepared to follow the original action as closely as possible."

Pausing to sip his drink, he gave me a knowing sneer. "Marlin bottoms for Noll. Twice. We both know you're quite accomplished in taking dick, but it may be an eye-opener for the audience. Another thing. Don't cut your hair. The reenactment will be in three weeks, and as you'll see, Marlin had long brown hair, to the bottom of his ears. Dye your hair dark to match."

Kip Noll was a gay porn legend. He reached that lofty status courtesy of late Seventies and early Eighties flicks directed by Higgins, including *The Boys of Venice* and *Pacific Coast Highway*. He had the classic California surfer look: lean muscles, smooth skin, and shaggy hair. And, of course, a big dick. In front of the cameras, he fucked with a frantic energy.

I wasn't too keen on the idea of staging a live sex performance. With a porn video the only audience was the director and the crew. This would be different. "So, um, you said this would be for an audience?"

Dmitri sensed my hesitation, but he wasn't buying it. He glared. "Hudson's private theater is small. It holds twenty, although the last time we did a reenactment, another ten or fifteen men stood in the back. All you gotta do is suck off Noll, let him fuck your ass—twice—and blow a couple loads of your own. Pretty much a night like any other for you. Or an afternoon." The muscle-bound Russian leered at me, and I wondered if his statement was an announcement of what he'd planned for my afternoon. "Lotta guys would love to swing on Noll's big cock. They'd do it for free."

He had a point.

Our lunch arrived, and I noticed Nico and a couple of his cronies across the street, watching me. Fuck. He wanted his three-hundred-dollar payday and had spotted me at the restaurant. I never understood how he discovered where I was, but he could be counted on to appear like clockwork every two weeks. I was a guaranteed paycheck for him.

Dmitri saw me looking at Nico and peered at the dealer. Frowning, he looked back at me with fury. "What the hell are you doing, dealing with that scum? Are you fucking crazy?"

I had no ready response. Reis had been connected with Nico, and I'd only gone along for the ride. "I-I knew him in high school."

"Even more reason you should know better. You're a fucking idiot." He disappeared for several minutes. Shortly after he returned, two beefy-looking men appeared and confronted Nico and his men. I couldn't hear the conversation, but from his body language, Nico was apologetic. He and his crew soon disappeared.

"From now on, I'll supply your marijuana," Dmitri said sternly. "You're off anything hard, effective immediately. If I catch you touching that stuff, you'll wish you'd never sucked your first cock. Nico won't bother you, but if I find you trying to contact him, you'll pay. It won't be pleasant. Do I make myself clear?"

I nodded dumbly.

Dmitri shook his head and exhaled. "Fucking blond airhead."

To my relief, it was the last time I saw Nico. I wondered, however, if I'd gotten myself into a deeper hole. I also wondered if Hudson knew about Dmitri's side business of peddling weed. True to his word, Dmitri delivered a fat baggie of dynamite dope every couple of weeks. He never asked for money in return. I was expected to pay in other ways.

After downing three martinis, I was beyond tipsy when I stumbled back to my apartment. I opened Dmitri's package, and Kip Noll stared at me from the cover.

I'd seen the photo before, although I couldn't place when or where. The image was iconic. Kip was shirtless, wearing a satin yellow letter jacket trimmed in dark blue that had Waipahu High written on the back. His shaggy hair was parted in the middle and fell over his ears. He had a serious expression on his face, his thick, pouty lips pursed. I fired up Reis's VCR player, ironically doing what I'd done at TPI—studying a porn video so I could mimic an actor.

As usual, the video quality was poor, and the plot was minimal. The real star was the famous letter jacket. Kip wore it in a solo scene at the beginning and another kid wore it in a solo at the end. In between, Kip and Marlin went through a box of Kip's stuff and Kip discovered the jacket, tried it on, and soon they were fondling each other's cocks.

The video was obviously filmed at different times. Kip had distinct tan lines at his waist and halfway up his thighs in his solo, while his skin was white in the scene with Marlin. Even that scene must have been filmed on several occasions, because Kip came three times with barely a break: once on Marlin's face, once on his back, and the final time in his ass. Marlin shot twice. I wondered how Kip would pull off three climaxes in our reenactment. I also wondered how I would pull off taking Kip's piece, which was mammoth.

Three weeks later Dmitri picked me up early, and I was surprised to find Noll in the back seat. We'd been told to come in costume, which for me meant only a pair of jeans. I wore a shirt as well because it felt wrong to show up at the Castle half-dressed. Kip wasn't as modest. He was bare-chested and wore what looked like the same tiny, frayed jean cutoffs he'd worn in the movie. They were unable to contain his junk. His soft cock and balls periodically made an appearance through the leg hole.

Kip acted like nothing was unusual. He introduced himself and we talked, chatting about movies and music. *Return of the Jedi* had been released several months earlier and we were both fans. He was eagerly awaiting the next *Star Wars* films, and I stifled the urge to warn him the next three wouldn't start appearing for sixteen years and would be generally regarded as disappointing, although the final three were better.

At the Castle, Hudson showed us the theater and produced the famous letter jacket, which he'd bought from the studio after *Roommates* was released. His interest in David's blue shorts now made sense. Kip smiled as he pulled on the jacket. Despite the passage of four years, he looked like he stepped out of the film. I'd dyed my hair brown and it hung to the bottom of my ears, but nobody would mistake me for Marlin. I was leaner and more muscular, couldn't match his sideburns, and was marked by Reis's tattoo.

We hung out before the guests arrived, and Kip talked about doing live shows at a gay theater in New York called Follies. "Money's better than shooting porn, but it's the porn that brings men to the shows. You could do shows now that Leo & Lance is out, but you should do some more porn first so everybody recognizes your name. All you do is dance on stage and keep an erection. No climaxes, though. That can get you in trouble. Go down into the crowd, let 'em kiss you and feel it. There's always a rich daddy or two who'll pay for it after the show, so if you're into that, you can get a double payday." He unexpectedly leaned over and kissed me, shoving his tongue into my mouth. Breaking the kiss, he laughed. "Yeah, you're into that stuff. With a cock and an ass like yours, you might as well sell 'em both." He planted another big kiss on my lips, slipping his hand onto my package.

Dmitri interrupted us. "The guests are arriving, so save that for later, girls. Mingle and show those happy faces. No booze until after you perform." He glared at me. "You're parading the goods in costume, pretty boy, so lose the shirt." Kip, in his satin letter jacket and frayed cutoffs, was ready to go.

By the time the show started, virtually every man at the party had pawed Kip's junk. It easily dropped through the leg hole of his cutoffs, and Kip did nothing to discourage the focus on his equipment. With mine stuffed in my jeans, I got less attention, although plenty of guys wanted to run their hands over my pecs and abs and feel up my ass. I might as well have been an animal in a petting zoo.

I was worried enough about taking Kip's big prong in front of the crowd that I'd loosened my asshole before Dmitri picked me up. I had no illusions Kip would go easy on my ass. I'd watched a couple of his videos, and he fucked like a mad man.

The theater was packed. Dmitri showed the video clip on the theater screen, and the feed helped me with timing, although my role was mostly to let Kip pound the shit out of me. In the video, Kip came on Marlin's face and then immediately grabbed a tub of lube, coated his cock and Marlin's ass, and powered in doggy style. He was soon administering a fast fuck. Dmitri stopped and replayed the tape frequently so our fucks didn't pass as quickly as they did in the final edit of the film. As a result, we performed for at least an hour. Kip had no trouble staying hard, despite three climaxes. The guy was intense and relentless, fucking like an animal in heat. I barely kept up. The crowd loved the action.

Afterward, we mingled and both of us collected invites for house calls, although Kip was pickier than me. As the party died down, he cornered me and gave me a sloppy kiss. "Fuck, that was the best sex I've had in years." I wondered whether it was the audience, the payday, or my butt that Kip liked so well, but he insisted it was my ass. "Perfect for my cock." He left no doubt he wanted me again. "I can think of better things to do with your big tool than letting it spew cum all over while I'm balling your sweet ass."

He pressed me to join him onstage in his theater act. "Man, the crowd in New York will love it. We can clean up. Plus, we'd have plenty of time to see the town and for you to ride my ass and for me to get my cock back inside your fabulous bubble butt. Whaddya say?"

I begged off, claiming I was afraid of airplanes. His offer was flattering, and I liked him, but even though Reis had performed in New York, my TPI assignment didn't include that stop. For better or worse, I was confined to California. Vacations weren't TPI-approved leaves, even if they were consistent with the original timeline.

The reenactment of *Roommates* was a hit, and soon Hudson wanted me back for another production. This time he planned a replay of my scene with Leo in *Leo & Lance*. We hadn't filmed together since, but I had no ability to resist making love to him again, even if the reason was a porn reenactment before a live audience.

Leo was quickly on board. "Sounds fun! They'll make it well worth our while. Boys like us need money, and men like Hudson's friends need to be reassured their money can buy anything. They want to see their fantasies come to life, and our cocks are magic. There's one condition. You can ball my ass for Hudson's buddies, but I'm gonna nail yours in return." Not a deal I'd reject.

I was nervous as hell, although I had no good reason to be. Things started fine, with the original scene playing in an endless loop in Hudson's packed theater. Being in Leo's arms again was incredible as we rolled around on the floor, reenacting the fireplace scene. Once in bed, I lost it when he whispered to me, "Let's give the audience a show they'll never forget. Don't just fuck me, make love to me. Make love to me like I'm the man of your dreams."

I have only vague recollections of the night. I'd memorized the movie, both the original version and my remake, and I didn't need the video screen to remind me. I was so emotionally into Leo, I kept being overcome by a pent-up desire to kiss, suck and fuck him. I could have run my hands over his body and sucked face with him for hours. I wanted him to fuck me, but I had enough of a grip on reality to know he wouldn't because he hadn't topped in the video.

The reenactment was a huge success with Hudson and his friends. When we finished blowing our loads on each other's faces, the audience clapped and cheered. Hudson pulled us aside. "You boys are natural pairs on screen. Higgins needs to make a whole series of flicks starring you two."

Leo was all business, lining up engagements with Hudson's wealthy friends. My dance card filled up, too, but by the end of the night, I was shaken, realizing how much I'd enjoyed making love to him. I wondered if he felt the same. If he did, he never let on. As Dmitri drove us home at the end of the night, he chattered about things he and Jamie were doing.

I had to move on. Leo was merely acting when we performed, putting on a good show because the rewards would be quick and tangible. I had a mission to attend to, and it did not include falling in love with Leo Ford.

CLASS REUNION

Leo called to tell me that Higgins had a new idea for a porn film. Rather than the typical series of duos, followed by a three-or-moresome at the end, the film would be one massive orgy. He'd gotten the idea from an earlier flick by J. Brian. Actors he filmed previously were invited to perform and, to his surprise, more than twenty showed up at his office on the day of the shoot.

Leo told me we were doing the shoot rather than asking if I was even interested. I wouldn't have turned it down anyway. It promised to be an easy way to make progress on my mission; plus, I could never say no to him. My only hesitation was I knew Reis hadn't been in the film, and I'd be changing the timeline. But I'd long since crossed that bridge.

We were bused from Higgins's office to a house in Glendale that had an incredible pool. The plot was that we were competing to win a motorcycle at Leo's birthday party. We hopped off the bus and admired the cycle, then raced down to the pool for the orgy. Guys paired off or got together in threesomes or foursomes in and around the pool, and at the end Higgins's boyfriend and Leo hatched the idea of a giant daisy chain. Not that anyone kept records of that sort of thing, but I surmised the event would be a slam dunk for the *Guinness Book of World Records*. In marketing the film, the studio advertised it as a "twenty-one-gun salute," a takeoff on the twenty-one actors shooting in the daisy chain, one after another. I questioned whether the venture would be commercially successful. Higgins had to pay an army of actors, so it was expensive to shoot, but at least it was shot in one day. Six hours to be precise.

I knew a good number of the actors, like Leo, Aaron, and a cute guy named Tim Richards, who'd been in *Leo & Lance*. Some had done older Higgins films and weren't involved in the ones I shot in 1983, although I'd hooked up with several of them anyway.

Having eight or ten couplings going on was distracting, but the group atmosphere got everyone in a good mood and it was an okay shoot overall. I was past getting turned on by sex with other porn stars, or for that matter sex period, so rather than a hot orgy with twenty handsome, well-endowed men, I viewed it as another day at the salt mine. But I stayed in eager-performer mode and with my reliable erection, I came off as sex-crazed. I did more than half a dozen guys, focusing on dudes I hadn't been with before, and was getting close to double figures when Higgins called for the daisy chain. I managed a good-sized load for the camera.

Impressed by my stamina and wouldn't-go-down dick, Higgins and the other actors awarded me the motorcycle. I rode it frequently since I never got accustomed to driving Reis's big boat. I would have happily bicycled, but in Eighties L.A. nobody past fifteen would be caught dead on a bike. The motorcycle was an ideal compromise.

Afterward, Higgins announced Studio One was hosting a post-shoot party for the entire crew, and we'd get free drinks. Studio One was a huge, exclusively gay dance bar that occupied an old factory building constructed before the Depression to manufacture cameras for Hollywood. The club had been around for most of a decade but was still going strong. On a good night, a thousand mostly shirtless gay men would hit the place, cramming the massive dance floor. The crowd was young, white, and hot. The admission policy ensured it. Blacks, Latinos, women, and older men were turned away unless they had three IDs. Nobody carried three IDs. However, a hot young man who was white could get in with a smile. If a smile wasn't enough, showing skin sealed the deal.

Higgins shot *Class Reunion* on a Sunday because some of the actors had day jobs during the week. Studio One hosted a late afternoon tea dance on Sundays that lasted into the night. Gay boys gathered to party, fueled by the triumvirate of booze, poppers, and drugs. While picking up a trick was the objective on Fridays and Saturdays, on Sundays the focus was more about partying with friends. Whether that was the result of the partiers having scored the night before or because they had to work the next morning was open to debate.

I couldn't help stifling a chuckle over Studio One's advertisement for the event with the *Class Reunion* actors: "Dance with the Stars." I was the only one there that knew of the "family friendly" show decades later, much different from a crowd of gay men oggling shirtless performers dance on stage, and then going home and watching them fuck on video.

Leo liked the motorcycle and insisted I take him on it. Jamie showed up and most of the cast did too. Aaron and Tim did their obligatory stints on stage, stripping down to their underwear and selecting different guys from the crowd to dance with. I tried to beg off, but Leo was having none of it. When it was his turn, he dragged me onstage with him and tossed my shirt into the crowd, getting a big cheer. He doubled down and did the same thing with my jeans, fortunately extracting my wallet first. I was tipsy from the free booze and got into it, mostly because it was only the two of us, swirling around on the stage, our bodies inches apart. If the bar threw me out for having an erection onstage—poorly concealed by my underwear— so be it. For a moment, I tasted what it might be like to be with him.

Jamie wasn't pleased, so he hustled Leo out of the club a short time later. I hung around in my underwear, talking to Aaron and Doug Cooper, another porn star with a hunky body who I'd gotten to know. It became clear the crowd and the bar's management were happy having me half naked.

Cooper's stage name was Tim Kramer. He'd fucked Leo onscreen a year or two earlier. He shook his head as he watched Jamie and Leo leave. "I'm not surprised Leo's a big star. He wanted it when we filmed *Style*. What surprises me is that he's still with Jamie. Jamie holds him back. It's only a matter of time until Leo wises up and gives the guy his walking papers." It hadn't occurred to me they might break up. The prospect intrigued me, although I told myself I shouldn't wish a breakup on Leo.

The bartenders kept feeding us free drinks. The actors had been given special wrist bands upon entering, but Kramer wasn't being charged either. When Aaron asked about it, Kramer shrugged. "A guy named Scott Forbes owns the place. I help him out with parties now and then. Be damn careful of him. He doesn't do favors without expecting three or four in return. Every waiter, bartender, and bus boy you see put out to get the job. If they want to remain employed, they put out whenever Scott wants. When Scott doesn't want them to put out any longer, their time here is over. Turnover is high, but Scott doesn't mind because he has an excuse to interview more cute boys and find out how far they're willing to go to get the job. If you're on Scott's good side, he has great private parties after the bar closes, like on Halloween."

Aaron introduced me to Bill Baker, a handsome porn star, acting under the stage name Buster. He'd done *The Big Surprise* back in 1980 and *Buster Goes to Laguna* in 1982. He'd filmed *Sailor in the Wind* in the summer with Leo and Aaron. Buster was a big enough star to get top billing with Leo. While he sported long, curly blond hair in his early films, by 1983 it was light brown, straighter although still wavy, and cut slightly shorter. It still covered his ears. The coming era of short hair was still several years away.

After fucking the afternoon away, I wasn't looking to hook up again. I hung around, talking to Kramer and Buster, who were engaging and interesting. They were Leo's age—Kramer was twenty-five and Buster was twenty-seven—and thus older than most of the hustlers and porn actors I knew. Kramer was from West Virginia while Buster was from Virginia.

We were chatting when Leo unexpectedly reappeared. He wasn't in the same happy-go-lucky mood he'd been in earlier. When Aaron asked about Jamie, Leo gritted his teeth. "He's probably sucking his own cock." He quickly downed a couple of drinks, and nobody pressed him for details. I had a bad feeling whatever fight he and Jamie had might have been triggered by our dancing together.

Leo wasn't pouting. "Hey, Buster, you still have that hot tub? I'm tired of this scene. Let's head there and relax." Buster said he was ready to split, and if we wanted to enjoy the rest of Sunday night at his place, we were invited. I endured an awkward ride on the motorcycle dressed only in my underwear with Leo's hands openly fondling my junk.

Once there, Aaron produced a couple of fat joints and soon we were drunk, stoned, and naked, crammed into an outdoor hot tub. I'd planned to take the night off, but Leo had other ideas. He leaned over and whispered in my ear. "I didn't think I'd get my revenge so quickly for you fucking my ass in Hudson's theater. Your time is up, baby."

He hauled me out of the water, slapped my ass and announced, "This hot boy booty is an asset that Higgins amazingly didn't tap this afternoon. Ever see a better bubble butt? Why he isn't on film with his legs in the air getting his brains fucked out is beyond me. Whaddya say, David? Between the five of us, we've got close to three feet of stiff cock. From what I remember, your tight hole won't have any trouble taking that. How'd you like to get butt fucked?"

Leo was at it again. I was so used to telling him "whatever" that I gave him the green light. "Whatever you say." In part I agreed because I'd yet to inoculate Buster or Kramer.

He bent me over the side of the hot tub, stuck a joint in my mouth and shoved some poppers under my nose. One by one, the big-dicked porn stars pounded my butt. Buster went first and thankfully was gentle until my ass got used to his huge shaft. Kramer followed.

Aaron, Tim and Leo each spent the afternoon blowing loads for Higgins's cameras, so they took a while to climax. By the time they jizzed my ass, Buster and Kramer were ready for sloppy seconds on my abused hole. Leo kept feeding me booze, joints, and poppers, and I didn't remember getting out of the hot tub.

I woke the next morning in a tangle of Leo's arms and legs on a futon in Buster's living room. Gradually working through the fog, I stared at Leo, trying to piece together what happened. For a second time, he'd engineered a gang bang with my butt as the entertainment and I'd wound up in bed with him. My head throbbed and my ass was sore, but I was happy to be in his arms.

What the fuck was I doing, sleeping with another guy's boyfriend? Playing the role of a homewrecker? Even if I swallowed those reservations, getting involved with Leo had never made sense. I'd been through this before and nothing had changed. I borrowed some shorts from Buster and took Leo home on the motorcycle, letting him off a block from his house in case Jamie was home.

Not long after the Studio One party, Leo, Jamie and I hit the town one night, starting at the Rage. It was a big bar, open to the sidewalk on Santa Monica when the weather was nice and populated by a young crowd. It had a well-deserved reputation as an S and S bar—stand and stare. After several drinks, Jamie announced he was bored and wanted some food, so we walked to an upscale hamburger joint on Santa Monica. We happened to run into Kip and invited him to join us. Hard to know if he'd slept with either or both of them; everyone in the L.A. gay porn industry knew one another in a sort of six-degrees-of-separation reduced to two, so it wouldn't have surprised me.

We'd ordered drinks and food and Kip was eagerly describing his act in New York when Jeremy Scott, a porn star whose real name was Troy Myers, happened by our table. Jeremy was tiny, even by the standards of porn stars, who often were short. He was a towering five feet, a California boy with a smooth, twinkish body, distinctive dimples and the requisite big cock. His porn calling card was an oversized mop of curls that often reached his shoulders. Sometimes blond but often brown, his curls were the product of a perm. He adopted the look after he and a lover made a pilgrimage to James Dean's grave in Indiana. They dyed their hair blond for the occasion and Jeremy's lover also tried the curly perm. Jeremy liked the look enough to adopt it.

His start in porn came in the summer of 1979 in a Higgins film, The *Class of '84*. Jeremy was underage, only seventeen, but hardly naïve about sex; he'd gorged on it since his early teens, hustling and hooking up in parks. After *The Class of '84*, he'd been Higgins's lover for a spell, danced and stripped in New York at a place called Gaiety, and continued to hustle and do porn. A 1981 scene with Kip in *The Class of '84 Part 2* became an iconic, blond-on-blond, twink-on-twink classic. Jeremy topped Kip, a turnaround from their normal roles and supposedly Kip's last time bottoming for the cameras.

Jeremy was drunk, but we all were. He stopped at our table on the way to the restroom and said to Kip, "Hey, Noll, you ever gonna take another dick in your ass onscreen? Or is it true you retired your sweet hole after my big cock destroyed it 'cuz you knew nothing could ever be that great?" We laughed and Jeremy added, "Well, you know where to find me, Noll. I mean if you want something better than these losers will give you." He groped himself, grinned and headed down the hallway.

Leo had been in a weird, combative mood all night, which I chalked up to another fight with Jamie. He watched Jeremy disappear and turned to me with a wicked stare. "I dare you to follow him into the restroom and do him. The dude loves sex in tearooms."

Kip chimed in, "Fucker played in them for years when he was jailbait, met his first lover in one when he was sixteen, and spends a helluva lot time in them while hustling. Your ass, your cock, and Jeremy in a john sounds like a deadly combination."

For reasons that can only be explained by me being drunk and unable to say no to Leo, I made a snap decision and blithely took him up on the dare. To prove what, I don't know. I followed Jeremy into the restroom, told him I fantasized about him fucking the cum out of me in a tearoom and begged him to dick me, claiming I loved his curly hair and couldn't resist little guys with big tools.

Jeremy happily obliged. Public sex was a silly risk, but the dude's cock was inside me before I contemplated what would happen if we got busted. Fortunately, he was turned on by the spontaneity, the setting and the fact a big porn star had begged for his cock. The hookup was quick; he shot fast and I made sure I got my load out while he juiced me.

Afterward I doubled down, broadcasting to the table that I'd joined the not-at-all-exclusive club of men and boys Jeremy had bred in a tearoom. "Anyone who wants dessert can lick it off the wall where I shot while taking a huge Jeremy Scott load in my chute!" I raved about his fat cock and how he'd turned me into his bitch, making him sound like God's gift to bottoms. I did it mostly to make Leo jealous, not that I had any hope of accomplishing that.

Jeremy grinned like he'd won the lottery and puffed up more with each bit of flattery. Nailing me was a badge of honor for him, and my gushing about his sexual prowess added to the mix.

My reckless gamble produced one happy result. In Jeremy's mind, you were either on his side or against him, and I was forever on his side. I instantly became his friend, and he practically adopted me as his little brother. He was only a year older, but he'd been hustling and doing porn so long that he was a jaded veteran and he took it upon himself to show me the ropes. He nicknamed me T2B—Top to Bottom—and connected me with some of his regulars.

As 1983 rolled into 1984, Leo tried his hand at producing his own porn videos and developed a bar act. He told me he got the idea from reenacting *Leo & Lance* for Rock Hudson, although the idea may have come from Kip's stints in New York. I never knew for sure, but I suspected Hudson funded Leo's ventures through a dummy corporation.

Leo started with a few shows in San Diego, and then took the act on the road. As a famous porn star, he was in demand. His special appearances packed the gay bars and bathhouses, and soon he was flying all over the country. His act pushed the boundaries. Depending on whether the local authorities could be expected to look the other way, he'd beat himself off at the show's climax—so to speak. Audiences went wild.

He pressed me to join him, saying we'd be great together. I was sorely tempted. I liked the idea of just the two of us together on the road. However, TPI had been certain the Alpha Carrier was in California, not New York or D.C. or Florida. So, despite wanting to hang with him, I gave him the same answer I'd given Kip: I was deathly afraid of flying.

As Leo toured, I stuck to my knitting. Hudson still invited me to parties and occasionally his bed. He liked how my dick stayed rock hard and how easily I took his cock, at least after I relaxed. It was a talent most of his conquests lacked. He was into newbies, but the other side of innocence was ineptitude, so few of his boys had much experience in gay sex, and they struggled to bottom. Not only that, most were so star-struck they had trouble getting it up and keeping it up. Sexually I was everything his other toys were not.

I saw him infrequently. Every few months, he had a fresh, new boy toy—always a big, blond, blue-eyed kid with ruddy cheeks, usually naïve and not the smartest boy on the block. Each looked like he'd walked off a farm in the Upper Midwest; more than a few had. They were in awe of Hudson and thrilled to get inside glimpses of Hollywood. In hindsight, it was no surprise Hudson took a fancy to Mike, the muscular blond in *California Student Bodies*. He was Hudson's type. For that matter, so was Dmitri. I needed to add twenty-five pounds of muscle to fit Hudson's sweet spot. Being a couple of inches taller wouldn't have hurt, either.

Hudson threw periodic pool parties, and his boy de jour often recognized me from porn. The more adventurous ones inevitably wanted a taste of what they'd seen on screen. It was easy to find discreet ways to accommodate them—and inoculate them—without Hudson knowing. Dmitri, on the other hand, missed little and inevitably detected my liaisons. He even arranged some. It was all part of the appeal for the parade of young men Hudson hosted: lounge by the pool during the day, sleep with a Hollywood legend at night, play with a porn star in between.

Despite Hudson having less interest in me, Dmitri had more. He continued to supply me with dope every couple of weeks. When he chased Nico away and took over supplying drugs, I initially thought he was doing it on Hudson's behalf, but as time wore on, I learned he had his own business interests and considered a blond porn star as a valuable resource for his ventures.

He picked me up late one night and chose an outfit that could only be characterized as sleazy. Rather than taking me to the Castle, we wound our way to a spectacular mansion in the Hollywood Hills. Upon arrival, he clamped a big hand around my neck. "Hudson's got a new toy to play with tonight. A blond airhead. The men inside have a blond airhead, too. You. You're gonna give them whatever they want, cheerfully and without complaining. Do you understand?" I nodded dumbly. His eyes glinted, and he clenched his jaws. "You better. Take your shoes and socks off and put your wallet and keys inside them. They're staying in the car, a little insurance policy against you thinking that you're leaving without me." It hadn't crossed my mind, but I dutifully complied. He shoved me inside, barefoot.

I was met by two fifty-something Hollywood agents and five twenty-something actors, outfitted with bottles of Dom Perignon, trays of caviar and a bulky, first generation camcorder. I gathered from the conversation the actors were in daytime soaps. Maybe if I watched TV, I'd have recognized them. Two were handsome enough to be matinee idols while the others were attractive enough, in a Hollywood way.

The night was anticlimactic, consisting of multiple rounds of bad sex in a haze of cigar smoke. I was taken for granted and treated as a piece of meat. While the actors inhabited handsome bodies, their sexual prowess didn't match their looks. So what? One of them might be the Alpha Carrier, and even if not they might spread the nanocell. When Dmitri collected me, the agents handed him a wad of cash and he pocketed it all. So much for a tip for good service.

Dmitri pimped me out several more times, each time collecting my shoes and keys before the event and pocketing big bucks afterward. I'd become an asset of his side businesses, for sale at the right price. While I'd overpaid in cash for Nico's dope, now I was vastly overpaying in sexual favors for Dmitri's deliveries. A baggie of marijuana every couple of weeks was absurdly cheap given what his clients paid him. Sure he was taking advantage of me, but the arrangement saved me the trouble of finding sex partners and involved men I wouldn't normally have encountered. I would have done it even without his weed, although it was good stuff and useful in my role as a sex-crazed gay boy.

Dmitri believed he'd stumbled across a dimwit who didn't understand how much sex paid in Hollywood and was docile enough to let himself be pimped out in exchange for trivial amounts of dope. I worried he'd get suspicious and wonder why I let him use me. As an insurance policy, I concocted a story and asked to see him one night. I did my best to act nervous and look terrified, claiming I needed his protection from a couple of men I'd crossed in the past. It was entirely plausible, given Reis's history, but maybe it worked too well.

Dmitri viewed his protection as a retainer that kept me available for whatever he wanted. He began pimping me out regularly, usually to Hollywood types, but sometimes he shipped me to Las Vegas where I'd entertain high rollers who liked gambling with a pretty boy in tow. While I was there, I found time to hook up with men I gauged as likely candidates to be the Alpha Carrier. As easy as it was to come by sex in West Hollywood, Las Vegas was in perpetual party mode.

As the summer of 1984 rolled around, Dmitri ordered me to cancel any plans I had for the last week of July and the first three weeks of August. The Olympics were in L.A. He had connections with the Russian delegation and big plans for me, but he was hugely disappointed when the Russians announced their boycott in May. He recovered quickly, working me day and night and pocketed a fortune. I was taken aback at how many male athletes wanted to cut loose and celebrate with a little gay sex after the competition, sometimes even before. Many of their well-heeled sponsors wanted to reward them by buying an American porn star. The spectators who flooded L.A. were flush with cash and in the mood to party, too. I'm surprised my balls lasted through the four weeks without falling off.

My porn career blossomed in 1984 and 1985. I did a string of films, none that Reis had done. Timeline changes for sure, but only small rocks tossed into the time stream; what could change if Lance did scenes in *Eureka Boys!* or *Special Delivery*? I was the dedicated performer porn directors dreamed about.

When I wasn't in front of the cameras, I slutted around L.A. with abandon. I had sex with kids of every flavor: college kids, street kids, homeless kids, rich kids, poor kids, black kids, white kids, Asian kids, and Latin kids. I did it with young studs, old studs, and daddies. I took on skinny dweebs, men who stank, guys who juiced. Despite the variety of fucks in bed, in cars, on the beach, in back alleys, the monotony began to wear on me.

By early 1985, I'd been at it for almost two years and I wondered how much longer the mission would last. Maybe I'd already inoculated the Alpha Carrier. Maybe TPI wouldn't extract me. Maybe the timeline was so messed up that I was totally forgotten.

SALT & PEPPER BOYS

The phone rang and I answered, hearing Leo's deep voice on the other end. "Hey, what's happening, David?" He sounded down, not his usual exuberant self, although his moods had been increasingly dour since the night at Studio One.

"Nothing much."

"You doing anything tonight? You mind hanging? I mean, only if you don't have something else going."

I seldom missed opportunities to spend time with Leo and the night wouldn't have good hookup opportunities anyway. A cold rain had washed out activity on Santa Monica and would dampen it in the bars. A rainy day had the same effect on hustling and pick-ups as on plants: things sprung to life afterward. Tonight, the boulevard would be dead, but once the dreary weather moved on and men emerged to hunt for sex, it would be much different.

"Sure. Everything okay?"

"No, not really. Jamie moved out this afternoon. Like ten minutes ago." He sounded tired and deflated, but I also heard a twinge of relief in his voice. Maybe I imagined that. "We should have pulled the plug months ago. Hell, years ago. We aren't right for each other. Time for both of us to move on. Past time."

I commiserated with him, assuring him it was for the best before telling him I'd swing by his house at eight. I hung up with an involuntary smile on my face. I should have felt sorry for him. I didn't. I was elated by the news. It gave me a warm feeling that he'd called me first and was telling me right after it happened. Would he want me to spend the night with him? Maybe we wouldn't have sex, but I'd provide company and distract him from his breakup. Or maybe he'd want to get drunk and fuck my brains out. I would have jumped at that opportunity, but I cautioned myself. Sleeping with a guy on the day he broke up with his lover was creepy. That course of action was a formula for disaster and would lead to nothing but trouble.

I dug through the closet to find a tight, baby blue polo shirt Leo liked, mainly because it was a size too small. Reis probably wore it in high school. My chest, shoulders, and biceps threatened to bust out of the shirt. The color was good with my tan and sun-bleached blond hair.

A couple of hours later, Leo met me at his house in his underwear, a pair of tiny bikini briefs incapable of corralling his big cock. I suppose that was the point. His earlier dark mood had dissipated, and he'd ratcheted to a manic, happy mood. He asked me to make drinks while he finished dressing, telling me to make his as strong as possible. From the looks of the kitchen, he'd been drinking already. He might have been doing drugs, too, although he didn't indulge in them at anywhere near the level most porn actors did.

The place didn't look much different. A few things were missing that I assumed Jamie had taken when he left. Maybe he was planning to retrieve more stuff later, but Leo owned the house, so he probably owned the furniture, too. The place was small, but because of the street configuration, it sat on an improbably large lot. Leo was savvy with money and with my inside knowledge of future real estate values, I recognized it as a fabulous investment.

Leo appeared, dressed in a vibrant yellow polo shirt and faded blue jeans. Yellow was totally his color. Like most blonds, he looked great in blue, particularly light blue, and especially when he had a tan, which he almost always did. But in bright yellow, he glowed. His hazel eyes, white-blond hair and tanned skin stood out. People were immediately drawn to him. The stud turned heads at any time, but he dominated the room when he was decked out in yellow.

He plopped down next to me on the couch and put his arm around my shoulders. My heart jumped a bit, and I wondered if he'd pull me into an embrace. Instead he said, "I'm ready to paaarty, man. Let loose, let off some steam. We need a night on the town. You and me."

"Sure." I was disappointed he wasn't making a move but relieved because it steered away from awkward issues.

Leo bent next to me, whispering into my ear as if he were divulging a top-secret mystery. "What I need tonight is a big, black cock." I glanced at him in surprise. He went on. "I wanna find a muscular black stud who'll slap my ass, knock me around and ram his big motherfucking dick so far into my hole I'll be able to taste his cum when he shoots. Maybe two or three big, black studs, back to back to back. I wanna get fucked so hard I forget everything that happened today."

Leo grabbed his cock and squeezed it through his jeans. "Whaddya say, man, how 'bout we go make history? Couple of blond studs swishing their hot asses around and making it known they need black cock, need to be bred like sluts, and need to be treated like bitches. Hell, the black studs in the ghetto will never stop talking about us."

I nodded numbly, puzzled by Leo's reckless mood and mystified by his sudden interest in black men. He'd only talked about interracial sex in passing, and none of his friends and hangers-on were black. I knew him well enough to know he wasn't prejudiced, unlike many in L.A.'s gay porn industry, but I'd never seen this side of him.

"You've had black cock up your ass before, haven't you?" Leo asked.

Not only had I had it, I'd gone out of my way for it. The incidence of AIDS among black men was high, so in my search for the Alpha Carrier, I'd made a point of seeking out bars, bath houses, porn theaters, and even parks black men frequented. Not all were interested in a white twink, but plenty didn't mind a tight ass and more than a few were intrigued by a big white cock.

There was, of course, my personal reason. Since the day I jumped to the Eighties, I'd carried on a quest to find my Uncle Ben's long-lost lover, Lincoln. I'd heeded Wells's advice to avoid contact with my relatives, but not with Lincoln. I wanted to immunize him from AIDS. It was the one task I could accomplish for someone I loved. If he'd lived, who knew if he and Uncle Ben would have stayed together, but I wanted to give my uncle that chance.

I didn't have much to go on, other than he was in the Marines and had been stationed in Southern California. My bigger problem was what to do if I found him. To immunize him, I'd need to sleep with him, which was creepy. Not as creepy as sleeping with my uncle, but the idea was vaguely incestuous. I'd have to suck it up and ignore my reservations to succeed. I told myself it would only be sex, like what I was doing for a living anyway.

When I didn't respond immediately, Leo leapt to the conclusion I hadn't done it with a black dude. "Man, you don't know what you are missing! Like they say, once you go black, you never go back. First time for me was a film a couple of years ago. I was getting started in the business, a couple of months after Jamie and I did our first shoot together. It was a three-way with Tim Kramer—you remember him from that night at Buster's house—and a black stud named Art. Sweet man and fucking hot! To look at him you'd think he was the meanest fucker in the ghetto even though he was skinny. His dick was smaller than mine and Kramer's, but still eight inches. They filmed us around a pool, and Kramer and Art took turns fucking my mouth and my ass.

I think my ass got permanently stretched. I took shit about getting fucked by blacks, but man, I'll do it again in an instant. I'm gonna do it again. Tonight! A big black cock attached to a motherfucking stud is what the doctor ordered for what ails me."

Leo downed his drink and gave me a dazzling smile. He was putting on the charm and whether he knew it or not, I could never resist him. I was quiet, soaking it all in.

We killed a couple more drinks and listened to an album by Grace Jones, who Leo loved and Jamie hated. In some sense, Leo's choice of the music was an announcement of his independence. I probed to see if he'd changed his mind about the night's planned activities. He was mercurial and could be intent on something only to divert into a completely different plan at a moment's notice. But he was adamant we needed to get balled by black dudes. He'd turned the project into something he was doing for me, having decided the absence of black cock in my sex life had to be remedied before the night was out.

"Black men are better at fucking. The fastest men in the world? Black. Every one of them. Dick work is the same. Black men instinctively know how to use a cock. Doesn't matter how big their equipment is, they're good at working an ass. You get a black cock inside you, and your prostate will be thanking you for years. If it's a big black cock? Damn, you're in for something amazing, boy. You'll be asking yourself, 'How come I never did this before?' Getting bred by a horny black man will open your eyes, not to mention your butt." Leo apparently subscribed to the stereotype of the virile black stud. I tended to believe the persistent image was damaging to black men, but it wasn't the time for a deep discussion.

Leo and I headed out, but after reaching Santa Monica Boulevard he decided it was too early for the bar he wanted to hit. It was still raining, and we were soaked. To dry out, we diverted into the Rage. Fittingly, "It's Raining Men" by the Weather Girls was playing as we entered.

Inside, Leo was surprisingly affectionate, finding excuses to keep his hands on me and hold me close. We were almost cuddling like lovers. He'd never been that way with me before, although he often was with Jamie when they were out on the town. I chalked up his change of behavior to the disruption of his breakup earlier in the day.

Still, I was enjoying being the focus of his attention. From the roomful of hungry stares, most of the bar patrons recognized us. While we got smiles and acknowledgments from the crowd, nobody came up to talk to us. The fact that we were all over each other probably made guys think we were fucking, and they'd be disturbing a soon-to-be intimate coupling of two blond porn studs. Then again, Leo might be using the occasion to publicly announce he was single again and ready for action.

He talked excitedly about his latest entrepreneurial idea. He wanted to open a yoga studio and was convinced he could expand it to be a chain with locations all over California. He was enthusiastic and eager, like he always was when he got an idea. I debated how much to encourage him. Yoga would become big, although maybe he was too early. In the end, I was noncommittal, suggesting that it might take a while to catch on in America, the land of donuts, dessert and Doritos.

After a couple of drinks, Leo announced it was late enough to head down the street, whispering to me, "The big black cocks in our future are about to appear." So much for changing his mind about the night's main feature.

Leo hit the restroom so I waited for him outside the bar. Standing on the street, I had the weird feeling I was being watched. That wasn't unusual—my face and body were plastered on the covers of enough porn videos that I looked familiar to plenty of men—but this time it felt different, like I was being stalked and not merely scoped out by someone who recognized me. I noticed a tall man in the shadows who I could have sworn was Vlad, the guy who'd wanted to film me in a porno but who Hudson had said was sadistic and into heavy kink. He took a step toward me, but Leo appeared and grabbed my arm, guiding me down the street. I was relieved. Vlad, if that's who it was, didn't follow us.

Leo and I ended at a sleazy bar whose clientele were mostly black. Midweek, the bars in West Hollywood were on the slow side, and on this night the crowds were further deterred by the nasty weather. However, on Wednesday night the bar offered twenty-five cent draws, and a crowd soon filled the place.

A white guy in the bar was either there by mistake, which was apparent in minutes, or there to get fucked by a black guy. The place had a couple of active back rooms. Black hustlers hung out in the bar and white guys often paid for the privilege of getting a black dick up their asses. A hot white dude might get a free fuck but had to be prepared to be roughed up and passed around. That was part of the appeal for the white boys who chanced the place. In my search for Lincoln, I'd been there and done that.

We were barely inside the dark room, waiting for our eyes to adjust, when I heard a deep voice. "Hey, hot stuff, what's happening?" I turned to see Cory, the young black stud who filmed the pool scene in *California Student Bodies* with me. He was skinny with a big cock and a smooth, handsome face. His afro wasn't super big but was still bushy.

I liked him. We got along while filming and he was great to be with. He was matter of fact about how black men were objectified and vilified at the same time, and he cracked me up with jokes. He'd dropped hints about how hot my ass was and how I owed him a go at my butt after I'd dicked him in the film, but I hadn't seen him since that afternoon at the pool.

"Hey, whazzup, Cory?"

"Jus' hangin'." A devilish look crossed his handsome face. "Aaannnd, wondering where you been keeping your big, white ass-buster and, more importantly, where you been hiding this awesome booty. Where'd you get a dick and an ass like this? You sure you ain't got a black great-granddaddy?" Cory pulled me into a hug like we were long lost friends, taking the opportunity to grab my ass cheeks as if it were a prelude to throwing me on the floor and fucking me.

Leo glanced at me with a bemused look as if to say, *Yeah, you claim you've never had black cock, but you know the first guy we see in the joint and he can't stop talking about your ass.* I introduced them, adding, "Cory filmed a three-way with Mike and me last summer. We turned him into a white bread sandwich." Why I didn't come clean and admit I'd been with plenty of black men, I don't know. Well, I knew. Leo was happy thinking he was showing me the ropes, and I didn't want to deprive him of that.

Cory smirked. "Yeah, you owe me for that. Big time. That blond bottom had a hot ass, though. Fucking hot." He leaned forward and whispered. "Not as hot as your sweet ass. You got me in that film, but now it's payback time, white boy." I don't know if Leo heard him, but Cory's smile left no doubt he assumed we were in the bar for the same reason every other white boy was there. Which, of course, we were. He put an exclamation point on his statement by slapping my ass and leering at me.

Cory introduced us to three of his friends. Two of the guys, Jay and Cott, were clean-shaven like Cory and looked underage, although fake IDs were easy to come by. Jay had short, shaved hair with coal black skin that made his teeth and eyes stand out like beacons. He was massive, at least six-five, with the biggest chest and arm muscles I'd seen in forever. Cott was slender and light skinned, with long dreadlocks. He could have passed for white, particularly with his pale green eyes, which made him look exotic. Cory's fourth friend was older and had a big afro, a trimmed goatee, and a major gut. I thought Cory introduced him as Ransom, but the din of the bar made it a guess.

Blacks wearing black was in, so the bar was a sea of black. With our surfer blond hair and our bright yellow and baby blue polos, we looked like misplaced Easter eggs. Cory wore a tight, charcoal-gray shirt that made his shoulder and arm muscles stand out. He was a black version of preppy, if that was a category. Ransom was in a tight tank top despite being the one guy in the group who shouldn't have worn it. Cott had a billowy, long-sleeved shirt. If it had buttons, they were unused, as Cott's smooth body was exposed down to his belly button, offering a hard-to-resist invitation to slip a hand inside and cop a feel of his ripped chest and tight abs. The contrast between his dark shirt and his beautiful tawny skin was striking.

Jay's short-sleeved black shirt had epaulets on the shoulders, which, along with his short hair, gave the muscle man a military look. He held himself rigidly, as if standing at attention, which made me suspect he might be a soldier. He was; he was the Marine buddy Cory mentioned when we filmed *Student Bodies*. I perked up and paid close attention, hoping he might have a connection to Lincoln, who, based on the faded photographs Uncle Ben showed me, could be his twin. Unfortunately, Jay didn't know him.

Cory disappeared to get drinks, returning with a couple of beers. We chit-chatted, Leo quieter than customary and looking bored. I scanned the bar, getting knowing looks from the crowd, both blacks and whites. Many of the knowing looks were from dudes who'd seen me in action at the bar before. The bar's back rooms were even better than the baths for quick and abundant fucks.

Cory was trying to convince Jay and Cott to do porn. We talked about filming, and Cory took the opportunity to script the night by describing a scene he shot in a bathhouse in San Francisco. "I never was into white boy ass until I shot this film in San Francisco. Director told this red-headed kid to go down on me on the dance floor, and he gave some damn fine head. The director pointed toward a side room and said, 'You know what to do.' That was all I needed. I took the carrottop inside and fucked the shit out of him. Kid didn't know what hit him. He'd never had that much cock inside him. Complained he'd be sore for a week, but the director told him to shut the fuck up and take it 'cuz he was getting paid good money. Kid had a nice, tight ass, though, and I loved how he squirmed as I fucked him silly. Only porn video that kid ever filmed."

He paused, giving me a lewd look. "Been into white boy butts ever since and lookin' for a repeat tonight." He slapped my ass and, snickering, slipped his fingers inside the back of my jeans. For emphasis, he slid them all the way into my crack, smiling like a cat cornering a canary.

Cory bought three or four rounds of beers, a waiter bringing them continually. I sipped while Leo glugged, drinking half of my beer, too. I was okay with that, given we'd started drinking at Leo's house and continued at the Rage. Cory probably figured a dollar of cheap beers was the price for my ass. It could be had for less.

The black men in the bar, several of whom I knew, stared at our group with undisguised interest. At the Rage, if you caught a guy looking at you, he'd look away quickly, pretending he wasn't staring. At most he'd give you an embarrassed smile, hoping you'd show some interest. In this place, men stared without a hint of embarrassment, daring you to look them in the eye, daring you to admit why you were there, and daring you to submit to them.

Cott was wearing two leather collars along with fingerless gloves like weightlifting gloves. With his long sleeves, they weren't that noticeable at first. I wondered why he was decked out that way. Probably a fashion statement that would be trendy among white boys in a few months.

Cory maneuvered his way behind me and wrapped his hands around my chest and stomach, fondling my tits and pressing his semi-hard cock into my ass crack. "You feel that cock pushing against your hot butt? It's ready for your ass. Nuttin' gonna stop that cock from getting inside it, baby." He pulled one of my hands behind me, sliding it inside the waistband of his jeans. He was going commando, and his dick was spongy and massive in my hand, already wet with pre-cum. "Cop a good feel, baby. My big black cock is takin' your tight white ass, pretty boy. I'm gonna fucking ride you into tomorrow!"

Leo had cuddled and been all over me in the Rage, and now Cory was doing the same thing. With, of course, the added attraction of shoving one of my hands into his pants and providing a graphic explanation of what he planned. In the Rage, Leo was merely playing and hadn't been serious. Cory was dead serious.

Cory whispered something to Cott and the slender man rook a thin leather collar off his neck. Cory snapped it around mine. "In case anyone is confused about who owns you tonight, white boy. And in case you forget." Like an animal in heat, Cory had targeted and claimed me. I wasn't complaining. As long as Leo was intent on us taking black cocks, I could do worse than the hot porn star humping my ass. Hell, even if Leo hadn't been intent on getting blackballed, I'd be hard pressed to do better than a fuck night with Cory, plus there was a good chance he'd invite some of the others to share me.

Ransom used a lull in the conversation to ask pointedly, "So, whaddya boys lookin' for in here tonight?" The answer was obvious, but he wanted to hear us say it.

"Just in the mood to party," Leo said brightly, suddenly paying attention to the conversation. He licked his lips slowly. "But this scene is kinda boring. We should move this party to where we can liven it up a bit. You gotta place?"

"I do," Cory volunteered. Leo and Ransom exchanged long stares, almost challenging each other. Cott and Jay downed their beers, signaling they were ready to leave and report for duty.

We piled into Cory's car, a big old boat Cory called his pimpmobile, and headed to south L.A. Not a great neighborhood for white boys, but I was comfortable Cory would take care of us. He gave every indication of liking me and clearly had claims on my ass. I worried about Leo, who was on a binge he'd regret tomorrow.

It was a wild night. The four black dudes got their fill of white boy butt. Only Ransom didn't get off multiple times. He did Leo and promptly passed out. Leo was out of the action next, never recovering after Jay rammed his huge cock into him in the second round. I was left to handle the brunt of the action, which was good for my mission, not that bottoming for a man two or three times— or in Cott's case four times—significantly improved the odds of transmitting the nanocell.

Rain was still falling when Cory deposited us at Leo's house close to dawn. It was painfully ironic Leo had gotten off lightly despite the whole fucking adventure having been his idea. I was too beat to tackle the walk to my place and was concerned about Leo, who was completely out. I didn't know what sort of drugs he might have taken and whether he would need help. So I made the call to spend the night.

I debated between curling up on the couch and crawling into Leo's bed. Fuck the couch. I slid next to Leo, who was face down, flat on his stomach. Despite the muggy night, I draped a leg over him and pressed my soft cock against his side. It didn't stay soft for long, not that it never did. I wrapped an arm across his back and nuzzled into his shoulder. It was nice.

We wouldn't have sex. Even if Leo hadn't been out of it, my ass was too sore to take dick, and his likely was in the same state. Still, I wanted to be close to him. Try as I might, I couldn't get mad at the dude despite the insane adventure he'd put us through. Hell, the fucker might not even remember it tomorrow morning. He'd probably ask me what happened after we left the Rage.

It felt like I'd barely fallen asleep when a pounding disco anthem woke me with a start. I squinted into the bright light streaming through Leo's bedroom windows. The storm had cleared out, and L.A. was once again basking in the bright California sun.

Seconds later, Leo ripped the sheets off the bed and was on top of me. The blond porn god was naked and his nine-incher was rock hard. His stereo was blaring one of his favorite Grace Jones songs, "I Need a Man," and Leo was singing along. He was using an empty Coke bottle in lieu of a mic.

I was on my side and Leo rubbed his boner against my hip in time to the music, sending my morning wood into a full erection. It didn't help that the bedroom smelled like a cum factory, likely caused by ball juice that even now was leaking from my ass.

Leo raced through the song. He finished with a shout, echoing Grace's lyrics and staring directly into my eyes. He bent down, fluttering his eyelids inches from my face, and softly echoed the last line of the song. "Perhaps that man...."

Holy shit! Was he serious? I didn't know what to do. Well, I knew what to do. Succumbing to the lure of a relationship wasn't an option, even in the unlikely event Leo was signaling he might be ready.

A moment later, he laughed and hopped up on the bed, flicking his hard dick a couple of times so it bounced against his washboard abs. It was exactly what he'd done in *Leo & Lance*, and the sight mesmerized me.

"Get up!" he commanded, grabbing my hand and jerking me out of bed. His eyes strayed to my hard cock, and he gave me a devilish smile before playfully jerking it down and releasing it. It hit my flat stomach with a resounding smack.

"I signed us up for a porn shoot! Not exactly a sequel of our first fuck show—different director this time—but close enough. We're gonna be balling on camera, getting paid big bucks to fuck and suck. Blond boy on blond boy sex scenes. It's gonna be called, *Blonds Do It Best*! If you think you'll get your hooded monster inside my bum again…you're right. But remember, what goes around comes around, fucker!"

Leo gave me a wide, happy smile, lighting up his tanned face. Damn, he was handsome. If our wild night of getting blackballed affected him, he wasn't showing it in the least. He was his usual cheerful, enthusiastic self.

"We need a recovery day at the beach. Yes, Venice Beach, here we come! Sun and fun, drink and dope. I wanna toast my buns on the warm sand. I wanna get drunk and high. I wanna enjoy the surf and sun. Maybe cop a little action if there's a hot prospect around." He frowned. "I might have to limit it to topping or oral. My ass is sore after what you talked me into last night."

"What *I* talked you into? *Your* ass is sore? What the hell about mine?"

Leo smiled happily. The fucker was batshit crazy. I stood blinking in the bright sunshine as he retrieved two tiny Speedos from his dresser, one baby blue and one vibrant yellow. His choice of swimsuits wasn't an accident. They mirrored our polo shirts from last night.

He draped the blue Speedo on my erection. "Blue is your color, stud. Get to work shoving that slab of horse cock inside this tiny Speedo." He aimed me toward the bathroom, slapped my ass and said, "Move that whore hole of yours, and let's get to the beach!"

PERSONAL QUEST DISASTER

Ironically, Leo's breakup caused us to draw apart as I saw him only infrequently for several months. Newly single, he toured the country with his bar act, flew all over the world for escort engagements, and had a brief romance with a fat drag queen named Divine who'd been in movies and had a stage act. Leo met him after one of his shows at Studio One. In between trips, Leo called and talked as if we were best friends, but we seldom got together and hadn't shared the same bed since the night he'd broken up with Jamie.

Cory wasn't around much either after our fuck fest, but I hooked up with Cott and Jay several times. Both men followed Cory into porn. Jay worked for a producer who specialized in filming military dudes, but he only did a solo scene and one where he fucked a white Navy boy. The kid had no idea what he was getting into, and his terrified reaction to having Jay's black python down his throat and up his ass made the scene infamous. Cott did a series of BDSM films, playing black doms, although with his slender frame he didn't particularly look the part. He also starred in a blacks-on-blonds, prison-themed film that became popular.

Cott periodically gathered a group and hit me up to bring booze and dope. He was into leather and had a well-stocked playroom where he hosted all-night sex parties. Often I was the token white boy at his bashes. He was totally using me, but in a sense I was using him, too. I would have been hard pressed to arrange better opportunities to spread the nanocell.

Jay was stationed at Camp Pendleton, and because of my search for Lincoln, I latched on to him, telling him I was into doing it with black Marines. I begged him to let me know whenever any of his bros wanted to party. He was noncommittal, but after a couple of months he called to tell me a group of Marines were meeting at a cheap motel near the camp and I could come if I wanted. I didn't quite appreciate how horny Marines got. They used my ass as target practice and by morning I didn't think I could walk. The orgy became a regular event. I recalled my ill-fated liaison with Maverick whenever I pulled into the motel.

I immunized a legion of Marines, but none of my nights at the motel gave me any leads to Lincoln. By the summer of 1985, I had all but conceded my quest to find him had failed. I knew he'd only be in Southern California until the fall. I'd likely saved scores of men from getting AIDS, but the one man who I'd set out to save had eluded me.

Jay was getting transferred in the fall, too, but shortly before his stint at Pendleton ended, he called and instructed me to meet him at Marina Del Rey on a Saturday afternoon and wear a red jock strap. Jay wasn't the type to ask if I was free or was interested; instead, he told me what I'd be doing. I never objected or claimed to have a conflict, so he probably believed he had a blank check. It never annoyed me.

I was puzzled about the red jock and had to buy one, but I understood its purpose when I arrived in Marina Del Rey. Jay and a bunch of his Marine buddies had invites to a red, white and black jock party on a big yacht. Black guests had to wear white jocks and bring white dates. White guests wore black jocks and brought black dates, and the dates all wore red jocks. We disrobed down to our jocks upon entering the ship, and sex was free and open, but with one rule. Whites could only hookup with blacks, and blacks could only hookup with whites. It was a floating interracial orgy, right up my alley.

The boat was well stocked with booze, drugs, and lube. Jay and his Marine buddies were quick to drink, quick to take a hit, and quick to fuck. No surprise. Within two hours, the interracial orgy had turned into a drunken, drug-fueled interracial orgy. It promised to challenge even my stamina for sex. I started off planning to stay sober, but as the afternoon turned into night, I surrendered and got trashed.

I was on the main deck with Maurice, a young Marine who was seriously interested in my cock, when a tall, muscular black Marine walked by. Maurice said nonchalantly, "Hey, Lincoln, how's it going?" My eyes flew wide open and I recognized the stud from my Uncle Ben's photographs.

Lincoln smiled and high-fived his buddy. The three of us talked for a while. Well, the Marines talked while I tried to flirt and signal how badly I wanted Lincoln, which didn't sit that well with Maurice. Trying to seduce my uncle's lover left me queasy, but it was the only way to pass the nanocell to him.

However, it became apparent Lincoln had no interest in me. Zero. Nada. None. I was intimately familiar with that reaction, having encountered it frequently before Danny remade my body. I soon had a hint of why he didn't fancy me. A white muscle stud who was at least thirty-five strode past us, and Lincoln gave his buddy a knowing grin. "I see something I'm gonna snack on," he said, leaving to pursue his prey.

Fuck! I'd spent two years searching for him, and now that I'd found him, I couldn't get over the goal line. I couldn't even get invited to the game. I watched him as the party continued, but every time I saw him with another guy, he was chatting with someone who had fifteen years and thirty pounds of muscle on me. It made sense that my uncle had the same muscular body Lincoln seemed to fancy.

Down and disappointed, I was out of options, except one I never thought I'd pursue. Late that night, long after most of the partiers had crashed, I slipped out of the bed I was sharing with a skinny black dude and made my way to the restroom. On my return I noticed Lincoln in a room by himself. He was asleep, flat on his stomach. In the dim light, the round mounds of his ass looked incredible.

I hesitated, staring at him for a long spell before creeping into the room, unable to resist one last effort to seduce the man. Sliding onto his bed, I cuddled and kissed him, hoping to get him horny enough for a round of sex before he was awake enough to tell me to get the fuck out.

I had no luck. He was completely out of it and I couldn't roust him.

I'll always hate what I did next. I was drunk and stoned, and the man's ass was fantastic. I was rock hard—what else was new—and I climbed on Lincoln's back, spread his cheeks, spat in his crack, and shoved my cock into his ass. He was passed out and totally relaxed, and his hole offered no resistance. I began to move in and out.

What I was doing struck me like a bold of lightning. *My God, I was raping him.* No other way to characterize it. The only thing that might keep me out of jail was that men in 1985 didn't report sexual assaults by other men. But I'd changed the timeline already, so maybe I was about to make history by being thrown in jail for a gay rape.

I fought with myself. I'd come this far and wanted to finish the job for my uncle. I mindlessly continued to thrust in and out, focused on saving the man's life and heedless of the way I'd chosen to do it.

Lincoln stirred, and I froze in panic. If the man woke up and discovered what I was doing, God knows how he might react. He could easily twist me into a pretzel.

He didn't wake, merely pulling one leg up so that, ironically, I had an even better angle on his ass. It didn't matter. My cock had deflated faster than a helium balloon punctured by a pin.

I was a shithead. No debate. I'd already fucked up, so I couldn't make things worse. I coaxed my flaccid dick back into an erection, fisted myself to the verge of a climax, and slid inside Lincoln. My dick erupted.

Unfortunately, so did Lincoln. He suddenly lifted up and flung me off his back like I was a feather pillow. My cock, not realizing the gig was up, still shot a final spurt of jizz. His eyes were blazing and he growled, "What the fuck?" With lightning quick reflexes he aimed a big fist at my stomach that caught me at the bottom of my rib cage. I heard a crack, felt a sharp pain and gasped for breath, bending over. I didn't know it at the time, but a couple of my ribs were fractured.

"Get the fuck out of here! You come near me again and you're history, understand? I'd beat you to within an inch of your life if we didn't have a boat of witnesses and I'd get kicked out of the Marines as a result. A black man can't touch a piece of white trash without paying the price. I never want to see your face again!"

In pain, I gasped, "I'm sorry!"

"Get out!"

I beat a hasty retreat, slumping onto a deck chair and crawling under a blanket. I'd had what was hands down my worst sexual experience ever, which was saying something because after over two years in the Eighties, I'd had scores of unsatisfying sexcapades. I immediately hated myself, a mood punctuated by my throbbing ribs.

I slept fitfully for a few hours. When the Bloody Marys and Screwdrivers started flowing and the sex ramped up again, I hid on the bow of the boat, trying to rationalize what I'd done. I told myself it was the equivalent of forced immunization. I'd faced an ethical dilemma and made a choice that was for Lincoln's own good. But I couldn't escape the harsh reality of what I'd done.

I heard heavy footsteps; Lincoln was glaring down at me, his massive arms crossed. "Somebody needs to learn that he can't take what he wants without permission," he said with an angry grimace.

I stood up and turned toward him, determined to face the music. "I'm really sorry. I've been beating myself up ever since. It was wrong and I'm an idiot for doing it. Whatever you want to do to me, I've got it coming." I steeled myself, figuring the odds of coming away with a broken jaw were fifty-fifty. I might be shark bait in seconds, my mission terminated early.

"Yeah, I lay a finger on you and it will be black man assaults white boy. I know what justice would await me. White men are all alike. You have a sense of entitlement when it comes to brothers, whether you acknowledge it or not. We're not smart, we're dirty, we're inferior. You've taken what you want for centuries with no repercussions, so why stop now? I should never have even set foot on this damn boat. But I've learned a lesson. Don't trust white men. Never." He strode off angrily, leaving me feeling like shit.

Perhaps I'd saved him from AIDS, but at what cost?

A LITTLE CASHE GOES A LONG WAY

Recovering from cracked ribs sidelined me, leaving far too much time on my hands. I couldn't work out, which removed one of the main ways I'd kept myself occupied. Television grated on me and reading books or newspapers bored me. I dreamed about Lincoln and woke each day depressed and dreading the day. I was lonely and isolated; the Eighties weren't home and I felt apart from everyone around me.

I'd hit a wall; tired of hunting for sex, tired of finding it, tired of getting it. Mostly tired of impersonating Reis, my twin who was completely unlike me. Or was he? I viewed him as the porn star and hustler, but after two years, isn't that what I'd become? Walk into any video store offering gay porn, and my face was plastered everywhere. Not to mention my cock. None of those pictures were Reis. They were me.

Reis did three films in 1983, a couple of solo scenes in 1984, and *Blonds Do It Best* in 1985. Along the way, he filmed a scene for Colt with Tom Littlewolf that was never released until 2008. I'd rewritten history in a big way, doing five times as many films. But I was out of gas and my time in the Eighties had become suffocating. The disaster of the night with Lincoln was the final straw, making me unable to continue.

Even after my ribs completely healed I couldn't force myself back into the routine of endless nights of stiff cocks and willing assholes; whatever enthusiasm I'd had at the beginning of my mission for hopping from one man's bed to another had dissipated. Tired of David's sad apartment, I finally hauled myself out and rode my motorcycle to the beach. I intentionally went late on a Sunday when I knew the gay crowd would have already vacated, heading instead to a tea dance. The weather was unusually warm so I pulled off my shirt and plopped on the sand, planning to stare into the sun until it slipped into the Pacific.

I'd failed. Wells and Lois were probably planning to swoop in and pull me out of the Eighties and move on to a better plan. Humanity would have to survive without my help. As for my personal goals, I might have saved Lincoln, but I hated how I'd done it, and while I had the hot body I'd wanted to open the world of gay sex, I was living the classic cautionary tale: be careful what you wish for. Being wanted only for my body was hollow.

A solitary figure walking down the beach, shirtless but carrying a jacket over his shoulder, caught my eye. As he got closer I got a better look at him. He might have weighed a hundred and ten pounds and been five-five with risers, although he packed a surprisingly muscular body on his diminutive frame. He looked like he was sixteen, with light brown hair parted in the middle that covered his forehead and ears. He had huge blue eyes highlighted by long eyelashes, a small mouth and an angelic face. The kid was the height of innocence and looked like a goddam choir boy. If the beach group had been in attendance he'd have attracted plenty of interest, even though he was likely in high school.

He looked vaguely familiar but I couldn't place him. He marched directly to where I was sitting and sat down next to me. I was annoyed. The beach wasn't crowded so it wasn't like he needed sit a foot from me, as if we were together.

I ignored him and he didn't say anything for a long spell before turning to me with a grin. "Should I call you David? Or Lance?" He paused for effect, raised his eyebrows and added, "Or Cody Montrose?"

I froze at the sound of my name. It had been two years since I'd heard it. The last person who said it might have been Kravitz when TPI kidnapped me from Maverick's motel room. Something was wrong, but likely nothing more than TPI arriving to pull me out of the Eighties and admit defeat. I wondered why Wells sent a kid to do it.

Seeing the surprised look on my face, he laughed and said, "Sorry, I couldn't resist. I'm Ty Cashe, or at least that's my name here in 1985. Lois and Wells sent me."

"You're here to tell me I failed."

"Yes and no. You haven't succeeded yet, but Lois says their simulations reveal you're close. Close enough so that the odds of finding the Alpha Carrier are considerably higher than when you arrived. But you need a course correction. That's what I'm here for. I've been with TPI for five years. This schoolboy look is courtesy of a makeover from Danny, although it's a little jarring to look like this when I'm twenty-six. Given my body before, I didn't have much to lose when they proposed the makeover."

"What course correction?"

"You were already close to burning out, but your bonehead stunt with Lincoln was the final straw. I've never seen Wells so angry. What the hell did you do?"

I took a deep breath and launched into an explanation. It was cathartic to get it out and I rambled for longer than I expected. Articulating things helped me put the incident into perspective, at least somewhat. It was still a disaster.

When I finished, he sighed. "I might have done the same thing. But we need to put that behind us, and we will. I wasn't quite expecting TPI to put me in the body of a teenager for this effort, but I'm looking on the bright side. Who wouldn't want to relive their teens but have a little more wisdom? I have to say, however, that I'd forgotten what it was like to be horny all the time." He groped himself and gave me a conspiratorial smile. I was having trouble reconciling Ty's twinky body with the adult inside.

"You and I will do a famous porn film together. *Blonds Do It Best.* I watched the damn film more times as you did at TPI headquarters. We'll stick to the same script, but we'll knock their socks off."

That's why he looked familiar. I recalled his name too. Both Leo and Lance had fucked him in *Blonds*, which was his first porn shoot. Taking it up the ass from the two reigning blond gods of gay porn was not a bad way to start a porn career.

"Beyond, that, we'll have fun and light up the town. You need to recharge your batteries and get back into the swing of things. Sex is your job, but you have to make it more than that; it has to be enjoyable and exciting too. I'm only here for four months, so I'm treating this as a sex crazed holiday during which we'll set the town on fire. Starting now. You've been moping around for weeks, so I bet you're hornier than hell. Time to get that famous cock back in action and massage that overly sensitive prostate Danny remade for you."

He looked at me, appearing to assess my reaction. I felt much better after having gotten the whole Lincoln disaster off my chest. And yeah, I was horny…

I could still do this. "When do we start?"

He grinned, looking like a kid playing a game. "Now would be good. Why not introduce your new fuck buddy Ty to the tea dance crowd? I'll need your help with things. TPI gave me a crash course in the Nineteen-eighties, but things like paper currency will be a challenge. If the Eighties were hard for you, think what they'll be like for me. I have to roll back the clock on seventy-five years of technology, history and change."

We headed back to West Hollywood, Ty wide-eyed about everything from humans operating ancient cars to how it was possible to function without a personal internet device. He asked questions nonstop. At the tea dance he flirted with every dude I introduced him to, then made them jealous by pulling my arms around him and telling them his night was spoken for. They didn't stay jealous for long; Ty made a point of whispering that he'd love a raincheck. He was a master of timing; play hard to get but send encouraging signals, letting men know they'd eventually score.

I was left wondering what he meant when he said his night was spoken for; was it simply his way of letting men down softly, or did he think we'd sleep together? He answered the question on the way out of the bar, confidently asserting that sleeping together and having a little fun after our day was done—or before it started—wouldn't detract from our mission and would help me treat sex as something enjoyable again. We were barely halfway home when he guided me into the alcove of a sandwich shop and worked my tool out of my jeans, giving me a hungry, excited look. "Stud, ever since I saw this slab of uncut manhood at TPI, I wanted it, and I've waited as long as I intend to. The fact that these huge balls are filled with pent-up cum is just the icing on the cake." He licked his lips. "Or... icing in my mouth."

With the expression of a sex-starved teenager, he wasted no time, using some impressive mouthwork to coax my dick into an erection. He played with my foreskin, muttered, "This is one awesome cock," and swallowed it, deep throating me and reducing me to a quivering mess despite the threat of passers-by. A long blow job would have been great, but that wasn't in the cards. He only sucked me for a few minutes before a massive load of cum exploded from my balls. He struggled to swallow it, finally coming up for air and saying, "Damn, you really hadn't milked those for a month."

I took it as a challenge to return the favor. When we reached David's apartment building, I cornered him in the hallway and pulled his jeans down, revealing an awesome looking cock. Admittedly that conclusion may have been unduly influenced by my self-imposed sex hiatus, but I was ready to go. I licked his dick until it was wet, took his hairless balls into my mouth and teased him by sticking a finger into his hole and working his prostate. He gurgled and moaned, letting out a big sigh when I relented and deep-throated him. Before long, he flooded my mouth with a huge nut. Panting, his eyes twinkling, he said, "How does 2060 taste?"

Still on my knees, with my finger in his hole, I licked my lips. "Very tasty. An excellent vintage. By the way, you're not done. I want this ass." I emphasized the point by poking his prostate.

He let out a couple of incoherent, "Uhhh, uhhhs" before recovering enough to say, "It's yours. I traveled seventy-five years and want the ride to prove it."

I kissed his ass cheeks, and he gave me a look of impish glee. "You realize you're old enough to be my grandfather."

I chuckled. "Me? I haven't even been born yet. Besides, I'll bet I'm not the first old guy to enjoy your ass."

"You been reading my C.V.? Guilty as charged. But you'll actually be the first man, period, to use this particular ass."

"So you'll be the only man in history to lose your cherry twice?"

He laughed and pulled up his jeans. Not a minute too soon, because a couple who lived in the apartment building appeared, puzzled as to why we were loitering in the hallway. Actually, only the woman was puzzled. I'd had her husband before so he had a pretty good idea of what we'd been doing.

Once in the apartment, we dropped our clothes and I picked him up. He wrapped his arms around my shoulders and his legs around my back, and we French-kissed for a long while. My arms were getting tired holding him but he kept teasing my bone by brushing his bare ass against it. I finally put him on the kitchen countertop, lifted his legs to my shoulders and worked my cock into his hole. It was tight but not a vice. A sweet ass. I began to pump in and out as he clung to my shoulders, whimpered, kissed me, and begged me to fuck him harder. It wasn't long before I dumped a second load, filling his tight twink butt.

Our night of sex wasn't over. Ty announced he'd looked at my bubble butt long enough and was going to test drive it. By the time we drifted off to sleep my hole was sloppy and dripping jizz.

After that night, it was easy to fall into being fuck buddies. Ty had no idea how day-to-day life in the Eighties worked, so realistically I was the only person he could live with. I was happy for the company, happy for his cheerful attitude, happy to have a confidant.

And happy to have a sex partner who was always ready to go, whether it was a quickie or an extended bout of love making. He was right. Sex could be fun.

Ty helped me balance my life and recharge my battery, and his presence gave me a much-needed boost. I mentored him on the Eighties and showed him the ropes, everything from how to use a manual toothbrush to reminding him to wear a shirt; like Danny, he wasn't used to them. He carried the nanocell but didn't share my rare blood, so his odds of immunizing others were much lower, but they weren't zero. He happily threw himself into the sex scene. He was cheerful and enthusiastic, wanting to do it all, whether it was porn, hustling, spur-of-the-moment trips to the baths, excursions to back rooms or spontaneous hook ups. We went to see a skin flick one night when only twelve or fifteen men were in the audience and he announced, "We aren't leaving until we've fucked or been fucked by every man here." He even did the kid selling popcorn. Twice.

Ty was an incredibly cute, voracious bottom, and when he took a dick in the ass his big eyes were bright with innocence and anticipation. Unlike many porn actors and hustlers, he genuinely loved sex rather than merely going through the motions. Almost overnight he outgrew his role as my apprentice and we became sidekicks. His happy attitude was contagious and I found myself enjoying life more than I had for a long time. It didn't hurt that for the first time in two years I had someone to talk to about the mission.

We settled into a pattern of meeting for breakfast at a greasy spoon diner near my apartment four or five days a week, after we finished a night of tricking and hustling. We'd show up at 5:00 a.m. and leave as the early risers arrived to search out coffee and start their days. Afterward we'd get in a final fuck before crashing. I'd shove my dick into one of his holes or he'd return the favor. He was a hot fuck and I understood why so many men were enamored with him. His small stature and cute looks condemned him to bottoming onscreen and in most hookups, but he was damn good at topping. I loved it when he turned the tables on me and rammed his shaft down my throat or up my ass. I often woke to feel him spooning me, his cock wedged in my crack or buried in my hole. For the first time in my life, I was sleeping with a man regularly.

BLONDS DO IT BEST

A month after Ty's arrival, we were on the set for *Blonds Do It Best*. Richard Morgan, a relatively new gay porn director, had decided to pair Leo and me again. Because of the success of *Leo & Lance*, it was odd Higgins hadn't done a sequel. In the original timeline he might not have wanted to work with the baddest of the bad again—Reis—but I was in his good graces. He wrote scripts and set preliminary shooting dates for a sequel, but before production started, he'd be off on some other project, showcasing some new talent. Maybe he didn't want to compete with himself.

The remake of *Blonds* followed the original script, and it was reassuring to be doing a film Reis had done, particularly after I'd rewritten his porn history. Given it was Ty's first experience in front of the cameras, he appreciated knowing what the final product was supposed to look like. For him, it was the same situation I'd been when filming *Leo & Lance*.

The action, except the first and last scenes of the film, took place at a lake house that Lance, Leo and the other actors supposedly rented. Morgan inserted a solo jack off scene with three actors at the beginning of the film, but it was something of an afterthought, unconnected to the rest of the movie and involving actors who weren't in any of the other action. To my chagrin, in the second scene Morgan put me in a Speedo like David had worn. Morgan filmed me enjoying the sun in the Speedo at the house as Ty showed up in a boat, having run out of gas. I obliged him by giving him a can full of gas and an ass full of cum. After living together and being fuck buddies for a month, Ty and I were relaxed and into the action, and some of that familiarity was reflected in the film. We produced an extremely hot fuck, playful and erotic.

The next scene had Mark Sheldon, a dark-haired kid who was in his first and only gay porn role, arrive at the lake house as Ty left. Lance was ready for more sex, but in the middle of the action Leo showed up. Lance was unfazed, telling Mark that Leo would probably join in. Of course Leo did, handing Lance a beer as he went down on him and Mark. Leo and Lance spit roasted Mark in front of the fireplace, with Leo doing the honors on the newbie's ass first, followed by Lance. As we filmed it struck me that Leo was into the action much more than I recalled from the original video. He'd watched my earlier scene with Ty, and knowing him he might have been jealous and competing to show he could put on an amazing performance for the cameras. Of course, he did. Hell, we both did. I loved being around him.

In the fourth scene, Leo was chilling by the fireplace when Shawn Michaels showed up with a stack of wood for the fireplace. Leo buried his cock in Shawn's ass but Ty appeared to return the gas can. Leo pulled out of Shawn's butt and answered the door with his erection pointing at the sky. Ty did what any red-blooded gay boy would do: followed Leo inside and gave up his twink ass to both studs. Again, Leo was different than I recalled. More dominant and eager to fuck Ty's brains out, but Ty was incredible too.

The film was head and shoulders above the original. Apparently Morgan sensed that too and wanted more. He proposed shooting another long scene at the lake house—Ty with Leo, then Ty with me. Perhaps he'd done the same thing originally but cut the scene, and perhaps he'd cut the new one in post-production. After all, it went against porn standards to have the same actors in two scenes, let alone the same actors in two scenes in the same film. Ty and I were thrust into filming without the benefit of knowing the end product.

Ty was the star of the new scene. He was shown arriving at the lake house to find Leo asleep on the couch. He wasted no time, going down on Leo, coaxing the stud's dick into a steely erection, and then sitting on it with a happy, dazed look on his face. Leo woke to find his cock imbedded in Ty's ass and pummeled the kid, eventually taking him in front of the fireplace and shooting a huge load on his back before ramming his cock back inside Ty and snowballing him. Spent, Leo fell back asleep peacefully in front of the fireplace.

Ty, still horny, was playing with his cummy asshole and jacking himself when I woke in the bedroom and decided to go to the restroom. Finding him with an erection, his finger in his ass and a sultry, come-fuck-me look, I went down on him before putting his legs in the air and pounding his ass with my uncut horse cock. It was wild to fuck him with Leo supposedly asleep only inches away; of course, we knew the stud wasn't asleep. In the middle of the fuck, I grabbed Ty and rolled backwards, putting him on top but keeping my dick in his hole. He rode me relentlessly before pulling off for the money shot. I jizzed my chest and Ty added a big load of his own to the cum pool. It was wildly hot sex, and I hoped it came through in

Morgan's camera. Ty kissed me as I fell back asleep, and the scene ended as he snuck out of the house while Leo and I slept peacefully in front of the fireplace. Morgan had us pump up our dicks so his camera caught us with matching nine-inch erections, as if we might have been in the midst of wet dreams.

The final scene of the remade *Blonds* followed the original. Morgan shot footage of Leo and me driving down a road in the mountains in a convertible, our blond hair streaming in the wind as we reminisced about the action in the lake house. We got so horny after talking about the sex-filled weekend that we stopped the car, hiked into the forest and fucked. Morgan interspersed short scenes of the car ride throughout *Blonds* as an introduction of the action to come. As porn plots go, it was actually effective.

Despite having been in front of the camera dozens of times, I was more nervous about the shoot than I'd been for any scene since *Leo & Lance*. I asked myself why I was so on edge, but the answer was clear. *Leo*.

In contrast Leo was relaxed as always, joking and comfortable being naked in front of the crew. He looked damn hot in the convertible, his blond hair blowing in the wind, and once we were in the woods I had a hard time not staring at him like a lovesick girl. He wore a black polo that fit him well and looked classy. I was in yet another of Reis's polos, a striped one that looked more discount store than Rodeo Drive. At one point, watching Leo's blond head bob up and down on my dick, I regretted not having had sex with him more often. But I knew why.

In *Leo & Lance*, I was an amateur compared to Leo. Almost two years later, I'd done more films than he had, but he was still light-years ahead of me when it came to playing to the camera. He controlled the action. He knew where the camera was at all times, knew what angles would film best, and kept my cock as the star of the show. He sucked me, dove into my balls, then come back to swallow my dick. After the shoot, I was drained, physically and emotionally, but he was full of energy, ready to celebrate. Morgan was ecstatic about the scene, claiming we somehow put something extra into it.

Leo called Ty a pocket gay during the filming because of his height, but the kid acquitted himself well, bottoming twice for each of gay porn's reigning big-dicked blond all-stars. It was a performance that rocketed him into porn stardom, and he quickly had offers for other films. He did them all, excited and enthusiastic about getting buttfucked by men who were seventy-five years older than he was.

Throughout the late summer and early fall of 1985 we went everywhere together. People who didn't know us assumed we were a couple, and those who knew better understood I finally had a fuck buddy, although I was accused of robbing the cradle. We tricked together, hit the baths together, played in back rooms together, and spend hours tossing back drinks at the Rage and assessing the crowd. He became an overnight sensation, and his face was everywhere. He filmed for half a dozen directors and we were paired in two of those films. That was a rarity, but there was some porn marketing magic in my big dick sinking into his tight twink ass.

For me it was a bout of sunny, calm fun before the stormclouds appeared. Ty's four-month assignment flew by, and all too soon I was confronted with the end of his time in L.A. On his last night, he wanted to see *Back to the Future* as part of a final bash and goodbye to the Eighties. He loved the movie, which struck me as odd because it had to look primitive compared to 2060's entertainment, but maybe it was like the enduring appeal of a *Casablanca*. He joked that TPI needed a DeLorean to add pizzazz to time travel. I'd always considered the movie to be a fun flick, but the time-travel angle only reminded me of his looming departure. We hit the bars afterward, got drunk and stoned, and went for an early breakfast at our usual diner. Early for us because we usually didn't show up until 4:30. As we finished, he leaned over the table and gave me a mischievous, eager and innocent look that was his trademark.

"I don't intend to take a single drop of semen back to the future with me; as soon as we leave here, I'm pumping it all into your holes."

Shaking my head, I deadpanned, "That isn't right. Your balls might be empty, but what about the whipped cum cream that I'll shoot down your throat to coat the pancake you just ate? And your ass will be leaking 1985 jizz for a week." He laughed. We spent the night flip-flop fucking.

The next afternoon, I drove him to Venice Beach. He kissed me goodbye. "I have a funny feeling I haven't seen the last of you…but then everyone at TPI probably says that before leaving the past."

"Who knows what the future holds?"

He grinned and headed up the beach, shirtless once again. I watched him until he disappeared. On my return to West Hollywood I began thinking of ways to explain to an array of disappointed hookups and producers that Ty had left town unexpectedly. And wouldn't return.

FLEEING NORTH FROM DANGER

Leo moved into the void that was created by Ty's and Kip's departures. He always came and went in my life, and he'd hit the road after we filmed *Blonds*, but when I returned from Palm Springs he was back, pitching his theater show to me. I'd resisted for two years, convinced it would hinder my mission. When he first broached the subject, I gave him the same excuse I'd given Kip, that I was afraid of flying. Leo claimed to remember the conversation differently and maintained that I'd ruled out flying but signed on for shows within driving distance. Out of the blue, a month or two after his return to L.A., he announced he'd scheduled four shows for us in San Francisco in November. I objected, but he wouldn't take no for an answer.

The day after he proposed the trip, I went to the gym as usual. I liked using long stretches on an exercise bike to help me think things through, and I needed to mull over Leo's offer. *Maybe it wasn't so bad.* I'd slutted around L.A. for over two years and hadn't found the Alpha Carrier. TPI inserted me there because that's where Reis lived in 1983, but Wells never narrowed the target area for the Alpha Carrier to L.A., merely to California, so maybe I'd been in the wrong place all along. I hadn't ventured to San Francisco in deference to the timeline, as Reis stayed in L.A. until 1986. But L.A. wasn't working, and a change of scenery didn't sound bad. Ty was gone and Dmitri was laying low, feeling heat from the authorities, so I had more time on my hands than I wanted. The more I thought about it, the more the trip made sense.

If I was honest with myself, spending a week with Leo sounded great. After more than two years, I couldn't stay away from him. I couldn't get close to him either. The intimacy I'd shared with Ty only whetted my appetite for something more with Leo.

I'd finished the cardio and was doing some light weightlifting when Jeremy appeared and pulled me aside, saying he wanted to talk. He'd never been in the gym before but had come looking for me. He was nervous and insisted we go someplace where we wouldn't be overheard, so we searched out a deserted section of the gym's outdoor pool deck and looked around furtively before taking a deep breath. "T2B, listen up. There's a million dollars on the street for anyone who'll deliver a snuff film starring you. You gotta be really careful! Don't accept porn jobs from people you don't know. If it were me, I'd stop hustling and lay low. Get out of L.A. A million bucks is enough of a lure that if you're in the wrong spot at the wrong time, someone will grab you in a heartbeat."

I'd come across references to snuff films at TPI, but law enforcement was convinced one had never been filmed and they were the stuff of urban legend. Of course, nobody involved in making one would broadcast it, so it was hard to know with certainty. "You sure?"

"Totally. The guy who told me this wouldn't make it up. He was approached to find you and although he's involved in some shady stuff, he's never killed anyone."

"Why me?"

Jeremy sighed. "All I know is that he's obsessed with you. Why? Why does anyone get obsessed with an image on a movie screen? Some reasons are obvious, like you're one of the biggest gay porn stars in the country and you have a big cock and a hot body. But some aren't so obvious, like he only wants a smooth-chested blond, and some are weird, like he insists on a guy who's uncut. He believes anyone who's circumcised has been maimed. But in his mind you're untouched and perfect. Plus, you're beautiful and you've never bottomed on screen. His fixation with blonds has to do with Hitler's master race thing. This fuck is Russian and wants to film a cadre of Russian soldiers getting revenge on a perfect blond Nazi boy. He wants to stage your first bottoming experience on film. After a gang rape he'll abuse you more before slitting your throat and watching you bleed to death. Did you see the sci-fi flick *Dune* when it was out last year at Christmas? Apparently, this sadistic fuck likes the scene where the Baron raped a blond boy as he bled to death. He's gonna reenact it and set it in World War II."

The visual made my stomach tighten. The bleeding-to-death aspect struck home, given that I'd bled to death after a bicycle accident in a prior timeline, and it was my weird blood that landed me in the TPI mission. The reference to a Russian punctuated the story with a nasty exclamation point. A Russian in the market for something blatantly illegal would certainly know Dmitri. He was laying low, and I suspected he was in financial trouble as a result. I didn't think he'd sentence me to death in a snuff film, but he might if he were desperate enough. A more likely scenario was that he'd deliver me thinking he was merely getting a fat payday for a typical night of pimping me out.

I pressed Jeremy for details, but he didn't know more, except one I would have preferred not to know. "The bastard's plan is even creepier than what I've said. One of his cohorts is into sex with corpses and wants to fuck you after you're dead, while your body is still warm and lying in a pool of blood." I was past the point of being grossed out.

I asked if I could talk to Jeremy's friend, but he shook his head. "Bad, bad idea. Like I said, he's never done anything like this, but there's a first time for everything. Some of the people he hangs with wouldn't have qualms about nabbing you, not when a million bucks is at stake. You don't want to be anywhere near those guys." I thanked him, promised to be careful, and finished working out, not knowing what to make of it all.

Still, his warning caused me to be cautious and pay more attention. Over the next week I occasionally had the feeling I was being watched and on more than one occasion I saw suspicious looking men who were out of place in West Hollywood. Maybe it was only my imagination. But I took precautions, not accepting hustling jobs from men I didn't know and confining my sexual escapades to places like the baths and back rooms where plenty of other men would be around. I wasn't hooking up all that much anyway because of filming *Santa Monica Boulevard*.

A week after Jeremy's warning, Nina, a Latin-Asian drag queen who lived in the basement of Reis's building and cleaned the public areas in exchange for reduced rent, invited me for dinner to pay me back for helping her move in a month earlier. Even though I barely knew her, after a couple of Margaritas, I mentioned the San Francisco excursion and my reservations about it. I didn't tell her one reason I'd never pursued a relationship with Leo was my temporary assignment in the Eighties, although after more than two years, my assignment felt anything but temporary.

Nina wagged a wooden spoon at me, giving me a stern look. "Honey let's review the facts. I may be ditzy, but I know a few things, and even though I've only seen the two of you in the same room a couple of times, I've seen the look you give that boy. When Leo walks in, you can't take your eyes off him. You positively glow inside. Your face lights up and you're stupid happy. You're fixated on him. Hypnotized."

Did I react that way around Leo? Nina was probably right. In the little time I'd known her, I'd learned she was often brutally frank.

"Now, you two boys may not be right for each other. Leo may not feel the same way about you, although I will say that boy is hungry for you in a way that makes my skin tingle. He jus' doesn't know what to do about it. Takes one step forward and immediately takes a step back as fast as he can. I've never seen the likes of it.

"Even if you're both madly in love with each other, that may not be enough. Lord knows, I've been infatuated with men before and they couldn't keep their hands off me, but we were oil and water. Fire and ice. Sometimes things are perfect for a year, and then they change and it's all wrong. That's no reason for you to deny what Leo does to you. You'd best own up to it and decide what you want. You're in love with that boy and nothing is gonna change that. Certainly not time."

Time was exactly the problem. Even if Leo and I were in love and right for each other, a long-term relationship couldn't happen. I could be recalled from duty at any moment.

I waffled. Maybe Nina was right. Why not explore a relationship with him during whatever time I had in the Eighties?

No. How many times had I been over this ground? The why not was obvious.

Without giving it a moment of thought, I said, "Sleep with me, Nina." Hell, she could be the Alpha Carrier. Even if she weren't, I'd immunize her from full-blown AIDS. Maybe she'd be the person to pass the nanocell to the Alpha Carrier. Aside from that, I was curious about what the multiracial drag queen would be like in bed. She had a slender, sexy body.

Nina gave me a look like I was crazy as fuck. "What, I tell you that you're in love with Leo, and your first reaction is to beg another man to sleep with you? Boy, you are one wild trip!"

"I'm serious! Guys tell me I'm good in bed."

"Honey, more men in L.A. know that than know the Ten Commandments. But this is all wrong."

"Why? I gotta big dick. It'll make your man pussy sing!"

"Oversized cocks and my petite asshole don't get along well. My curse is getting enamored with big-cocked tops before it becomes apparent that our physical equipment isn't compatible."

"Okay, so fuck me! Guys say I have a sweet bubble butt. Tight ass. I don't care how big your dick is. I can take it."

"That's another thing I hear on the street, honey. Odd that a boy who will only top in front of the camera turns into a hungry bottom when the bright lights are off. Why do you suddenly want to do it with me? What gives?"

I sighed. "Life's too short not to have fun when you can, and something tells me I'm looking at a lotta fun in bed."

Nina laughed. "Damn, boy, you sure know how to sweet talk a lady."

I hopped to my feet, bent over, and flexed my ass. Running my hands over it seductively, I tugged my shorts down to expose the top of my crack. I looked over my shoulder to give her my best come-fuck-me look and purred, "What do you say, sweetheart? I've got buns of steel, made to take a stiff dick. Made to milk your balls until they're dry."

She cracked up laughing. "Don't think I haven't noticed that amazing bubble butt you got working. Hard to look at that and not wonder what it would be like to ride it into the sunset. If you're offering, I'm happy to be on your one-and-done list." In a moment, I was smothered by a deep, sensuous kiss.

Nina fucked like a banshee and was damn fun in bed. But she wasn't Leo.

The next day, she fixed an awesome breakfast, although by the time we ate, it was too late to legitimately label it breakfast. Brunch was stretching it. However, when I made my way back upstairs to David's apartment, the door was slightly ajar, and the lock was busted.

I should never have ventured inside, but I crept in, not chancing the lights. The place hadn't been ransacked, but some things had been moved. My eyes went to a small brass cannon of Reis's that Dmitri played with every time he picked me up. It wasn't in its normal resting place, although I remembered planting it there when I'd cleaned a day earlier.

My stashes of cash and dope weren't hard to find and were undisturbed. I grabbed them, not bothering to check whether anyone was hiding in the bedroom or closet. My heart thumping like a drum, I raced back to Nina's. I wasn't the victim of a normal robbery; thinking I was home someone had apparently come looking for me rather than my stuff. I'd escaped only because I spent the night with Nina.

Thank God she was still in her apartment. She looked puzzled when she opened the door. "What's this, honey? Last night was great, and I totally mean that. Your tight ass is everything it's rumored to be. Maybe better than advertised. But isn't it a little soon for an encore? I mean, you're one-and-done, remember?"

"It's not that," I said, slipping inside. I hurriedly explained Jeremy's warning about the snuff film and the break-in of my apartment. For the first time I'd known her, she looked shaken.

"Oh, my heavens! Sit down, honey."

She left to check the front of the building and came back even more alarmed. She flipped the locks on her door, lowered the shades and paced back and forth.

"There are two men outside who are scary. I'm sure they're armed. There's something else, too. Three nights ago after our drag show, the girls were talking about some less-than-savory characters who were looking for a blond porn star to do a snuff film. It never occurred to me that it might be more than talk and you might be the target! Jeremy is spot on that you need to leave town for a spell. Go to San Francisco with Leo or somewhere else."

Nina's confirmation of the snuff film only made the knot in my stomach worse. I took a deep breath. "Can you make me look like a woman?"

She scanned me up and down. "Not a pretty one, darling. I can work with your baby blue eyes, but I can't hide that jaw line. Or those shoulders. It would help if you weren't almost six feet tall. Don't worry, though. I'll make you up so that those men outside won't give us a second glance. They probably couldn't care less who *leaves* the building anyway. They're waiting for you to return. I can take you to Santa Barbara. I have a friend there who'll help us out. That should be far enough away to be out of harm's way for the moment. Don't come back to L.A. anytime soon. I'll keep an eye on your place."

Two hours later, Nina had worked miracles, and I was a passable drag queen. Admittedly a tall, graceless one. She had a pair of heels that fit me, but after a failed lesson on walking in them, she gave up and put me in flats, shaking her head. We sashayed out to her car, and as she predicted the men keeping surveillance on the building paid us no attention. I didn't get a good look at them, but they might have been two of Dmitri's thugs.

When we arrived in Santa Barbara, I hid a stack of bills in Nina's purse without her knowing. She'd rejected my offer to pay for her help, but I was grateful and she could use the money. She bid me a tearful goodbye. I was comfortable that we hadn't been followed, but to be safe, when I called Leo to accept his offer and tell him to pick me up in Santa Barbara, I used a pay phone. Before saying too much, I asked him to call me back from one. Pay phones had proved to be remarkably handy devices in the cell-less Eighties.

I had ten days of down time before Leo arrived. I wasn't eager to stay in a dress for the duration, so Nina's drag queen friend took me shopping, outfitting me in much better clothes than I'd have found on my own. She had a great sense of style, was fun and interesting, and knew virtually everyone in Santa Barbara's small gay community. My stay happened to coincide with an annual underwear party that attracted gay boys from miles around. I dutifully slutted the event, making the most of the opportunity to spread TPI's nanocell to a roomful of new men. I don't know how many recognized me from porn films, but plenty were eager to play.

A few days later, Leo picked me up and we drove to San Francisco amidst some spectacular fall weather, detouring through Big Sur. He was booked into two bars and two bathhouses. The bar shows were on Saturdays, with the bath houses on Monday and Thursday in between. He was a performer first and foremost and maintained doing back-to-back shows wasn't good because he couldn't get a big climax without a day in between.

I loved San Francisco. Unlike car-centric L.A., it was walkable—perhaps hikeable was more accurate, given the city's infamous hills. By day, I happily explored the city. By night, I continued my needle-in-a-haystack quest to neutralize the Alpha Carrier.

Although Leo wanted me to perform in his shows, I begged off, figuring it wouldn't be wise if people looking for me got wind I was in San Francisco. He still wanted me at each show, and after performing at the baths on Monday, he was exuberant and claimed he was too wired to go to bed immediately. We hit a couple of bars and when they closed, we found a diner that served breakfast twenty-four hours a day. It was almost like my breakfasts with Ty. By the time we got to the hotel, it was close to dawn.

We shared a room in a gay hotel. One of the bars had arranged it, although the hotel likely comped the room for the advertising and probably rented some rooms because we were there. The place was as cruisy as they come, with a communal living room that served as ground zero for pickups. Leo didn't play there, but it was a quick and easy way for me to score. Watch TV, scope a guy out, accept a silent invitation, follow him to his room. Fuck, return, repeat.

Our room had twin beds and as soon as we were inside, Leo plopped on his, making no move to undress. Instead, he wanted to watch me to disrobe. "Yeah, baby," he cooed, "give me a little hint of the hot performance that room of horny men missed tonight. Show me what you got. Work it."

He groped himself and was only playing, or so I thought, so I did a strip tease for him. I pulled off my shirt, jeans, and underwear and gyrated a bit. "That's right. Shake that big ass buster hanging between your legs."

My reliable boner soon made an appearance.

"Fuck, yeah. Get it hard for me baby. I wanna see Lance's famous, uncut porn cock in all its glory." It didn't take long before my shaft was pre-cumming, although it never took long.

"Why haven't you taken it onstage? You're a natural." Compared to him, I wasn't a natural by any means. But showing off for him was somehow different. I gave him what I hoped was a beguiling look and licked my lips as I slowly rolled my foreskin up and down over my shaft. He watched me like a hungry cat stalking a canary.

"Show me that ass, baby. You know I think the porn directors have it all wrong. They should be filming your amazing butt. The hottest bottom in the business is right in front of their noses, and all they see is your big dick."

I turned around and flexed my glutes a couple of times, then bent over and spread my ass crack, exposing my hole. Leo growled, "Fuck yeah," and pounced. He shoved me onto my bed and was on top of me in seconds.

I always liked being naked beneath a clothed man, but this time there was a bonus—the man was Leo. I felt his erection, separated from my ass only by his jeans, rubbing against my crack. "I never got a revenge fuck for you doing me in *Blonds Do It Best*. You gonna let me use your tight ass?" I mumbled yes and it wasn't long before he pulled his jeans and jock down to expose his cock and began dry humping me, sliding his tool between my crack.

"This ass is as beautiful as it was the first time I fucked it in the snow after *Leo & Lance*. Fuck, it's better." That afternoon was crystal clear in my mind, but he'd never mentioned it before, and I was surprised he remembered it.

Leo spit in his hand, coated his cock, and began to work it into my hole. "Fuck, I almost came watching you shimmy and wriggle this amazing bubble butt just now. After the first time I balled you, I don't know why I didn't chain you to my bed and fuck your brains out every night, every morning, and every afternoon."

"You were with Jamie."

"Like I said, I don't know why I didn't grab you right then and there." With a sudden thrust, he penetrated me. I melted.

The sex was rough and erotic. Leo balled me twice, once face down and once on my back with my legs on his shoulders. He never removed his clothes. Afterward, he stayed in my bed and was soon asleep. I was wide awake, happy to snuggle with the blond porn god and sleep with him for the fourth time. Not that I was counting.

The next morning, Leo acted as if nothing happened. Maybe he didn't want to admit what we'd done. He never mentioned it and was back to his usual self. Probably wishful thinking, but I thought I detected a difference in the way he reacted to me, and I spent a couple of days in a happy, euphoric mood.

A MAINE
FALCON

Three nights after sleeping with Leo, he performed at a different bathhouse and told me afterward that he was leaving with a friend. The happy mood I'd been in for the past days vanished. Rather than return to an empty hotel room, I said I'd hang at the baths for a while. He gave me a knowing smirk.

I wandered back to the hotel close to dawn after hooking up with at least a dozen horny guys. How many men had I been with in the past two and a half years? A thousand? I probably reached that milestone in 1983. Three thousand? Likely. Five thousand? Maybe. The numbers were staggering. The saving grace was that I'd immunized virtually all those men from AIDS, and the ones who could retransmit the nanocell had immunized many more. Still, compared with the fifty thousand people who died of AIDS annually in the early Nineties—deaths reflecting infections during the mid-Eighties—I was impacting the timeline much less than I wanted.

When I woke late on Friday, I had a pounding headache. It took the what left of the day to recede. Feeling like crap, I moped around the hotel. It was November fifteenth, ten days before the birthday Reis and I shared. I'd be twenty-five, pretending to be twenty-three going on eighteen.

I begged off hitting the town with Leo Friday night, escaping the hotel only to grab takeout Chinese and a newspaper. I still couldn't get into Eighties TV; *Dallas* and *Dynasty* hadn't aged well. I leafed through Leo's copy of the first anniversary issue of *Advocate Men*, which pictured a bunch of porn stars, many of them my friends and acquaintances. It seemed like a goddam high school yearbook. If I hadn't had sex with a dude who was pictured, I'd had sex with someone who had.

A quiet night cooped up in a hotel room wasn't like me. When Leo was around, I followed whatever he proposed. Even if I wasn't hanging with him, I could have explored San Francisco. I'd loved wandering through its neighborhoods, but I had no energy.

The headache was better on Saturday, but I had a nasty hangover despite not drinking. Leo knew something was wrong and told me to stop feeling sorry for myself. "Regardless of how much you're wallowing in self-pity, we're going to Falcon to meet Chuck Holmes, the head of the studio. Get with the program!" I reluctantly agreed, realizing I needed to snap out of it.

Falcon Studios was the gold standard of gay porn. The studio's production quality was assured, which allowed it to keep prices high. The flicks were formulaic—mostly older, muscular guys in somewhat vanilla scenes—but what porn wasn't formulaic? Falcon might be predictable but was always quality. Customers kept coming back.

Leo turned twenty-eight the prior summer. His enduring ability to pull off the young, blond surfer look was amazing, but he needed to reinvent himself or move on. The meeting with Holmes was to explore that. My situation wasn't much different. Everyone thought I was Reis's age, twenty-two, although I was often mistaken for nineteen or twenty. Yet I was a few days short of being twenty-five.

Falcon's offices were in the city, not the usual suburban strip malls or warehouses used by producers in L.A. They were decorated with posters of successful releases of the last few years. One caught my eye. It was a vision that wouldn't go away, even more iconic than the photo of Kip Noll in his letter jacket. A beautiful, curly-haired blond in a baby-blue polo shirt stared out from a poster advertising *Splash Shots*. His head was bent slightly as if he was studying me. I'd seen the picture many times while surfing the web for porn.

The actor was Kurt Marshall. I'd seen his photo the night before in *Advocate Men*. Another poster, for *The Other Side of Aspen II*, a new release, featured Marshall as well. There he wore a red, white, and blue ski sweater. His curly blond hair, square jaw, and the cleft in his chin made him look fresh and sexy. In both posters he was clothed and not bare-chested, a rarity in porn advertising.

We gave our names to the young receptionist and had barely arrived when an older man, balding and overweight, stepped from an office. "Ah, Leo, good to see you. Could I have a word with you before you meet with Chuck?" They disappeared into the office.

The receptionist gawked at us when we entered and he continued to stare and give me beguiling smiles. He abandoned any pretense that he was working. "God, I am one of your biggest fans!"

"Uh, thanks." The kid was painfully skinny and gangly. His skin was so pale it didn't look like he ventured outside during daylight, contrasting starkly with his mop of curly black hair. If his hair had been straight and he had a piercing or two, he'd be perfect as a Goth, but I didn't think they existed yet. Maybe in England.

A door opened and a deep voice said, "Chuck, I appreciate the offer. I'll give it overnight, but I can't imagine not doing it. Thanks again." The man with the deep voice closed the door and looked at me. He was Kurt Marshall.

There was a disconnect between Marshall's deep voice and his youthful appearance. He sounded like a forty-year-old businessman and looked like a teenaged athlete. He was my height, five-ten, with blue eyes peering over high cheekbones. He had full lips and wore a bright yellow polo shirt that highlighted his dark tan and broad shoulders. The sports themes of his Falcon films gave him a fresh, athletic image that was marketing gold. With *Aspen II* coming out, the face of young gay porn was either Kurt or Leo—or me—but Kurt was new.

Kurt was better looking in person than in the posters, as surprising as that was. For a moment, neither of us spoke.

He smiled faintly and broke the silence. "You're Lance."

"Yeah. Actually, David Reis. You're Kurt Marshall."

He gave me a bigger smile. "Actually, James Rideout. Friends call me Eric." He crossed to me and extended his hand. We shook, James—or Eric or Kurt—staring into my eyes. "Someone who filmed you three or four years ago said you had hazel eyes. Recently somebody else said they were blue. Definitely blue."

I was taken aback that anyone studied the color of my eyes, let alone one of the era's biggest gay porn stars. "Uh, yeah, they're blue," I said. Mine were blue, Reis's were hazel. In two and a half years, nobody had noticed the difference. It was mystifying Kurt of all people detected it.

He continued to stare, his eyes twinkling. "Have dinner with me. Tonight."

I was speechless. I started to explain that I couldn't because of Leo's show. I'd agreed to go onstage with him for the final performance after he came up with a way to do it without anyone knowing who I was. The club was erecting a glory hole, so only my hard cock would be exposed. He spent several days planning scenes around my boner. However, the bars wanted to sell plenty of booze to the waiting crowd before Leo went onstage, so the show wasn't until eleven, probably more like midnight. I was free for dinner.

"Sure." I was intrigued. Yes, Kurt was gorgeous, but the way he carried himself, his deep voice, and his presence in the room were riveting.

He grinned and asked where I was staying. "I'll pick you up at eight." He gave me a firm handshake and turned to leave. As he passed the receptionist, he leaned down, looking back at me with a knowing smile. "Joey, tell Chuck he needs to hire Lance to fuck me silly. Make us baseball players. Lance can pitch, and I'll catch. He can play hard ball with me."

Joey's eyes got big. "I'll make sure he gets the message, Eric. Absolutely sure."

Eric—or Kurt—disappeared through the front door, but not before glancing over his shoulder and smiling at me again. Damn, he was beautiful. I took a deep breath and asked the receptionist, "How old is he?" His face made him look like a teenager, but his demeanor and the way he carried himself suggested a much older and more experienced man.

"Old enough to think he knows more about pornos than Chuck, but young enough to star in them. He turned twenty-three days ago. He's exactly a year older than me; we share the same birthday, but that's about all. He's twenty going on thirty-five."

I was feeling like a giddy high school girl with a crush on a guy five years younger than me. He may have been gorgeous, but his strength of personality attracted me more than anything. The crummy mood I'd been in for the better part of two days evaporated. I was excited about the date.

Leo returned, and we met with Holmes. The meeting started as more social than business, a meet-and-greet with some vague discussions about working together down the road. Leo's first couple of flicks had been for Falcon, but I got the impression some bad blood existed between him and Chuck, although Leo got along with everyone so maybe that wasn't it. Perhaps it involved Jamie. Reis's final film—*Splash Shots II*, a sequel to Kurt's film—was for Falcon, so I assumed Chuck had at least some interest in me, but he was noncommittal. Maybe he viewed me as overexposed.

His interest level changed after Joey slipped him a note. Chuck read it and asked with a frown, "Was he serious?"

Joey shrugged. "Seemed like it, but I can never tell."

Chuck sighed. "Me neither. Even if he was serious, he could've changed his mind already. The baseball angle is good, though."

He turned his attention to me and asked questions about who I'd filmed with, would I be interested in working with Falcon, and so on. I took the opportunity to get his reaction to me having a different look—short hair dyed black, maybe a full armful of tats—and a different stage name. I'd contemplated the changes to reduce the risk of being recognized and targeted for the snuff film. If the Russian behind it wanted a blond porn star, I'd become a black-haired one. I'd even thought about getting circumcised but that was a bridge too far.

Chuck was eager. Pairing two smooth blonds wasn't Falcon's style but pairing a blond with a heavily tatted, dark-haired guy might be. If Lance were overexposed, I'd start over with a new look. As Leo and I started to leave, Chuck asked what I knew about baseball. Go figure.

Leo smiled during it all. Once we were on the street, he asked, "What was that about baseball?"

"Falcon's doing sports-oriented films, so baseball is probably next." That satisfied him.

However, Chuck's comment about Kurt changing his mind made me worry he wouldn't show for my dinner date. I hadn't gotten his number, so I had no way to contact him. It occurred to me that maybe Joey would give it to me. Not perceiving a good excuse that would explain going back to Falcon, I told Leo about Kurt inviting me to dinner.

"Fuck, hot stuff, of course you should go out to dinner with him!" Leo clapped me on the back. "Just remember—show's at 11:00 and you gotta save your first climax of the night for that. After the show, you can fuck Marshall's ass all night long. You won't be the first guy who's enjoyed that little delicacy, but that boy is beautiful." I thought I detected a hint of jealousy in his voice, but he'd be jealous one moment and set me up for a gang bang the next.

I circled back to Falcon, worried nobody would be there since it was late. Joey was still around and surprised to see me. "You're out of luck, David. Chuck and everyone are gone for the day."

"I'm in luck, because it's you I wanted to see." Joey gave me a puzzled look, like 'that can't be right.'

I explained about needing Kurt's phone number. Joey gave me a big sigh and with a conspiratorial voice said, "Well, I'm not supposed to give out phone numbers or addresses. Especially Eric's. I could get in big trouble. Maybe lose my job. I mean, every gay man in the city would be calling him if they could. But...*for you*...I suppose I could break the rules once. As long as you don't tell anyone!"

I assured Joey that I wouldn't and he looked up Kurt in a big rolodex behind the reception counter. They still seemed quaint.

Joey had over-the-top, queenie mannerisms, but I liked him. Watching him, it crossed my mind that his sex life couldn't be all that great, although I chastised myself moments later for giving into unfair stereotypes. Still, thinking about his sex life gave me a sudden idea. Leaning over the reception counter and giving him a warm smile, I said, "Thanks. I really, really appreciate this. And, um, what time do you get off?"

Joey frowned. "Why?"

"You, uh, doing anything after work?"

He appeared to be perplexed, viewing the obvious conclusion— that I was making a pass at him—as unthinkable. "No..." A puzzled note of caution sounded in his voice.

I smiled and winked at him. "I'll hang around until you're ready to go."

"Uh, w-well, I-I was about to close u-up," he stammered.

"Good. You said nobody else is here?" He nodded. I spotted a bolt lock on the front door and stepped over to shut it. Fucking at Falcon had a nice ring to it and it wouldn't be the first office where I'd done it.

"So I guess we're alone and you're off duty."

"Yeah?" Joey replied, frowning. I circled around the reception counter, staring down at him. His caution hadn't disappeared; perhaps he was thinking I would beat him up. I figured jump starting my seduction of the kid was the right move and pulled my polo shirt over my head, dropping it into his lap. His eyes got huge and he gawked at my chest and abs. I reached down, undid his tie, and started to unbutton his shirt.

"What, what are you doing?"

"I like thin guys. Curly black hair, dark eyes." He was a step or two beyond thin. His chest was flat, with no pecs to speak of. His ribs made him look like he was on a starvation diet.

"Oh, fuck," Joey said as it dawned on him what I was doing. He wasn't about to let the opportunity go to waste. He leaned forward and fumbled with my jeans, dropping them and pulling down my underwear. He reached for my cock, putting his hand on it and saying, "Oh, God. This cock is beautiful." He bent forward, licked my dick, and in record time had it all the way in his mouth and was deep throating me.

Maybe I was wrong about his sex life. The kid was a masterful cocksucker. Most guys struggled to get my piece down their throats, but he swallowed me like he sucked big cocks for a living. The dude's skinny neck didn't look big enough to accommodate my tool, but his nose was pressed into my pubes and he was deep throating my dick like he was born to suck cock. Looking down I saw nothing but a curly mess of black hair bobbing back and forth on my crotch.

Admittedly it had been a couple of days since I came, a rarity, but his hot mouth had me rock hard in no time. I closed my eyes, relaxing and enjoying every sensation as I spread my fingers through his curly hair and guided his head back and forth.

However, I began to worry that I'd blow my wad. I pulled him off my dick. "Damn, you know how to suck cock!"

The kid grinned. "Thanks. When we're shooting, my job is to get the actors hard before a scene. Chuck hired me when I was fifteen—I told him I was sixteen—and he says I'm the best fluffer he's ever had."

Huh. The kid sucked cock for a living after all. Unfortunately, I couldn't let him finish the job; Leo would be pissed. Instead, I dropped to my knees, saying, "My turn."

"Seriously? You're gonna suck my cock?" He'd sucked plenty of dick in his life, maybe given up his ass frequently, but I surmised that the guys he'd been with didn't reciprocate. He was barely nineteen, probably just out of high school, and his slight build and effeminate mannerisms would have caused him nothing but trouble in school, particularly if boys got wind that he was a cocksucker.

I pulled him into a deep kiss. "Hell yeah, I'm gonna suck your dick. I want it rock hard when you pound my ass and fuck my brains out."

"You're a top," Joey said mechanically, still not believing what was happening. "You've got a fucking huge cock."

"I top when the cameras are rolling, but offscreen..." I shrugged and pulled his pants down to his ankles. His chest, stomach and arms were completely smooth, and his underarms had only sparse hair. But his skinny, pole-like legs were covered with silky, dark hair. His legs were hairier than mine. The contrast above and below his waist was striking.

I leaned forward and swallowed his tool. He wasn't big but not small either. Normal sized and cut. His balls were big, however, and his sac was almost hairless. I enjoyed playing with it as I sucked on his cock.

Joey kept repeating, "Oh, God, oh God," over and over. I couldn't tell how close he was and didn't want to push him too far, so I pulled off his cock, leaving it dripping, and worked my way up his body, kissing his stomach, biting his tits and driving my tongue into his mouth. Thankfully, he wasn't a smoker; I'd never gotten used to the number of men in the Eighties who smoked cigarettes.

We kissed for a spell, fisting each other's cocks off and on. I whispered, "Where are you gonna fuck my ass? Take me wherever you want."

Joey swallowed, but he knew what he wanted. "On Chuck's desk. No, wait, on the reception couch. Every time I look over there I want to remember you with your legs in the air and your big dick halfway up your abs." I chuckled and got to my feet, pulling him up and pushing him in front of me. As we neared the couch, I wrapped my arms around his slender body. My cock slid between his hairy ass cheeks, and I dry humped him several times. My cock looked huge next to his narrow hips and small butt.

"You gonna fuck me? I can take it. I've had huge dicks before."

I nuzzled into his neck while slipping a fist around his boner. He was already pre-cumming. "Rain check on your ass. Right now I'm putting my legs in the air, and you're gonna fuck me into tomorrow."

Joey growled, "Hell yeah!" and put me on the couch, legs up. I pulled my ass cheeks apart to expose my hole. Joey fished lube and poppers out of a small table next to the couch. The evidence suggested I was on one of the infamous casting couches where young wannabes showed up looking for a modelling or acting contract left with a load of cum in their asses. I'd heard enough stories about guys getting fucked at porn auditions to know it was more than an urban legend.

"God you're hot," Joey said as he greased his cock and my ass. "I can't believe this is happening." He eased into me and started off gentle, but soon we were both breathing poppers and he was fucking me like his life depended on it, pulling all the way out, slamming back in and panting and moaning. Sweat covered his smooth face and dripped from his curly hair. The kid wasn't much to look at, but his excitement and enthusiasm were great, and I was having a better time getting fucked than I'd had in a while. Probably since Ty did the honors, except, of course, for the night with Leo.

Joey grabbed my cock with both hands, one on top of the other, and started to slide my foreskin up and down. His hands were so small that even stacked they didn't cover my pole. The kid was good with his cock; I had to revise my earlier theory about his sex life. He might be a skinny nineteen-year-old, but it wasn't the first time he'd pummeled a man's ass. "God you feel good inside me," I moaned. He gasped, "Oh fuck!"

When he blew his load, he was shouting, "Oh fuck, oh fuck!" His cock lurched a good ten or twelve times and he must have shot a mammoth load, because he left my ass wet and sloppy. He stayed in me and, panting, gasped, "That was incredible." I pulled him into a deep kiss. "You were fantastic. You delivered exactly the butt pounding I needed. I'm so fucking glad I came back to find you." He gave me a big smile, but I had to disappoint him when he wanted to jerk me off.

I was in a good mood as I left Falcon and headed to the hotel to shower and change. As bad as I felt yesterday and earlier in the day, I was past that. And Kurt loomed in the future.

He picked me up wearing a navy blazer and a blue dress shirt. I'd put on an aqua polo shirt I'd bought in Santa Barbara. It was classier than anything Reis owned, but not in the same league as Kurt's getup. I asked if I was underdressed.

"Nah. We're going to a small place, no dress code. I wear a jacket to look older. If I dress like this and ask the waiters to recommend an expensive bottle of wine, they never card me. I have a fake ID, but I like seeing if I can get away without it."

The trendy restaurant was perched on the side of a hill, but so was much of San Francisco. The place was packed when we arrived, but the maître d' knew Kurt and seated us immediately at a table in a bay window facing the street. Kurt gestured to the sidewalk outside and the tables in the restaurant. "I hope you don't mind being in a fishbowl. Being mildly famous, at least within a tiny circle, means it's easy to get a good table but hard to find one with any privacy."

He asked the waiter to recommend a nice Cabernet, rejecting the waiter's first suggestion and requesting something "a little bigger." I suspected the waiter was calculating his tip by the time Kurt settled on the third suggestion. As predicted, the waiter didn't card us.

I thoroughly enjoyed dinner. Kurt was from Maine and came to San Francisco for the same reason most gay men did. Unlike many porn stars, he had no regrets and didn't feel the industry had taken advantage of him. "I went in with my eyes wide open, and I don't mind it. But it feels like a dead end. On-screen sex is not what I want to be remembered for."

Probably too late for that. His image was destined to become ubiquitous, iconic even in the 21st Century.

He was beautiful. More important, I liked him as a person. I liked his presence, liked his confidence, and liked his maturity. He was optimistic and, by all appearances, well-adjusted. Our dinner conversation was intellectually invigorating and fun at the same time. He had a clever, engaging sense of humor and was excited when I mentioned I skied and cycled. He wanted to do a ski trip to the Sierras, and I had a vision of him in his red sweater from *Aspen II*. Eighties ski equipment would be a challenge, but I was ready.

It was hard to reconcile the starving college student with the boy who ordered expensive bottles of wine. The food was great, but the place was for special occasions and pricey. I asked him about it. He gave me a beguiling smile. "How often do you get to take a man out to dinner who you've dreamed about ever since high school?"

I was flattered and embarrassed. His reference to high school reminded me how young he was. He changed the subject, but I was bothered by him spending that much money on me. Even if we split the bill it was too much.

Unlike Kurt, I could afford to pick up the check. I'd saved plenty over two plus years as a porn star and hustler, partly because I had ready access to the TPI-funded bank account. I slipped away to the restroom, found the waiter, paid the bill and left a generous tip. The waiter took my gesture wrong, hitting on me and telling me he got off shortly. The dude wasn't bad looking and I didn't reject overtures from men who might be the Alpha Carrier, but between Leo's show and Kurt, I had to propose another night. He readily agreed, pointedly mentioning I was welcome to bring my boyfriend too.

When Kurt asked for the check, the waiter gave him a knowing smile. "It's been taken care of."

Kurt frowned. "How?"

"One of your admirers. Young man, blond hair, quite fetching if I do say so myself." The waiter glanced at me with a hungry smile.

Kurt scanned the room. The restaurant was small, and nobody fit the waiter's description.

"The gentlemen in question is wearing an aqua polo shirt. Looks quite nice with his tan. You make a delightful couple. Quite extraordinary."

Kurt fixed his gaze on me and the waiter retreated. "You weren't supposed to do that!"

"Character flaw. Everything I do for fun is something somebody else thinks I'm not supposed to do. I like going against the grain." He stared into my eyes, his jaw clenched. It only made him more beautiful.

Dinner had taken a long time, so I had to go directly to the bar for Leo's show. Kurt laughed when I mentioned it and said he wouldn't miss it for the world. The crowd was already overflowing when we arrived and he asked me to take his blazer backstage, saying he was overdressed even without it. While I didn't think he'd disappear on me, having custody of his jacket gave me a warm feeling.

The show was hugely successful. Leo did his usual act at the end except he added a twist. He kept me on stage, behind the glory hole, and used his big boner like it was a sword fighting with mine. He fisted himself to a climax, shooting all over my dick. The crowd went nuts. It wasn't exactly the cum explosion from *Leo & Lance* but close. The dude could shoot more than anyone I knew, pumping a bucket out every other day. He spurted a good eight or twelve inches.

Leo used his cum as lube and fisted me off, collecting my jizz with his hand and then smearing it on my face. Even though I was behind the glory hole, the crowd knew exactly what happened and roared approval.

Backstage, as I wiped my face, I asked, "Why the hell did you use me as a cum rag?"

"Because you fucking deserved it," he spat.

"For what?"

"For being a dickhead!" He *was* jealous. Nina was right about Leo: warm one moment, cold the next. I was too excited about Kurt to ponder Leo's mood, so I told him I was splitting. He had autographs to sign and would work the room for another hour. Perhaps neither one of us would use our hotel room.

I found Kurt. He smiled. "That was quite a performance. I was planning to invite you back to my place, but I suppose you're probably beat after the show. No pun intended."

"That little warm up won't slow me down one bit. I'm good until dawn. The first load takes the pressure off and makes the next three or four better." He grinned.

We walked back to his place through the damp San Francisco night. Inside his tiny studio apartment, he pushed me against the wall and kissed me for a long time as we ran our hands over each other's bodies. He broke the kiss, lust in his eyes. "We have one small problem."

I wasn't in the mood for problems, small or otherwise. I ignored him, using the break to unbutton his shirt.

"On screen, I only bottom and you only top. That's not tonight's script. I want your ass. I don't know why you've never been filmed bottoming. You have an amazing bubble butt, and I want to see your big cock flop around while I'm drilling it."

"I haven't heard anything yet that sounds like a problem. Unless you're saying that you're only fucking my ass once tonight. *That* would be a problem." He grinned. Problem solved.

We stripped, leaving a pile of clothes next to the door, and Kurt fell onto his bed, spread-eagled on his back. I crawled on top of him and wrapped my hand around his hard cock, ready to swallow it. He was uncut like I was and a good nine inches.

"You touch it, you own it," he purred.

I didn't think anything could make me want him more, but that statement did. I went down on him with abandon, licking his balls and cock and gradually deep throating him. I loved playing with his foreskin.

Kurt stayed still, his hot body stretched out for me. I was into sucking his manhood, hearing his moans, feeling his rigid shaft. Despite his announcement that he was fucking me, I wanted his ass. I pulled his legs up, positioning them on my shoulders, and aimed my rock-hard cock at his hole.

"Did you forget you're not filming? I'm supposed to fuck your ass, remember?" Flat on his back with his arms outstretched, he made no attempt to stop me, giving me a knowing smirk instead. He was a perfect vision of vulnerability and desire.

"I specialize in doing things I'm not supposed to do. A character flaw. I'm about to give you an excellent reason to take revenge on my ass and get even. After I dump a load in you, you'll have all night long to use my holes. All night."

I was turned on and rammed my cock into Kurt's hole harder than I intended. His ass felt so fucking great I didn't stop, sliding in and out of him, breathing deeply as his tight hole clamped on my dick. "Oh, yeah," I gasped. "You're fucking beautiful."

Kurt peered at me through half-opened eyes. "Have your way with me, stud. One rule. Pound me with all you've got. Show me how much you want to own me. Fuck me silly."

Fucking him silly was exactly what I intended to do, and I slammed into his ass, leaning over him and pushing his knees down until they touched the bed on either side of his head. I piledrove my dick into his hole. I couldn't resist kissing him, forcing my tongue into his mouth as I dominated his hot body.

"Take me," he gasped. "Use me. Own me." I was too horned up to stop. I slammed into his ass, staring at his beautiful face. "Do anything you want to me," he whispered. At that point, I was thinking solely through my dick, and all I wanted to do was ram his sweet ass until I climaxed. That's what I did. My body went rigid, my cock spasmed, and as wave after wave of cum exploded from my balls. I closed my eyes and panted.

When I opened them, he gave me a half smile. "I think you enjoyed that."

"Fuck, yeah!" I collapsed on top of him, kissing him and running my hands over his body. He rolled over on me, my cock still inside him. My still-hard boner plopped out when he lifted up. He grabbed it and squeezed. "This assault weapon should come with warning labels. Do you destroy all the boys' asses the way you ruined mine?"

"Only when I'm insanely turned on by a hot, amazing man."

Kurt grinned. "I'm glad you set the tone for the rest of the night, stud, because I won't have to show you mercy when I extract my revenge. You promised you're mine until dawn. I'll give you a brutal demonstration of what it's like to be owned. What it's like to be a sex toy." He crawled forward and fed me his hard cock. "Suck like your life depends on it, porn boy. I know you've been with hundreds of men. Thousands. But I'm the man you're gonna remember. You'll never forget tonight. Never forget me. Never!"

Kurt took full possession of my holes for what remained of the night. He was tireless, fucking until he came and then starting up again ten or fifteen minutes later. He showed a raw edge, almost like he was competing and the goal was to thoroughly subjugate me, turning me into a cum dump. I was totally at home. That had been my role for two and a half years.

Despite—or maybe because of—the way Kurt dominated me, sex with him was incredibly sensual and passionate. Most guys I fucked or who fucked me fit the typical stereotype, wanting to get their rocks off quickly. I didn't mind, because quickies meant opportunities to score again later. Kurt took his time, enjoying the moment, and was both tender and tough. I was enamored. Strangely enough, the wild sex reminded me of reenacting *Leo & Lance* in Hudson's theater.

Through the night, I sensed a dark undercurrent in Kurt. I wondered if he'd been seriously hurt in the past. Once I focused on that possibility, I couldn't shake the feeling he still carried the scars of something deep. He talked of his fourteen brothers and sisters and how they were mostly supportive of his being gay, and he hoped they'd understand the porn stuff. Whatever it was went beyond that. He dropped a couple of references to a prior relationship with an older man in Maine. I didn't press although I suspected that affair was the source of his wounds. When I got to know him better, I'd have plenty of time to understand him.

Which, of course, was exactly the problem. Kurt was one of few guys I'd been seriously interested in. Maybe the only guy aside from Leo. My reaction was odd given he was five years younger than me, but he was more mature than his age suggested. I remembered Joey's comment about him being twenty going on thirty-five. He was right. Kurt's maturity and the deepness of his personality was part of what attracted me.

When I pulled myself from his bed at midmorning the next day, we were both spent. I kissed him, explaining I had to get back to the hotel and check out. Even before meeting him, I'd planned to remain in San Francisco rather than return to L.A., given that it was far too soon to venture there given the snuff film risk. I'd arranged to stay at the hotel while looking for something more permanent, but I had to change rooms.

He gave me a lazy smile and grabbed my shoulders, pulling me into another kiss. "Don't go. Stay with me. Don't ever leave me."

He looked beautiful and vulnerable. I was sorely tempted to check out of the hotel and move in with him, but I pulled away, promising I'd call. I needed time to think things through. A single night of passion with a guy hardly meant we were right for each other and destined to spend the rest of our lives together. But damn, I was excited and happy in a way I hadn't been since my first experience with Leo. Actually, each of my experiences with him, but those were going nowhere.

Kurt was persistent. We showered, and he was still naked as I got ready to leave. His curly blond hair was damp as he pulled me into a kiss at the front door, wrapping a bare leg around my jeans. He had a devilish look in his beautiful blue eyes. "Meeting you was destiny. Come back to me. Or I'll follow you wherever, until you tell me to go."

Leo ran the other direction every time we got close, but Kurt was taking the opposite approach. I broke the embrace reluctantly. "I'll call you. I promise. Free for dinner tonight?"

He smiled. "This time, my treat."

On the spur of the moment, I ran the makeover I'd been contemplating past him. After Holmes green-lighted it, I'd scheduled a session with a tattoo artist to begin concealing Reis's tiger tat in a forest of other tattoos. My arm would be covered in ink. "What if the man you take to dinner tonight has short black hair and an arm covered with tattoos?" Kurt looked puzzled, so I added, "Same blue eyes, hungry asshole and uncut dick."

His face lit up. "You've stolen my fantasies! I love tats. I'd like nothing more than to help you ink your entire body from your neck to your feet. Short black hair, crew cut like the military? Bring it on! The anticipation of fucking the lights out of that stud will keep me hard all day!" My last sight of him as I left his apartment was his beaming face.

Sunday morning was damp and chilly. As soon as I was outside and the cool air hit me, I knew what I'd do. I almost returned to tell him, but I'd dallied in his bed too long as it was and had to hurry back to the hotel. I'd leave the hotel without checking into my other room, visit the tattoo parlor and return to Kurt's with what luggage I had. I'd checked my personal life for two and a half years, but no longer.

VLAD THE IMPALER

Walking through the San Francisco fog, I was lost in my thoughts and almost in a trance when a black car slowed and halted next to me. I was so used to men soliciting me from cars that I instinctively stopped. That was a mistake. I watched numbly as the car doors flew open and three burly men jumped out.

Belatedly realizing it wasn't a Sunday solicitation, I took off at a full sprint. I outran them, but three more men emerged from a second car stopped in front of me. I was trapped. One man tackled me and as soon as I was on the ground, another planted a knee in my back, grabbed my arm and wrenched it behind me. I struggled to get free, which was my second mistake of the morning—if I had given up, I might have escaped injury. Instead, a man aimed the handle of a gun at my head to subdue me. I saw it a split second before it struck my skull. Pain exploded in my head, and I blacked out.

I woke much later in a dark room as a heavy door creaked open, letting light stream in. My head ached, my ribs were bruised, and I had a fat lip. I felt a wound and a row of stiches on my forehead where I'd taken the handle of the gun. I had no idea what time it was but I felt I'd been out for a while.

A big, muscular man filled the doorway. He was backlit so I couldn't make out his features. His voice was gravely. "Well, pretty boy, I see you're awake. I hope the accommodations are to your liking."

I was locked in a cage meant for a large dog. It was too low for me to stand up. I shook the walls, which were solid even though they rattled. "Let me out."

He laughed. "You'll get out when the cameras are ready to roll. You're used to cameras, aren't you? This will be your final performance. One that people will talk about for years. You'll be famous. Well, you're already famous, or should I say infamous? A gay porn legend. But you'll be giving your command porn performance, although it's too bad you won't live to see it on film."

He'd confirmed my worst fears about why I was being held captive: the rumors about the snuff film were real.

I'd been a complete idiot. I'd gotten complacent, blinded by spending time with Leo and exploring San Francisco. San Francisco was an obvious place to look for me, even more obvious with Leo doing shows in the city. I'd painted a target on myself by rooming and hanging out with him. I should have cut my hair, dyed it black, and covered my tattoo like I'd planned, but done it in Santa Barbara. I should have gone anyplace but San Francisco. I should have stayed clear of Leo.

My jailer opened the cage long enough for me to use a filthy john. At least I was able to stand up and stretch, but, shackled by a heavy chain around my ankle, I wasn't going anywhere. Pissing was a challenge because my dick had been imprisoned in a metal cock cage. The reason was obvious enough, but he confirmed it. "Do you like the cock cage? A cage for you and one for your piece. Looks a little snug on that big tool of yours. The boss doesn't want you spilling any juice before the filming. He wants those balls full before he milks them dry and then cuts your throat. That last part is gonna be messy, with blood gushing everywhere."

Fuck my damn blood. It kept coming back to haunt me.

I had to try something. "I'll suck you off if you let me go. I'll let you fuck me, too. Never been done on camera." A long shot, but I didn't have anything better.

The man laughed. "I'm not into fag sex."

"I've got money. You know I'm a famous porn star, and I've made a ton. I'll pay you. Name your price."

He snorted and shook his head. "The boss would throttle me. Money won't do me any good if I'm dead." All too soon I was back in the cage. The man left some food and water, but I had no appetite.

Alone in the dark, I had a chilling thought. What if my death in the snuff film was essential for neutralizing the Alpha Carrier? Jeremy said a man wanted to fuck my ass after I was dead, and maybe that sicko was the Alpha Carrier. My nanocells wouldn't enter his bloodstream until I was history. If my captors slit my throat, maybe the nanocell would be transmitted to the poor soul tasked with cleaning up the bloody mess. The odds of that type of transmission were low but could happen.

The cage was cramped, and for the next several days I only saw light three times a day when my jailer opened the door for a few minutes to let me use the john or bring some food and water. I sunk into a deep depression. I wasn't cut out to be a prisoner.

I was in the cage for what I thought was a week. Sufficient time for my head wound to heal so the stitches could be removed, but I found it was excruciatingly long. I wracked my brain trying to think of ways out but had nothing.

I thought about Kurt. His last words echoed in my mind. *Maybe it's my time to find someone to be happy with.* For a fleeting moment, I seemed to be that someone, but it wouldn't happen. Was he angry I'd stood him up? What did Leo think when I failed to check out of the hotel? Was anyone was worried about me or looking for me? Maybe that was an added reason I'd been tabbed for the snuff film; after a few days, nobody would miss me.

As much as I dreaded what was to come, it was a relief when the cock cage was removed and I was hauled out of the dog cage and thrown into a shower. I was handed over for makeup, and my hair was cut short, the way I should have cut it myself after escaping L.A. Then it and my eyebrows were bleached to an unnatural yellow, and my cheeks were made up to a rosy red. I asked why, and was shown a Nazi propaganda poster picturing a young blond man in a uniform. My German was good enough that I understood it: *The German Student Fights for the Führer and the People.* Fuck. Jeremy was right; the snuff film was set in World War II. The hair color and the ruddy cheeks looked fake, but they matched the picture. I was told to put on a tight-fitting Nazi uniform and ushered onto the film set.

It had been constructed in the old warehouse I'd been held in and was far more elaborate than any porn set I'd seen before, not that most porn sets were much more than a mattress or a blanket. The set was a grim prison cell stocked with various instruments of torture. Gazing at them, it occurred to me that getting my throat slit might come as a welcome relief compared with what I might be facing.

The crew was far larger than anything I'd seen on a porn shoot. Half a dozen cameramen milled about, making final preparations and waiting for the action to start. Another three or four men busied themselves with lights and props. Several tough-looking men were dressed as Russian soldiers, and I assumed they were actors. Whoever was behind the snuff film was sparing no expense. That brought home in stark terms what I was up against—a man with money to spare and a massive organization.

Nobody on the set appeared to be the ringleader until a tall, gaunt man entered and everyone fell silent. He wore long black boots and what looked like the billowy breeches of a Cossack soldier. He should have ridden in on a horse, but he was carrying a riding crop so maybe he had one elsewhere in the warehouse. He was shirtless, out of place for a man on the wrong side of fifty, but his entire costume was out of place, even for a film set.

With a start I realized who he was. I was staring at Vlad, who I'd spoken with at the Roman soldier party. Hudson warned me away from him, saying he was dangerous and sadistic. That fit the profile of a sick fuck who would stage a snuff film. Ironically, he might have been the only man I'd ever turned down.

He strode over to me, grabbed my jaws, and held them tight as he glared into my eyes. "You should have agreed to my offer two years ago. I would have tortured you a little and raped your faggot ass, but I would have released you. You would have recovered easily and gotten paid plenty for your trouble.

"No one rejects my offers without suffering the consequences. When you turned me down, you forced me to turn you into an example. Initially I merely planned to teach you a lesson. Oh, I'd still enjoy your ass, but after that you'd get away with a routine beating, maybe a gang bang, conceivably a few scars to kill your porn career. But as I watched you again and again onscreen, this event grew bigger and bigger. I've planned it for two years now. I was angry when you rejected my offer, but I am now quite pleased with the way it turned out. You gave me the impetus to develop this marvelous plan. This whole glorious idea. I'll torture you for days, rape your ass over and over, and let my men do whatever they want with you. You'll never get a dime. You'll never recover.

"Soon you'll beg me over and over to stop. When it becomes apparent I won't, you'll beg me to end your misery. That request I'll grant. I'll slit your throat and let your life pump out on the floor while I'm breeding you one final time. I want to feel the moment of your death, when your body goes flaccid. I want to see how long that big cock everyone is so enamored with stays hard."

He gave me an evil smirk. "I *always* get what I want. Sometimes I *take* it."

To emphasize his point, he pulled a sharp, curved knife from his breeches and raised the blade. I held my breath as it hovered inches above my right eye, fearing he would blind me. Time seemed to stop.

At the last second, he lowered the knife in a quick move and nicked my cheek with the sharp tip, just below my eye. I felt almost no pain but blood began trickling from the wound. Vlad stood mesmerized, gazing at it. His eyes shown with maniacal excitement that was chilling and frightening. In that instant, I knew he'd happily cut my throat without the slightest hint of remorse. He'd enjoy doing it. I might as well have been dead already.

After a week in the dark cage, I'd been so despondent that I was ready to give up, curl into a ball and wait for the end. But Vlad's speech and his knife work made me change course. He wanted me beg and whimper; a woeful, desperate, pleading victim probably was key for snuff film fanatics. I wouldn't give him that. I wouldn't cry out, I wouldn't beg, I wouldn't whine; I'd be stoic and determined. He enjoyed inflicting pain, but if his victims' reactions were the source of that enjoyment, I'd deny him that pleasure.

Shackled by a heavy chain, any chances of escape would be few and far between, but I'd watch and wait for any opportunity. That would keep me going. I wanted to see my uncle again, wanted to know how the mission turned out, wanted to live the rest of my life. I wanted to see Kurt again. Leo…

I clenched my jaws, hoping my resolve was evident. Whatever Vlad read in my face elicited only a sneer. "I'll enjoy seeing fear in those blue eyes, then the pain, and then the last bit of life being wrung from them." I continued to stare defiantly, but I had a knot in my stomach and was anything but confident I'd withstand what I was up against.

Vlad ordered the crew to start. I was slated to play the evil commander of a Nazi prison who'd been captured after viciously torturing scores of Russian prisoners. Looking like an innocent teenager, with my red cheeks and yellow hair, I scarcely resembled a prison commander. A naïve kid who got lost on his way to a local Hitler Youth meeting? Quite possible. A grizzled veteran in charge of a prison on the Eastern Front? Not a chance. Vlad either didn't focus on the incongruous casting or didn't care.

The film would start with half a dozen Russian soldiers dragging me into the cell and taking revenge for the wives, children, parents, and boyfriends they'd lost in the war by raping me repeatedly. A plain vanilla gangbang I could handle, but that would be merely the beginning of my ordeal. Filming would continue for three days as Vlad and a parade of sadists took turns using various instruments of torture on me and fucking me at will. Three agonizing days followed by a slit throat wasn't much to look forward to. I had to hope I'd endure the pain and that Vlad didn't want a bloodied, bruised, and battered victim for the final scene of his snuff film.

When the shackle around my ankle was released so the filming could start, I almost wished it were still attached. How had it come to this? I'd left 2060 thinking I was headed for a hedonistic, carefree visit to the Eighties. Instead I was staring at an ugly death.

Suddenly the doors to the warehouse flew open amid shouts of, "Police! Hands up!" Men in blue uniforms carrying assault rifles stormed the room. Most of the crew stared dumbly and raised their hands above their heads, but Vlad and a couple of his henchmen made a run for it. They were quickly corralled.

It took me only a moment to get over the surprise. I was elated as it began to sink in that I'd been rescued. But a beefy policeman pointed the barrel of a big handgun in my face, glared at me and shouted, "You deaf, boy? Hands up!" He wasn't interested in my mangled excuse that I wasn't one of Vlad's team. I complied and, as the cops lined us up, patted us down, took our names and fingerprinted us, it sunk in that they weren't there to save me. I was merely the beneficiary of a happy coincidence. I'd take it.

The cops were anything but friendly. I was a suspect and, with my Nazi uniform, not the most sympathetic one, but I was too thrilled by my good fortune to care. If it came to a real jail cell over Vlad's staged one, I'd take the real one, although it was hard to imagine a bigger target for other inmates than a blond boy dressed as a Nazi.

Three more men entered the warehouse. It took me longer than it should have to recognize them: Kravitz, Anders and Kato. I'd seen them before in police uniforms, at the beginning of my journey. Kravitz's body tipped me off; his latest uniform fit his musclebound body no better than the one he'd worn the first time I saw him.

Between the trauma of getting kidnapped, the dread of the snuff film, and the exhilaration of being rescued, I struggled to process what their presence meant. Either they were making a temporary visit to change the timeline so my mission could continue, or...my mission was over and they'd come to take me with them.

Kravitz flashed a badge to the officer in charge and said confidently, "FBI." He gestured toward me. "We have some questions for that one—the Nazi—on an unrelated matter of considerable importance. Get what you need from him. We're taking him."

"He's yours," the cop said with a shrug. "We have his particulars, and he isn't a suspect we're arresting."

Anders crossed to me, frowning. "Your, uh...uniform...might attract unwanted attention on the street. Do you have other clothes? We can talk when we're alone." Fortunately, my jeans and polo shirt remained in the small room that served as my prison. I quickly changed, discovering with surprise that my wallet was still in my pocket. I was only too happy to bid the place adieu. A week in the cage was a week too long.

As soon as we were outside, Kato introduced himself and the other agents. "We're here to take you back to the future, Cody."

I was Cody again. It was a jolting reminder that things were about to change, but Kato's introductions were a clue of what was to come. At last we were in a timeline in which the pandemic never happened, which meant the three agents never kidnapped me and thus had never met me. "The operation was successful?"

"That's what Lois says."

I felt a massive sense of relief. "When do we leave?"

"Less than an hour." He glanced at a watch, but even in my era nobody wore watches. I suspected some sort of Dick Tracy device used to communicate with Lois.

Kravitz held up a set of car keys and looked at me. "We need to get to San Francisco. Would you mind driving? I'd rather not risk my life again with Anders doing the honors."

The older man glared at him and snorted. "Don't forget it's been thirty years since I drove an automobile. At least I've actually driven one."

It was almost the same exchange the two men had when they abducted me originally, but only I heard it. The original exchange was in a timeline that no longer existed, wiped out by my venture to the Eighties.

I focused on the job at hand, eager to get as far away from the film set as possible. I surmised we were in a warehouse district near the Bay in Oakland. It was Sunday and with traffic light, the trip didn't take long. As I drove, my mind raced. *Did I want to leave?* With the specter of Vlad's snuff film behind me, I wasn't so sure. The entire time I'd been in the Eighties, I'd wanted nothing more than to fulfil my mission and go home. I'd dreamt of this moment and longed for it. But now it was upon me, I had second thoughts. Perhaps I wanted to reenact my incredible night with Kurt. Reenact it repeatedly. I'd given up on that tantalizing thought during my week of imprisonment, but was it possible?

It wasn't. I wouldn't even be able to say goodbye to him, or to Leo for that matter.

Anders interrupted my thoughts. "You gave us quite a chase. Your disappearance in L.A. might be textbook. Even after we pinned you down here in San Francisco, Pavlov beat us to you. It took a week to arrange your rescue. Fortunately, Lois knew the authorities were looking for him, so we clued the police into where he was. We could have avoided all that if we'd taken Kravitz's suggestion of busting in and kidnapping you ourselves before you ventured out that morning."

Talk about an awkward end to my planned romance with Kurt. Of course, being abducted by Vlad was bad for the relationship anyway. Kurt probably thought I ran off.

The jump place was a deserted parking lot off Polk Street. Kravitz explained the site was chosen because TPI was bringing Reis back at the same time. Upon arrival he'd be drugged, and shortly thereafter a man TPI hired to play a good Samaritan would chance upon the passed-out Reis and call an ambulance. Conveniently, a doctor—also a TPI plant—would diagnose him as suffering from a drug overdose with a side effect of severe memory loss. That would explain why he had no memories of the previous thirty months. No memories of *Leo & Lance*, Leo Ford or Kurt Marshall. No memories of Rock Hudson or Cory Jacobson. No memories of Vladimir Pavlov or his threatened snuff film. I was taking those back to 2060 with me.

Polk was deserted on the cloudy, drizzly morning. We stopped at a narrow lot wedged between two buildings, and Kato and Kravitz took up positions at either end, even though the likelihood of anyone venturing by at this time of day was remote. Far too early for Polk's usual seedy crowd, particularly on a Sunday.

The exhilaration from pulling off the long-shot mission tempered my ambivalence about leaving. I chewed my lip, dreading the jump. Even after two and a half years, my memory of the searing pain from the jump headaches was fresh. Still, it would be a walk in the park compared to what Vlad had in mind for me. I shivered at the recollection, touching the wound on my cheek.

Anders placed a blanket on the ground. A bluish light flashed and Reis appeared. My twin. Anders checked his vital signs and I stuffed his wallet into a pocket of his jeans. It was oddly symbolic. He was getting his identity back.

On the spur of the moment, I asked for a minute alone with him. After masquerading as him for years I felt strangely tied to him and responsible. He was likely destined to throw his life away unless something changed.

His eyes betrayed fear. The last thing he probably remembered was being alone in his apartment; now he was staring at his twin in San Francisco. "Look at me, David. You know who I am. I'm here only temporarily, but I'm here to tell you you've been given a second chance. Few people get one, but you have the opportunity to change your life and avoid the course you're on. You're headed to a life of drug addiction, floating in and out of jail. That doesn't need to be where you end up. Use your head. Nothing you've done in the past dictates the future. I've left you enough money that you can start over. Take control and live a good life. I promise there is someone in your future to love and spend your life with. You can be happy. The porn, the hustling, you don't need to do it now. You're free." He didn't respond, staring dumbly at me. I bent forward and gave him a quick kiss on the lips, adding, "Someone cares about you David. Me. Trust me." I thought I detected a flicker in his eyes, but it was probably only my imagination. I nodded to Anders, who injected him, and David was soon unconscious.

It was probably silly to think that my speech would make a difference. David might not even remember it, and if he did, he'd likely chalk it up to a drug-induced hallucination. After all, who has a conversation with himself? Still, I had to try.

With my stint in the Eighties ending, I stared at the gray San Francisco sky, fearing what I'd feel like on the other end. Anders motioned for Kato and Kravitz to join us and the light flashed again. Suddenly I was inside a white room, wondering if I was still alive and feeling so bad that I wasn't certain I wanted to be.

BACK TO THE FUTURE

I remember little of my first day back in 2060. I spent it in a bed that could have been the same one I'd occupied before, administered to by a woman rather than Danny. During my few waking hours I somewhat came to grips with the events surrounding the snuff film and my quick exit from 1985. I was still numb from the suddenness and permanence of my departure and my memories were bittersweet. Of Kurt. And Leo.

I woke the next morning after a fitful sleep. My massive headache had receded and I felt good enough to get up, surprising the TPI staffer watching me. It was before five in the morning. I showered, enjoying once again how great the 2060 showering system was. Who'd have thought the experience of taking a hot shower could be improved?

By the time I finished, Wells appeared. Other than being sleepy and disheveled, she didn't look much different. I studied her closely, noticing a scar below her left eye I'd never detected. I resolved to ask her the story behind it. Sometime.

"Welcome," she said with a small smile as she embraced me and we sat down in a small conference room. "You pulled off an incredible long-shot mission. Gave us quite a scare, though."

"Scare? How?"

She exhaled. "Lois lost you in the first timeline. It's by far the most disconcerting event in the history of TPI, although history is a fluid concept when time travel is involved. I'm not certain they're capable of what we consider emotions, but if they are they are profoundly embarrassed."

I frowned, wondering what being lost in a timeline meant. Maybe my vision of Scotty losing a doomed soul in a *Star Trek* transporter beam wasn't so far-fetched after all.

"They had you until November of 1985, but then you disappeared. No sign anywhere. Not a trace. In fairness, the Eighties and early Nineties preceded the era of digitizing and recording of vast amounts of data, but that's no excuse. Most TPI agents were convinced you were dead."

Maybe I was, bled to death in Vlad's snuff film, under hot lights with a camera stuck in my face.

"It turns out you were right under our noses the entire time. You lived in San Francisco for more than a decade."

So I hadn't met my end in the snuff film. I wondered how I'd escaped from a situation that seemed hopeless. After I'd made it out, I had a suspicion of what happened. I'd hid from Vlad but hid from Lois and TPI as well. A black-haired dude covered in tats wasn't the man they looked for.

"We should have known what we were up against. Being invisible comes naturally to you. It's instinctual, heightened by growing up gay and hiding your sexual orientation. Lois caught a lucky break a few days ago when they unearthed an obscure scientific report about a man who showed up in a morgue in 1997. His blood was unique, Rh-null, and he carried the HIV-3 nanocells. You."

"A morgue?" Dying might have been a lucky break for Lois, but it didn't sound all that lucky for me. I was once again confronted with a story about dying in a different timeline. Apparently I'd avoided it in the snuff film only to succumb to another form, although that's what always happens when one avoids death.

"Ski accident. Back country avalanche. Either it's a huge coincidence or something strangely tied to time travel, but you died on November 25, 1997."

"The day I was born."

"Exactly. That juxtaposition of events has opened a new area of research for Lois. Your death was probably a bizarre twist but perhaps a hint of time travel's limits. We may never know. However, with that data point, they triangulated to 1985, when we pulled you out."

She took a deep breath. "We're incredibly grateful for what you did. I'm incredibly grateful. You saved my family, friends and probably my life. To say nothing of humanity itself."

I'd saved humanity but what had I lost?

I wondered what happened in the timeline I'd been in, apparently until 1997. Was I with Kurt? Leo? Someone else? It didn't matter now. That was in the past. Not even in the past; it never happened, although the memory of my night with Kurt was fresh in my mind.

"There's some unfinished business. Lois wants to identify the Alpha Carrier. His identity might matter in a future timeline. By triangulating, we narrowed it to someone who received the nanocell between Friday, November 15, 1985 and Sunday, November 17."

I thought back. I spent the early hours of Friday at the bathhouse after Leo's show late on Thursday and had sex with a dozen men. I didn't remember any names, probably never knew most of them in the first place, let alone any particulars. "What time Friday morning?"

"After 5:00 a.m. In our final triangulation efforts we nabbed you entering your hotel then."

That ruled out the regiment of men from the baths and also explained why I felt awful when I woke Friday afternoon: a triangulation time jump headache.

Friday night was one of the rare nights during my time in the Eighties when I hadn't had sex. I spent Saturday night with Kurt. He had to be the Alpha Carrier. I recalled his beautiful face and, with some sadness, how excited he'd been anticipating a second night with me. It never happened, at least not in the current timeline. "Kurt. James Rideout, actually. His friends called him Eric. He used Kurt Marshall in porn videos."

Wells was taking notes. "Any others?"

I almost said no, but it dawned on me Kurt might not be the Alpha Carrier. "Uh, Joey."

"Joey?"

"Yeah." I didn't have many details about him. I was like a woman who didn't know the father of her baby.

"Last name?" Wells asked.

"I uh, don't know." Wells raised her eyebrow. Why was she surprised? My mission was to fuck as many guys as I could. It wasn't like I asked for full names and biographies before the semen flowed. At least I knew his first name.

"We'll need more than that, Cody," Wells said with a sense of disapproval. I couldn't put my finger on it, but she was somehow different than the version I'd known before.

"He was young. Probably graduated from high school in 1985. Worked as a receptionist at Falcon." I tried to think of what else I knew about him but came up with a blank. He hadn't mentioned anything about where he lived or grew up.

"Falcon?" Wells asked.

"Uh, yeah. Falcon Studios. Made a bunch of gay porn in the Eighties. Still did in my era." I wondered if Falcon was still going strong in the new 2060 timeline. Wells wouldn't tell me even if it was.

Suddenly I recalled that Joey saying he and Kurt shared birthdays. Kurt turned twenty only three days before the fateful day we met; Joey was exactly a year younger. "Joey's birthday was November 13, 1966, if that helps."

Wells raised an eyebrow. "It will." Her fingers flew over her digital placemat. She looked up a minute or two later. "Tax authorities have payroll records showing that a Marco Joseph Reyes worked for Falcon Studios during 1985 and for a number of years after that." In another minute a grainy high school picture of a young, curly-haired Joey arrived on Wells's placemat.

"That's him."

"Any others?"

"No. So one of them was the Alpha Carrier?"

"A good possibility. Not a certainty. We've pinpointed the period during which the Alpha Carrier was neutralized to those forty-eight hours. However, you weren't the only person carrying the nanocell by then. You'd passed it to a number of men, any of whom could have neutralized the Alpha Carrier by retransmitting it during that time frame.

"Also, it's possible multiple carriers of HIV-3 existed at that point. The Alpha Carrier may have passed it to a hundred people, and during those forty-eight hours the last of those hundred people were inoculated with the nanocell." After all the effort I'd spent searching for the Alpha Carrier, it was anticlimactic to realize he remained unknown.

For next few days, TPI ran extensive medical tests and grilled me over countless Eighties details. With the debriefing complete, I met with Wells again. She was still the mashup of Whoopi Goldberg and Oprah Winfrey she was in the prior timeline, but she was different, too. I didn't feel as close to her. I felt barely any connection with Kravitz, Anders or Kato, who were distant and treated me like an assignment. Even more jarring was Ty. In the current timeline, he'd never had his body remade and never spent four months with me in the Eighties. Nice enough guy, but we were strangers.

"I have a choice to offer you, Cody. As you recall, we staged your death in 1985 and with your remade body you wouldn't have your old identity anyway. If you return to your time you'll have an alias and an assumed identity. Lois hates tinkering with timelines and because any trip into the past creates a new one, I'm surprised that they are willing to send you back. However, they let it slip that they think you have an important role to play if you return. Regardless, that is what we promised."

Huh. A government agency that kept its promises. What would they think of next?

"Your other option is to remain here in 2060. You'd have a learning curve to get up to speed on technology, but you're bright and your background in engineering physics and computer engineering would help. Unfortunately I can't show you much about what life here would be like. If you chose to return, Lois doesn't want you to take knowledge of the future with you."

I didn't take long to decide. "I'd like to go home. To my own time."

Wells nodded with a small smile. "I understand. I'd do the same thing in your shoes."

Her answer didn't surprise me. Going home for her would mean returning to her wife and kids, assuming they hadn't disappeared when I changed the timeline. For me, I'd be home only in the temporal sense. My staged death and remade body meant my friends and family were gone, not that I had many of either to begin with. Seeing the changes in 2060 would have been exciting, but I would have been like a caveman thrust into modern times. With a little more luck than I'd had in my last two timelines, I might live to see those changes anyway. It felt right to stop being a time traveler.

Wells continued. "Lois insists on one requirement if you return. That is absolute confidentiality about TPI, time travel, and your mission. They have the capability to do extensive memory sweeps, but if we use that we'd erase all your memories, not only those related to TPI. I've convinced them your performance in the Eighties is hard evidence you can be trusted, but they'll monitor you. If I were you, I wouldn't do anything to arouse suspicion."

Before returning, I had to forget the history I knew and instead assimilate years that I'd never learned about or experienced. My history lessons were delivered in sterile, textbook fashion courtesy of Lois's data banks. The world wasn't all that different from what I'd known, but I never anticipated which things varied and which remained the same. Lois was deeply interested in my reactions, as my trip offered the first opportunity to study an extensive timeline change.

The biggest difference in the new timeline was that many young gay men never died of AIDS, particularly in California but across the country as well. Unlike the original timeline, gay porn stars hadn't been devasted by AIDS. Instead, they became the nanocell-carrying brigade that saved humanity from disaster in 2060.

Some men who survived went on to great accomplishments. Others found different ways to kill themselves. The fight against AIDS had better funding—it was no longer only a disease of promiscuous gay men—but progress been delayed because scientists hadn't quite figured out what the nanocell was or how it worked. That had thrown them off the trail of anti-HIV drugs; PrEP was still in development. I'd saved thousands of men from AIDS only for thousands of others to die from the disease instead.

The first people I searched out were Uncle Ben and Lincoln. I didn't find much on Ben. Lincoln was easier. He was married to a handsome black man who he'd been with for years. After leaving the Marines, he was instrumental in the effort to repeal "Don't Ask, Don't Tell," and went on to be active in Black Lives Matter. The news left me with mixed emotions, happy I'd saved him despite my methods, but apprehensive about Ben.

I redoubled my search for him. Nothing connected him to Lincoln. I eventually found a reference to him in a list of men who'd died from AIDS, along with a solitary news article that suggested he'd suffered considerably and died when I was young. I was left with the hollow conclusion that Ben contacted AIDS because he'd never been in a monogamous relationship with Lincoln. I'd succeeded in saving Lincoln but condemned my Uncle. I had a hard time dealing with the disappointment.

I hoped the guys I'd known in the Eighties met better fates. Leo's porn career—and apparently his hustling days too—wound down shortly after I left in 1985. With the fortune he made on the bungalow in L.A., he opened a travel agency in Hawaii catering to gays, and expanded it to become the biggest gay travel group in the country, offering cruises, biking, hiking, cultural trips, you name it. He sold the company for a boatload of money.

Kurt also dropped out of porn. He got a degree in business administration and took a job at a small charity, eventually heading it and moving on to become the chairman of one of the largest charitable foundations in the country. Along the way, he invested in a high-tech Silicon Valley startup and made millions. He invested the millions in another startup and made hundreds of millions, then did it several more times. I wondered if something I might have revealed during our night together clued him into the coming success of internet companies. He was regularly listed as one of the wealthiest and most influential gay men in America. The media was fascinated with him, partly because they could dish about his past porn stardom.

David apparently had steered away from drugs. He never shot porn after returning to 1985 and owned a successful antique store in San Francisco. He'd married his longtime partner in 2008. His seemingly happy ending made me feel a little better. Maybe I'd helped him.

Tim Kramer became a successful real estate developer under his real name, Doug Cooper. Buster, as Bill Baker, served on the West Hollywood City Council and was elected to the California legislature. He married a man who was a judge and moved to the Sierra foothills. Rock Hudson was alive and still living in the Castle above Beverly Hills. I found nothing on Dmitri, but I never knew if that was even his real name.

Some stories didn't have happy endings. Cory Jacobson died of AIDS in the early Nineties. He was on the unlucky side of the near-certain odds that I would transmit the nanocell. Kip Noll had reportedly married a woman and died of natural causes in Salt Lake City, although some reports suggested the Thomas Earl Hagen who died there wasn't Kip. It was discouraging how little information existed about guys I'd known only months ago.

After putting it off until I'd run out of other people to investigate, I checked on Cody Montrose. He was me, never having been kidnapped by TPI or taken that ill-fated bicycle ride. Indeed, he apparently wasn't into bicycling, as I didn't find him listed in any of the races and other events I'd done. I wondered if we'd become friends when I returned, the equivalent of twins who'd grown up experiencing the same things, even though neither of us had a memory of the other.

As I dug deeper, however, what I found left me feeling ill at my stomach. He was still in college, the head of a fraternity that had been accused of blatant anti-gay harassment. Worse, he appeared to be the ringleader, having been disciplined twice and kicked out of school after one particularly nasty episode. He'd been readmitted after two years only following pressure from his stepfather, a notoriously anti-gay evangelical preacher who my mom—our mom— had married before she passed away. I read the information over and over, telling myself it couldn't be as bad as it appeared. If it was, maybe getting kicked out of college taught him a lesson.

With my re-indoctrination complete, I readied for yet another painful time transition. Before the jump, Wells said she and Lois had a proposition for me. "We've been talking. It's given me a hint as to why they are willing to let you return. We'd like you to join TPI. Having an agent in the past who understands and has experienced time travel appeals to them. Likely there would little or nothing to do for years, so for your own sanity you'd want a day job.

"We'll pay you, of course. It's easy to access the government's antiquated computers of the era and arrange for money transfers that will never be traced. Those systems got better over time, so we'll do it only once, when you return. You'll receive a lump sum in advance that will include thirty months of pay for your time here and in the Eighties. The sum will be sizeable."

I readily accepted. Big bucks for a minimal job? No brainer. It was a huge amount for a guy only recently out of college and with virtually no expenses. As for the job, it was hard to see a downside, and having a permanent connection to what I'd experienced by travelling to the future and the past had an appeal.

Wells asked what name I wanted to use in my new identity, since Cody Montrose was taken. I thought about keeping David Reis, but I'd taken enough from him and Wells pointed out, correctly, that using his name and looking exactly like he did decades earlier might not be wise. Lance was even more problematic for the same reason; the fictional Lance was better known than David. I settled on Linc Montrose, the first name being a mashup of Lance and Lincoln, along with a new identity as my long-lost cousin. I'd get credentials for the college degree I'd originally earned, not that anyone would actually remember Linc Montrose attending school.

As I readied for the jump, Wells took me aside. "Cody, I have some advice for you. Between your time here and in the Eighties, you've spent almost three years on an endeavor with a clear purpose and the biggest of stakes. Once the excitement of returning to your time wanes, you'll inevitably feel empty, as if you have no purpose in life. It's a common problem. Soldiers returning from war inevitably face it. It's a type of withdrawal syndrome. We're confident you'll handle it. But recognize the problem and don't hesitate to get help."

It was a problem I hadn't considered. She suggested I take some time before looking for a job after I returned and encouraged me to travel, particularly to L.A., saying it would help me treat the Eighties as a distant memory rather than something that happened months ago.

Kravitz took the jump with me. The man was incredible, shaking off physical effects that I struggled with. He hadn't exactly been warm and fuzzy when I first met him, but the new version was worse. I told him to give Danny my regards.

I returned to my time a week after I'd left, even though I was almost three years older. I had a complete set of paperwork, a passport, birth certificate, driver's license, and credit cards. I had a sterling credit history and a massive bank account.

The first thing I did after recovering from the time jump was to drive to Grand Lake, where Uncle Ben lived. It took me a while to find anyone who knew him; he'd been dead for over ten years. I finally ran across a gay man who, for over fifty years, had owned a shop specializing in American Indian jewelry.

"I remember him," the man told me over coffee. "Sad young man. His family disowned him and his illness wasn't pretty. He lingered a long time, and his death was painful. I'm afraid he died alone. A handful of us helped him at the end, but nobody he knew visited him."

I felt hollow inside.

I'd been on edge about my next stop, fearing the worst but hoping it wouldn't be that bad. I drove back to Boulder and for several days scoped out Cody, watching him come and go from his fraternity house. It was eerie. He wasn't fit and carried an extra twenty pounds of flab, but aside from that—and some trendy face fuzz that totally wasn't working—he had my old looks, mannerisms and movements. It was like peering into a mirror, albeit a distorted one.

Late one night, I tailed him and a pack of his frat brothers on their way to the Hill, a small commercial strip that catered to college students. They were drunk and obnoxious, insulting every coed they passed. That wasn't the worst. They accosted a young man, hurling anti-gay taunts at him before instigating a fight. I watched in stunned disbelief as seven frat boys punched and kicked the kid. I was never much of a hero, but, heedless of the danger, I waded into the fight, succeeding in stopping the assault with the help of several outraged bystanders. The victim was curled into a ball on the ground and he picked himself up, blood streaming down his face. Looking stunned, he mumbled thanks and took off running, fear showing in his eyes.

The crowd dissipated, but the drunk, angry frat boys remained, glaring at me. Cody's eyes were blazing. "Stay out of this, bro."

That was my angry voice and my face, twisted in rage. I took a deep breath. "You jerks are lucky if I don't call the cops and have you thrown in jail. What the fuck did you think you're doing?"

Cody gave me an evil grin. "You're queer too, aren't you? You suck dick and take it in the ass like that faggot. You're a fucking fairy!"

"Damn right I am. You have a problem with that?"

A sneer crossed his face, but there was something else, too. Lust and sexual hunger. The realization jarred me. He was as gay as I was, but deeply closeted. Like too many men, he'd fled from his own sexuality to become an anti-gay bigot rather than dealing with it honestly.

He snarled, "Yeah I have problem with that. Faggots like you are ruining the country on your way to hell."

One of the frat boys looked uncomfortable. "Man, we better get out of here. You can't afford any more trouble."

Cody reluctantly turned to his brothers. "Let's go. Don't want to keep the sorority ladies waiting." He gave me a final smirk, hissing, "This sissy can go suck his own dick." The group laughed and hurled insults at me as they walked away.

I couldn't quite fathom what I'd seen and heard. Only one thing explained what Cody had become: the absence in his life of Uncle Ben coupled with the presence of his new, evangelical stepfather.

I spent a week digesting the jarring reality of what I'd seen and planning my next move, taking long bike rides up Boulder Canyon. The water in the creek was high and fast due to the spring runoff, and sound of the rushing water helped cleared my mind.

Cody was a consummate jerk and an insufferable asshole. I was sorely tempted to write him off, but he was the closest thing to family I had. My time in the Eighties had brought home what it was like to be alone and isolated, and I instinctively wanted to keep the minimal family ties I had, even if they were unorthodox. On top of that I felt directly responsible for what had happened to him. Maybe I could help him; deep down, he was me and perhaps I could reach that person.

I could also protect him against AIDS, although immunizing him would require that we have sex, a thought I found to be a long walk bordering on eerie. Was it incest or masturbation to fuck yourself? In the end, if there was a problem, it was only in my mind.

I'd seen the look he gave me on the faces of other men, and I knew what it meant. But I had to get him alone, which posed a hurdle because he never seemed to step outside the fraternity house without one of his frat brothers.

I resumed my surveillance of him, but this time making it easy for anyone who was paying attention to spot me. His frat brothers weren't paying attention, but he was. After a few days of crossing paths and exchanging glances, he took the bait and solved my problem of getting him alone. He and three of his frat brothers emerged from the Sink, an infamous watering hole on the Hill that had been around for years. Even though it midafternoon, the frat boys were drunk. Cody looked at me, and I stared directly into his eyes. They flickered with anticipation, and ten minutes later he reappeared, alone.

"So faggot, why are stalking me?"

"Why would you think that?"

"Because you just accidentally keep turning up wherever I am." True, but he was the only one who noticed, and that was because he thought I was hot. Admittedly I'd done what I could to look the part, dressing to attract the attention of a horny man like I'd done for three years. I was in tight jeans that highlighted my bulge and a muscle shirt with deep armholes that gave a wide-open view of my abs and chest to anyone who cared to look.

"Okay, so you got me. I thought maybe we could, you know, talk."

"Talk? You don't want to talk to me. You wanna suck my cock, just like all the queers. You're desperate for a Greek dick."

He was playing into my hands, making the sex part of my plan easy. "So, you wanna go somewhere?"

Excitement shown in his eyes. Just as I hadn't questioned Maverick's interest in me, he wasn't questioning my interest in him, instead assuming I had some sort of fetish involving abusive frat boys. "Follow me. But stay behind me. I can't be seen with you...."

We ended a small garage nearby that was barely big enough to hold the car inside. I sensed he was nervous and excited. He practically was panting. "You just won the lottery." He groped himself and his eyes sparkled.

"Yeah."

"Take off your clothes first."

Only gay boys want their trick to be nude; straight guys don't want to see all that hard, hot flesh. Poor deluded Cody. I'd stripped for men a hundred times, so it was business as usual. I quickly pulled off my shirt and dropped my jeans and underwear. Cody's eyes raked my body, lingering on my dick.

"Damn, you're big. Shit." He reached for it and began pumping.

"Thanks. You like?"

That was the wrong thing to say. He took his head away as if burned. "I'm no faggot." He looked ready to spit at me. Or kiss me.

"What do you want me to do?"

He looked around, nervous. "On your knees. Suck me."

I did what he ordered. He was rock hard even before I unzipped his jeans.

He started to bark more orders when I began swallowing that cock I knew only too well.

"Oh, man, yeah, gonna make you gag on my dick."

I pulled off his cock and looked up at him, staring into the same blue eyes I saw in the mirror. "You gonna fuck me?"

He looked startled for a moment, then a sick smile spread across his face. "Yeah, I'm gonna hit your faggot ass! Turn around and spread your crack."

He might have been in a fraternity, but by the way he fumbled at my hole, it was clear he hadn't fucked anyone much. I had to tell him to spit on his dick. His entry was clumsy, and I winced, thankful he couldn't see the pained expression.

He remained still, his dick wedged in my hole, catching his breath. After a few long minutes he began to move in and out once more.

He broke the silence, "How do you like having a real man's cock inside your shitter?"

I figured the nanocell had been passed to him. With that goal accomplished, it was time to turn to the second part of my plan, considerably more challenging. "Feels so good...especially when the real man...prefers another dude to vag."

He stiffened and almost slid out of me. "Shut the fuck up," he muttered. He grabbed my hair, jerking my head back. He snarled but didn't choke me, instead he brought his face close. I could smell the beer on his breath.

"How many times have you bent over and taken it up the ass?"

I took hold of his free hand and moved it to my cock. He didn't resist. "How many times have you wanted to fuck someone like me?"

The kiss was more of mashing his lips against mine. I forced my tongue inside his mouth. He whimpered then, as he began a renewed poinding my ass. After a couple of minutes of labored breathing, sweat gluing him to my back, and he thrust into me a final time and jizz spurted into my hole.

He almost collapsed against me. I pushed him off, stood up, and leaned against the garage wall. He crouched staring at my body, especially my big cock. I played with it lazily, keeping his attention.

"Come on...you know you want this, too."

He shook his head but hadn't moved. He seemed enthralled but paralyzed.

I took a few steps closer.

"I-I'm not a faggot."

"No, you're a real man." I closed the distance between us. I reached down and took hold of his hair this time. "And a real man gets what he really wants." I slapped my dick against his cheek.

He whimpered. And then his desire chased away all hesitattion.

I've had worse blowjobs. He gagged, spit, seemed ready to quit, only I held his head down. And all the while I pumped into his mouth, stretching his jaw, I spoke in a soft, gentle voice. Telling him how good he made me feel. It was only a half-lie, because, for I felt sure that when I came in his throat, he would eagerly drink and realize that there's so many ways to derive pleasure, and none worthy of shame. s felt good.

And when I was through, when he sat back on his heels and his mouth hung open, lips slick and dripping saliva and spunk, I told myself that he, a version of me, didn't looked defeated. More awe-struck over what he had just done.

If only he knew the truth. That would mess any college kid up.

Seeing L.A. helped me put my time there in perspective, but the changes were disquieting. I needed to get back into life rather than being a bystander. I posted a plain vanilla profile on Grindr that attracted much more attention than I ever had as Cody. It was a reminder that appearance votes early and often in the gay world; in four days—hell, four hours—I had more traffic than in four years as Cody. I met a few guys, a couple of whom were interesting. Try as I might, I couldn't cross the line and hook up. Despite my new body,

I got as much sex as Linc as I had as Cody. None. I was a man with a body built for sex who had zero interest in it. A hot body didn't make life wonderful and being wanted only for it was hollow. Whether I was ignored because of my looks or desired only for them, men didn't focus on who I was.

Who was I anyway? In a prior timeline I'd been a Cody who nobody now recalled except me. I'd been David and Lance for almost three years but I was under a confidentiality edict about that. Now I was Linc, an invented person with a history I couldn't tell anyone. I'd always felt different from people around me because I was gay, but now I was fundamentally different from every person in my world. Perhaps I should have stayed in 2060 where at least I could talk about time travel.

Maybe I was suffering from the lack of purpose and withdrawal syndrome Wells warned me about. I had to build a life, making friends along with way, but the task was daunting and I wasn't certain what life I wanted. I was eerily like Frodo Baggins in *The Lord of the Rings*, having saved the Shire, but not for himself.

Leaving L.A. to return to Denver, I picked up a copy of the *Los Angeles Times* and read Rock Hudson died. He was in his nineties. The news story recounted his leading-man history from the Fifties and Sixties, his hiatus during the Seventies and Eighties, and then his reemergence in the Nineties as a beloved character actor. He'd finished filming a short role for a superhero action flick only weeks before his death. He was vocal in his support for gay rights but never officially came out. Hudson still owned the Castle where I'd played in the pool and performed in the theater years ago, although it was recent in my memory. His lengthy obituary made no mention of Dmitri. Not a surprise. Even if he'd been with Hudson at the end, the press wouldn't have reported it.

The story was a wake-up call. I had some unfinished business before settling down. When I got to the airport, I changed flights and flew to San Francisco.

SAN FRANCISCO ECHOES

In San Francisco, I found my way to an antiques store in the Mission District. Staring at the sign that read, "DAR Antiques," I wondered how many people mistook the store for a shop run by the Daughters of the American Revolution rather than David Alan Reis.

I saw him the instant I stepped into the store. He was close to sixty, still with most of his hair, although it was shorter and had darkened from the beach-blond color that I still sported. He was in good shape, not overweight. He still had the same crooked grin we shared. The wrinkles around his gray-green eyes and the lines in his face showed his age.

"Can I help you?" he asked. He hadn't focused on our resemblance.

"I, uh, wanted to meet you. Everyone says I look exactly like you when you were my age, and I wanted to see for myself."

Surprised, he stepped closer. "They're right. You look like me, at least the way I used to look." He smiled and reached for my chin, turning my head sideways a bit. "Scary. You could be my identical twin, if I weren't more than three times your age." *More than three times? How old did he think I was, eighteen?*

"You used to be in porn, didn't you?"

Reis gave me a weary nod. "No reason to hide it." He pointed to a basket of dusty VCR tapes and DVDs. On the front was a copy of *Leo & Lance*. "That's me, in my porn days."

Actually no. That's me instead.

It was weird seeing VCR tapes in an era of streaming content when even DVDs were disappearing. I flipped through the basket. *Leo & Lance, Blonds Do It Best, Class Reunion*, even *Eureka Boys!*—they were all there. Seeing the cover photos was odd. They were faded and looked years old. Ironic, because I'd posed for some of them recently. Even the oldest, *Leo & Lance*, was less than three years ago.

"To tell you the truth, I remember little of my porn career. I recall the first couple of shoots, and then there's a big gap. I was hugely into drugs and major-league overdosed. I woke up in a recovery clinic. Plenty of people remember me during my porn days, but I don't remember a thing about them. Nothing.

"For years, complete strangers would tell me we'd screwed, or they'd filmed sex scenes with me, or we'd hustled together. I had dudes thank me for convincing them not to get into porn and hustling. I heard stories about how I was the biggest sex-crazed, gay slut in L.A. I heard them often enough to be certain they weren't made up."

Not made up. They merely had the wrong guy. That slut was me.

"You seem to have emerged unscathed."

He nodded. "I met my partner, Luis, in rehab. He worked at the clinic and was into young blonds with big dicks, and I had a thing for Latin guys with tight asses. We were a match, but beyond that something clicked between us right away. He may have been the only gay man in San Francisco who hadn't seen my films, so for him I was only a young kid strung out on drugs. He helped me a ton. I left rehab, moved in with him, and never left.

"I never went back to porn. I didn't need the money. I had a sizable bank account, which I didn't remember at all. I had offers from directors and could have done a dozen films in six months. But Luis hated it and convinced me there was no future in it. In a few years, I'd have been old enough that nobody would have wanted to see me anyway. I never regretted getting out when I did. It worked out well with Luis."

I felt better after talking to him. Objectively, TPI's involvement in his life had helped. He didn't die of AIDS or get in trouble and seemed quite happy. I wondered if my speech to him had helped or if he even remembered it. I'd never know; it wasn't something anyone would discuss with a stranger.

I bought DVDs of *Leo & Lance* and *Blonds Do It Best* and asked Reis to sign them. He brushed me off at first but relented, scrawling, *To Linc* on the covers and penning *Lance...David A. Reis.*

I had another stop planned. I wanted to see Kurt Marshall, although he hadn't used that name for years. He was James Allen Rideout, Jr. He'd been into IV drugs—I hadn't detected that when I slept with him—and went into detox shortly after my night with him. He reversed course on porn, dropping out and never going back. His porn career consisted of only seven scenes in four Falcon films. In some sense that was a plus, because his beautiful, teenaged face on the covers of *Splash Shots* and *Aspen II* made him a gay icon who never aged. He lost his youthful look over the years but was strikingly handsome.

My requests through his secretary to set up an interview were politely but consistently rebuffed. As I hung around San Francisco devising a plan to contact him, I had a series of eerie experiences. Looking to grab lunch, I found myself staring at a vacant storefront on Castro Street. I'd been certain a great café was there. I could almost hear diners inside and smell the food. I asked a woman in the shop next door about the space, and she told me a restaurant beloved by the gay community had occupied it for many years, closing recently. *How could I have known a restaurant had been there? A restaurant where I knew the menu inside and out?*

Parts of the city I'd never set foot in became hauntingly familiar, but only at the fringes of memories I couldn't quite grasp. I found myself at a hole-in-the-wall Mexican joint off the beaten track, but I knew exactly how to find it and worse, I knew the place offered dynamite carnitas burritos. They were delicious.

Strolling through an area near the Castro one afternoon, I was lost in thought when I found myself on the front steps of an old Victorian townhouse, searching for the key to open the door. I'd never been on the street before, yet I remembered walking down it a thousand times. For a moment, the townhouse's interior, even the color of the walls and the placement of the furniture, was vibrantly clear in my mind. A bright, sunlit bedroom overlooked a flowering magnolia tree in the backyard. The vision faded, leaving a bittersweet sense of longing.

I was subconsciously recalling another timeline. Or several timelines. Wells had warned that was a possibility. In one of those erased timelines, I lived in San Francisco for twelve years.

The ghostly recollections hadn't occurred when I visited L.A., only San Francisco. I couldn't shake the feeling I'd been with Kurt during my stay there. One night I saw a slender young man with curly blond hair on the street, and my heart jumped. I was certain he was Kurt, wearing an old brown leather jacket he loved and looked great in. As I caught up to the man, he laughed at something one of his companions said and kissed a slender young black man. The group was enjoying a *night on the town, but he wasn't Kurt.*

I redoubled my efforts to talk to Rideout, reading everything I found on him. I wished I had Lois's endless data banks, but the internet was vastly superior to what the Eighties offered. I talked to journalists and other people who knew him. I compiled his daily routine, and one day I camped outside his office in downtown San Francisco, knowing he often went to the gym at noon. To bolster my chances of catching his attention, I'd tracked down an aqua polo shirt in the Eighties section of a vintage clothing store. The shirt wasn't the exact shade of the one I wore on my date with him, but close enough. It was tight across my chest and arms. I was back to dressing to attract attention from a gay man.

I was about to give up waiting when he emerged and I caught him on the street. "Mr. Rideout? My name's Linc Montrose. I'm terribly sorry to bother you, but I'm doing research on the Eighties and I would really appreciate it if you would spend a few minutes to talk to me."

Rideout stopped and stared. His hair was darker than in 1985, but from studying his films and pictures, I suspected the golden-blond curls of his porn days were helped along by a bottle. He had a light, scruffy beard that looked great on him. His blue eyes still sparkled, highlighted by the wrinkles around them.

The only thing I had going for me was the possibility that the polo and my face might trigger memories from a single night decades ago. It was a long shot. We'd been together barely twelve hours and perhaps he'd forgotten me.

However, as he studied me, I knew he recognized me. Of course, for him, I was merely a kid who bore an uncanny resemblance to someone he knew long ago. If we'd been together in the alternate timeline, it had been erased and for him it never happened.

He started to say something, stopped, and started again. "Have dinner with me. Tonight."

His words took my breath away. Eerily, the same ones he'd spoken to me when we first met. Years ago for him, months ago for me. I quickly agreed. He told me to contact his office later, after he got back from the gym. "Wear this shirt tonight. You look good in it."

This time his secretary didn't put me off, rather giving me a restaurant's address and telling me to meet Mr. Rideout at eight. It would have been impossibly ironic if the restaurant were the same one he'd taken me to in 1985, but, not surprisingly, that place had closed.

Over dinner, I asked about his current life, most of which I knew from studying him. He'd never married or had a long-term relationship. "I was hopelessly enamored once, but I never met another man who I felt the same way about. It was a mere infatuation that saddled me with unrealistic expectations. At this point in my life, I'm too set in my ways to accept the compromises necessary for a successful, monogamous relationship. I'm comfortable with that."

Was I the mysterious boy he'd loved? We spent all of one night together, so it was far from certain, although my faint memories of living with him in the alternative timeline suggested I might be.

For years, Rideout engaged in a quixotic quest to legalize sex work. His crusade was on the verge of success in California and a few other vanguard states, which was one of the changes that surprised me upon returning. He laughed when I asked about it. "I can't escape my porn past regardless of what I do. It's not like being associated with such a scandalous issue can damage my reputation. The whole idea of prostitution being criminal has been used for too long to exploit sex workers. The voters who legalized marijuana will eventually look at sex work in the same light. It's a victimless crime that causes far more damage to society by being declared illegal than it ever would otherwise.

"Of course, the public assumes my goals in this undertaking are personal. They're right to an extent. I'm not at all interested in paying for sex, but I was selling sex in the Eighties to pay for college; pornography is essentially the same thing. Who's to say that young men today shouldn't be able to take that one step farther? So what if wealthy men want a trophy boy or girl to show off to their friends for a night or a weekend or a month? Why shouldn't that be an option for men and women willing to take the job?" He'd pushed that line in his many interviews on the subject, intentionally coy about whether he'd hustled to pay for college along with filming porn.

He'd broached the subject of his porn days, and I was there under the pretense of interviewing him about the Eighties, so I asked about Falcon. It was well-worn ground for him, and he gave me lines he'd rehearsed repeatedly. He told me the oft-repeated story about moving to San Francisco from Maine and agreeing to film with Falcon to pay for a college textbook. It was a sterile, clichéd final version of the story he told me four months earlier, lacking the color and feeling of the first version.

When I asked why he went into detox, he gave me a long look. "Oddly, it was another porn star. I happened to meet a guy who had worked in L.A. under the name of Lance. That wasn't his real name, but Kurt Marshall wasn't my real name, either. We slept together one night. Maybe the stars were perfectly aligned, but it was incredible.

I wanted that night to last forever. I desperately wanted him to remember me.

"I was convinced I was in love. I was barely twenty at the time, and I'd never felt that way about anyone. Actually, I've never felt like that since. Lance was attractive and smart, wonderful in bed, and had a great personality. He seemed to be looking for something. Or someone. I was convinced I was the ideal man for him, and I'd found someone to be happy with.

"After that night, I was on cloud nine, happy and excited. In love, or so I thought. I began to have doubts when he didn't call me the day after we slept together, but I was impossibly enamored and couldn't contemplate that it wouldn't work out. When I didn't hear from him for a week, I knew something was wrong. I didn't discover what happened for a while. He had a serious drug overdose and turned up in a clinic with no memory of me.

"Still convinced we were meant to be together forever, I was ready to nurse him back to health. He was a different person. Same looks, but an entirely different personality. His voice was the same, but his words were different. He confessed he didn't remember me. There was no spark, nothing. I visited several times, but it was worse each time. He was a stranger. If he hadn't looked exactly like the man I'd slept with, I'd have been convinced he was someone else.

"The detox was brutal, because he'd lost a good fifteen pounds of muscle and had a haunted look in his eyes. Seeing Lance like that was a big wake-up call. I checked myself into detox, stopped doing drugs, and got out of porn, even though Falcon repeatedly begged me to come back. I started thinking about a career. In some sense, Lance saved me. As disappointed as I was about losing him, he delivered my life back to me."

I wondered why Rideout had avoided the obvious point that I looked like Lance, indeed that I *was* Lance. "I've been told I look like him."

Rideout stared into my eyes. "You do. You bear a remarkable resemblance. You look like him, sound like him, and your personality and intelligence remind me of him, too. The Lance I spent the night with, not the Lance who emerged from detox. If they remake his old porn videos, you could star." I laughed, although being in front of the cameras again sounded like torture.

Rideout was melancholy after talking about our night together. He went back inside his shell, giving me well-rehearsed answers to my questions. We finished dinner, and I thanked him several times for talking to me. He clearly didn't want to delve any deeper into that single night, such a long time ago.

Outside the restaurant, I asked a final question. "Is there anything about your college days and your life in porn that you regret?"

Rideout gave me a quick, canned answer. He'd been asked the question before. I'd even read his response. "I only regret things I could have done and didn't." His look turned wistful as he gazed at me in the moonlight and paused. "I regret I didn't meet Lance earlier. I regret his overdose meant I only had one night with him. I've lived for years and years wanting a second night."

For an instant, I thought he would pull me into a kiss and take me into his bed. The moment passed, and Rideout's look turned wooden. "That overdose saved my life. Sometimes bad things have a silver lining. The episode saddled me with a hopelessly romantic and flatly unrealistic vision of being in love. If we'd spent more time together, it would have quickly become apparent that it wouldn't have been like that one night forever."

He didn't necessarily believe what he'd said, but he wasn't looking back. That chapter of his life was closed. He'd moved on. Deep inside him, I recognized the boy I'd slept with in San Francisco, but I didn't recognize the man he'd become.

I was convinced that in the alternative timeline we'd enjoyed the years together he longed for, living in the Victorian townhouse and eating at the shuttered restaurant on Castro and the Mexican dive. All of that was wiped out when Lois located me in 1985 and triangulated me back to 2060. Perhaps one day I'd have access the trove of erased timelines they stored and confirm my suspicions. That wouldn't happen any time soon. Time travel hadn't been invented yet.

What would that accomplish anyway, other than confirming something I was more certain about each day I lingered in San Francisco? Meeting Rideout triggered an avalanche of faint half-memories. When my mission had first been described, I feared people thinking I was crazy—mentally divergent—because only I remembered earlier timelines. It was worse than I'd envisioned.

I had to escape the ghosts of the past and get out of the city.

THE PAST IS PRESENT

From San Francisco, I flew to Honolulu, rented a car and drove to the North Shore. I found the house I was looking for without trouble. It was a dramatic, modern space built of stone and steel with expansive floor-to-ceiling windows. The views were incredible.

I was nervous as I knocked on the door. When Leo answered, I realized I'd been holding my breath. He was in his early sixties, but I would have known his face anywhere. If Reis and Rideout had aged well, Leo had aged incredibly well. He was trim, clearly in shape, and more muscular than I remembered. His hair still had a little curl and was light brown rather than the white blond it had been in the Eighties, although his hair color in that era wasn't entirely natural.

He quickly recognized me, or rather recognized my resemblance to the Lance he'd known decades ago. His eyes widened. "You look exactly like someone I knew a long time ago."

"I hear that all the time." I extended my hand. "I'm Linc Montrose. I'm doing research for a project on gay porn in the Eighties, and I was wondering if I could interview you. It would really help me."

Leo gave me a skeptical look. "That was a long time ago. I can't imagine anyone would have an interest in reading about it, let alone writing a book about it."

I shrugged. "I got into the subject because everyone thinks I look like Lance. The more I saw his picture, the more I got intrigued."

Leo's eyes melted as he stared at me, but maybe it was only my imagination. He smiled. "Sure, come in. I'll tell you what I can remember. It wasn't all glamour, fame, and riches. It was pretty mundane for the most part."

That's the way I remember it, too.

He started at the beginning, describing his first porn shoot in San Francisco with Jamie in 1981. They were lovers at the time and Jamie and Leo fucked each other next to a pool in Marin County. It was a hot scene, and Leo's porn career was off and running.

Leo hit the big time later in the year, filming *Spokes* for Falcon, which was one of the studio's first releases with a theme. It became a porn classic. He shortened his last name to Ford for the first time—he'd been listed under his real name, Leo Hilgeford, in his first porn shoot—and got second billing behind Lee Ryder, a guy with a huge ten-inch cock. *Spokes* was still streaming in the 21st Century and stills and pirated copies were easy to find on the internet.

I recorded everything Leo said, taking notes on my iPad, but mostly I only wanted to watch him, taking in his blue eyes, the shape of his nose, the cleft in his chin and the familiar gestures. I found him more handsome.

I knew most of what he was telling me anyway; I'd experienced much of it first-hand.

"Many men doing gay porn in those days refused to bottom, particularly the gay-for-pay boys who began getting into the business in the early part of the decade. In *Style*, the second movie I did for Falcon, I got paid more for bottoming and the director said they'd pay even more if I'd bottom for a black guy. I figured my asshole couldn't tell the color of a dick and a black one would feel the same as a white one. Why not? The director put me in a three-way with Art Williams and Tim Kramer. Kramer's real name was Doug Cooper, and he later did a bunch of porn down in L.A."

I remembered Leo mentioning *Style* the night we hooked up with Cory and his friends. Hearing him talk about Kramer as if we were strangers was weird. I knew exactly who he was; he'd been part of the hot tub orgy Leo engineered at Buster's house.

"I don't know which part of *Style* was more controversial—the blond boy getting fucked by the black stud or the blond boy getting double-penetrated. Like they say, there's no such thing as bad publicity. Guys complained about the film but couldn't stay away. It became a big hit."

We talked most of the afternoon and into the evening. Leo showed me his house, including a spectacular wine cellar mirroring the house's stone, steel and glass construction. He offered me a glass of wine. "Red or white, David?"

"Red," I said, barely noticing he'd called me David. I didn't know myself who I was. My life as Cody was over, I'd spent two and a half years as David and been Linc for a few months. If you asked a random sample of gay men who I was, they would have uniformly said Lance.

Leo handed me a glass of wine and pursed his lips. "I called you David just now, didn't I?" He shook his head and didn't wait for my answer. "Sorry. You could be his twin."

I couldn't resist pressing him for his perspective of our relationship. He gave me a wistful smile. "I was still living with Jamie when I met David. Lance was a stage name, and I never knew where it came from. My relationship with Jamie was about over then, although it wasn't apparent to me. I knew David did porn work and had seen him at a party a year or two earlier, but I didn't get to know him until the day we shot the opening scenes of *Leo & Lance* at Big Bear. It was a solo where I jacked off in the woods, and after Higgins cut David threw a snowball at me. I was pissed as hell but Higgins loved it. He adopted the idea and added a snowball fight to the film.

"The scene with David in *Leo & Lance* was incredible. He had a great body and a huge cock and came off as sorta happy-go-lucky on screen, ready to try anything. I was into him more than I wanted to admit and got off on the shoot. The scene at the end where he floods my face became an instant classic. For years, you would see photos of that everyplace.

"After that, David hung around all the time, but I liked that. I went out of my way to invite him to things. We did all sorts of crazy stuff. Hustling, you name it. I introduced him to men who had a thing for lanky, rough-looking blonds, and with his tattoo, he fit the bill. Today, a smallish arm tat would be nothing, merely indicating a guy was young and slightly hip. Then it was a novelty, implying he was from the other side of the tracks. The contrast of his blond hair and lean body against his tattooed arm and bad boy image made men hunger for him.

"Looking back, I had a crush on him, but something about our personalities and the situation wouldn't let me come out and say it. Maybe it started with him being a jerk the first time I met him at the beach in San Diego and then that damn snowball fight. I treated him like shit, making him bottom for groups and putting him in awkward sexual situations with johns and other dudes just to see what would happen. I got off on controlling him. He'd do almost anything I suggested. Once I challenged him to have sex in a restroom with another porn star, Jeremy Scott. He showed no qualms. None. Ten minutes later Jeremy was boasting about it!

"David was the biggest gay slut in L.A., and that is saying something. I suppose that put me off a bit, which is weird, because I was making my living hustling, doing porn videos and taking my clothes off on stage. Go figure.

"Some of what I did to him was to watch him have sex. It turned me on. I regret I didn't recognize my feelings for him. Deep down I knew what I felt, but it scared me. I only fucked him a couple of times, and I completely regret not doing that more. That boy had an incredible combination of a beautiful cock and an amazing ass, and I could have had both anytime I wanted. But we were competitors in a sense, and I never let myself see him as a boyfriend.

"Looking back, I understand what held me back was knowing deep down if we got any closer, I wouldn't have been in control. I was terrified of that. Silly, completely silly. I couldn't stay away from him, but I couldn't get closer to him. I was afraid I'd fall helplessly in love. Talk about a missed opportunity.

"The overdose that ended his career came out of nowhere. I knew David better than anyone and never saw him do hard drugs or even suspected that. He'd drink some or smoke dope when he was in a group, and we got trashed far too often, but he didn't abuse drugs. He'd been worried about being targeted by someone supposedly doing a snuff film, and I wondered if he was set up and the overdose was related. It happened in San Francisco. We'd spent a week in a hotel together and were supposed to check out, but he never appeared. Later he showed up in a clinic. He was never the same.

"The weird thing is when it happened, I'd come to the realization I wanted to pursue a relationship with him. If he would've had me, but I think he would. I hoped so. We'd spent the week doing shows, and I loved being with him. I was planning to propose we move in together. It never happened."

Leo paused, a faraway look in his eyes. "After the overdose, he was completely different. A stranger. He didn't even sound like himself. His voice was the same, but he talked completely different. I'm sure he suffered brain damage. Whatever spark existed between us disappeared. I think he lives in San Francisco, but I haven't seen him in years."

We killed the bottle of wine. He opened another and fixed a steak salad for dinner. We continued talking, but as it got late he said, "You shouldn't be driving after drinking this much wine. I have a guest bedroom that you're welcome to use." I happily accepted.

I didn't go to sleep immediately but lay awake, listening to the waves. The hours I'd spent with Leo left me with a warm glow. By morning I had an idea. I told him I was using my research to write biographies on a handful of porn stars, and I wanted to write one on him. Would he meet me again? He laughed, again expressing skepticism about the project, but agreed.

We settled into a routine. I met him two or three times a week, sometimes at his house, sometimes in Honolulu, sometimes on the beach. Increasingly our conversations veered away from his porn history. I enjoyed being with him regardless of what we were doing or talking about it and looked forward to our meetings.

Six weeks into my supposed research, Leo fixed dinner at his house and afterward I wandered outside onto a huge deck that faced the Pacific as he fetched a bottle of ice wine. It was a clear night with close to a full moon, and the waves breaking on the beach in the distance looked like tiny silver ribbons that appeared and disappeared in the dark water.

I'd had a terrific evening with him and it dawned on me that for the first time in my life I'd been dating a man. Six weeks wasn't an eternity, but I was in love. Still in love. Whatever flame I'd had for him in the Eighties hadn't burned out. Time had softened Leo's raw edges and removed whatever barriers had separated us. He held more allure for me now, a combination of the young man I'd known and the mature man I knew now. I'd been very cognizant of the difference in our ages six weeks ago, but that issue had receded far into the background. I wanted him.

I heard the door open behind me but didn't turn around. I hoped he would come up behind me, wrap his arms around me and kiss my neck. I wanted to feel him next to me.

He didn't. A minute went by and I turned to find him leaning against the wall of the house, staring at me with a slight smile.

"It's beautiful here," I said.

"That's why I built the house. I fell in love with the location and the view. It's peaceful, but at the same time the ocean is constantly moving. The storms moving in from the North Pacific are spectacular."

I stood staring, leaning on the deck railing. He took a sip of his wine. I had an eerie feeling I was standing on a precipice of time and whatever I did next would send me down an unalterable path. I crossed to him, put my hands against the wall on either side of his head and trapped him. "Make love to me, Leo."

He gave me his signature smirk. "You don't want to have sex with me, Linc. I'm old enough to be your father. Probably your grandfather. Definitely your grandfather."

"I want you. I've been obsessed with you ever since *Leo & Lance*. I think you're better looking now than you were then. More importantly, I love who you are. You're the man I want."

Leo shook his head. "You're a third of my age. I'm not interested in fulfilling some fantasy you have about having sex with an old porn star. If that is even why you're here. Why are you here?" He furrowed his brow, his eyes turning dark.

His response set me back. "I know you're rich, but that doesn't have anything to do with this. I have more money than I can ever spend. I want to make love with you. Not because you were a porn star. Because you're you."

"You hardly know anything about me, kid."

On the contrary, I know a great deal about you.

Ignoring his comment, I pressed my body against him, staring into his blue eyes. "I'm not leaving, Leo. I'm never leaving. Ever. We both know I belong here. I belong in your arms."

His resistance faltered. I brushed my lips against his. I probed with my tongue, and he opened his mouth, letting out a soft moan as we locked lips together. He moved a hand to the back of my head, pulling us closer.

I wanted to feel his body next to mine and unbuttoned his shirt. His chest was no longer shaved as it had been, but now had a light, almost invisible spray of blond hair. Maybe it was white. I didn't care. I ran my hands across it. He didn't have the hard body of years ago, the firm body of a twentysomething man, although he was more muscular and his skin felt wonderful. I had waited for this far, far too long.

I slipped my shirt over my shoulders as Leo and I continued to kiss. His eyes strayed to the tattoo on my left bicep. Lance's tat. He frowned. "That's the tattoo David had."

"I know." I didn't try to explain, not that I had a coherent explanation. I used the pause to slip out of my jeans and underwear. Standing naked, my dick was rock hard, pointing at the sky and leaking pre-cum. Maybe seeing my stiff cock made him forget about the tattoo. After all, he was confronted by another coincidence; I had the same dick he remembered David having.

"You're hung, Linc. Fuck, your dick looks like David's." I saw a look of desire cross his torn face. I'd won.

I pushed him into a deck chair and crawled onto his lap, pressing my stiff hard-on against his abs. I regretted having lost the years I could have spent with him, but that only made my desire for him more intense. I pulled his hands to my ass cheeks, and we French-kissed again.

I didn't remember ever feeling so horny. Granted I hadn't even whacked off since my night with Kurt months ago, but this wasn't simply physical desire. My deep emotions and my feverish longing for Leo had pushed me to place I'd never been before. I was light-headed and intensely focused on sex.

"Fuck me, Leo. I want you inside me. Fuck my ass!"

Leo broke our kiss long enough to pull his pants and underwear off. His cock was hard, the same cock I had sucked in front of Higgins's cameras, the same cock that had taken my virginity, the same cock that had been inside me a few months ago in San Francisco. I dropped to my knees and swallowed him, struggling with his size. I always had to work to get his nine inches down my throat.

He moaned as I sucked, his hands holding the back of my head as he started to thrust forward. I stared up at him. His eyes were closed. I still saw the young guy I'd spent so much time with during the Eighties, but I loved the older man who stood over me.

I worked on Leo for a long time before he pulled me off. "You better stop that unless you want me to blow my load in your mouth." I wanted to taste him, but I wanted his cock in my ass more. Plenty of time for me to savor his cum later. Now I wanted him inside me, to possess my body completely.

He led me to his bed and put me on my back. Lubing his cock and my asshole, he raised my ankles to his shoulders and positioned himself at the entrance to my hole. Before he penetrated me, he bent over and kissed me again, deeply, his tongue exploring my mouth as I ran my hands along his side and legs.

"Fuck me, Leo. I need you inside me. My ass is yours."

He entered me slowly, far different than his first venture into my ass. Despite Danny's work on my sphincter muscle tone, it often took me a little time to adjust to big cocks, but either because Leo knew what he was doing or because I was so insanely horny, I didn't feel any pain. Maybe the wine helped. He slowly worked his cock into me and began to pump, pulling out and sliding back in relentlessly, hitting my prostate each time he entered. Watching him, his face intent as he fucked my hole, drove me crazy. My dick was leaking pre-cum like a faucet, and I resisted the urge to stroke it. I knew I was only a couple of fist pumps away from a climax, and I wanted the fuck to last.

Leo breathed deeply and stared into my eyes as he pounded my ass. I pulled his head down, shoving my tongue into his mouth. I was in heaven. I'd wanted to be in this position ever since I first kissed him almost three years ago, and it was happening.

I thought I could take his cock all night, but my dick had other ideas. With little or no warning, I came spontaneously, shooting a giant wad of cum that arched into the air and caught Leo in the face. My balls weren't done. Wave after wave exploded, coating my abs, my chest, my face and the headboard.

Leo grinned and quickened his motion. "Been a long, long time since I fucked the cum out of a hot man."

Despite climaxing already, I didn't care how long he rode me. It took a while longer before he shot, blasting his load deep inside me.

Leo chuckled as he came to rest, his cock still wedged in my ass. "I'll say this. You share more than looks with David. You shoot like a fire hydrant and so did he, and your bubble butt is amazing and so was his."

"That was incredible," I murmured, still high from getting fucked and having Leo inside me. "I've only cum hands-free once before." *You did the honors then, too.*

Leo laughed, smearing jizz across my chest and then collapsing on top of me, ensuring both of our chests and stomachs were cum-coated. He kissed me again, long and slow.

He broke the kiss, scooping a blob of cum and feeding it to me before sucking the last bit off his fingers. "Now tell me why you're here."

The romantic moment shattered. "I told you everything." Of course, that was a lie. "At first I was curious. I admit I'd studied you, but I had no idea what you'd be like in person. When we met and began talking, I felt like I'd known you for years. I want you more than anything. I've never wanted a man like I want you." I wrapped my arms around his shoulders. "I'm never leaving."

"You're a kid, Linc. How can you know what you want at your age? Isn't this idea that you and I will settle down together a little premature? A little unusual? I'm forty years older than you, and we've known each other for what, six weeks?"

Almost three years. We'd lusted after each other the entire time we'd known each other in the Eighties. I knew that full well and

Leo knew it too, if he overcame the rigidity of his timeline. "We were meant for each other, Leo. You feel the same way I do, that you've known me for years. It's not merely that I look like Lance. It's something deeper. Don't tell me you feel I'm someone you only met a few weeks ago."

Leo's eyes showed he sensed our connection. He shook his head. "God, you're exactly like I remember David. Except he never admitted that he wanted me. He pulled away when I was moving toward him and vice-versa, I'm afraid."

Leo rolled on his side, cum still glistening on his chest and stomach. He put an arm under his head, staring at me. His other hand drifted to my chest, and he absentmindedly swirled my drying load around my pecs. "What if I lock you up and keep you as my personal sex toy?"

I laughed. "I'll find the key and throw it away. You won't need to lock me up, except maybe for sex games now and then. The only key you'll ever need will be to lock me out. I meant it when I said I'm not leaving. Ever."

"Kid, you've got an incredible cock and a hot bubble butt. You're cute. Handsome. But I'm over sixty fucking years old. Too old to keep you satisfied."

"I'm not a virgin. Far from it. I've taken enough dick and fucked enough ass to last a lifetime. I'm done with all of that. The only cock I need now is the one between your legs."

"You're persistent, I'll give you that."

"I fell in love once. I thought then, and know now, the guy loved me, too. But the timing was all wrong. We never told each other how we felt. I lost that man, but I've been given a second chance. I don't mean to let it happen again."

Leo smiled, the cleft in his chin becoming more noticeable. "Fuck. I've lived long enough to know I don't know what tomorrow will bring. I've reinvented myself before. Why not try? There have probably been stranger relationships."

Probably not.

I moved in with Leo and we settled into what I can only describe as a blissful life. We were happy and contented. We traveled extensively. He taught me about wine and cooking, and I taught him how to ski and bought him a bicycle. I took a telecommuting job, actually began writing his biography and undertook a long-term, long-distance reclamation project: Cody. I wasn't making much progress, but I wasn't giving up hope.

My tranquil life was interrupted one evening after Leo and I made love on a deserted beach. I always liked doing it outdoors because it reminded me of losing my virginity to him in the snow at Big Bear and the first time I saw him naked and boned, before the snowball fight. Fucking on the beach is tricky because of the sand, but we'd mastered that and this time had been magical. Sex with him only got better.

Leo left to clean up and start dinner, while I stayed to watch the sunset. We were in an isolated location, so I was surprised to see a solitary figure appear, wandering down the beach, shirtless and carrying a jacket over his shoulder.

As he approached I reached for my swimsuit but stopped when I realized in disbelief who he was. He sat down next to me and grinned. "What should I call you this time? David? Lance? Cody? Linc?"

Ty looked the same when we went to see *Back to the Future* in 1985. The same mop of brown hair, big eyelashes and innocent eyes. He still looked sixteen. Our journeys to the Eighties had left the current timeline with two of each of us; Cody and the Ty I met in 2060 were products of the current timeline, while the Ty on the beach and I were renegades from a previous timeline.

"It's Linc now; I'm done with the other three. It's been a while, but you look the same."

"Well that slab of manhood in between your thighs looks the same, too. Which is to say, luscious. But for me it's only been two months since the last time you slid that uncut horse cock into my tender ass, fucked me silly, and then offered up your amazing, tight butt. That flip flop combination was always nirvana."

I laughed and gave my friend a hug. "I suppose this means my stint with TPI isn't quite what Wells promised, a job with little or nothing to do."

"Something like that. There's been a small glitch we have to fix."

I wondered if turning down the assignment was an option, but without asking I knew it wasn't. I should have thought things through more carefully before accepting the too-good-to-be-true job with TPI. "Look, I don't want to disrupt the timeline and risk destroying what I have with Leo."

"Well, with time travel there are no guarantees—as you learned painfully with your Uncle—but nothing we're charged with doing has any likelihood of impacting Leo. If everything goes as planned, after a year—or two—you'll be back in time, pun intended, for the dinner Leo is fixing you. You may not feel like eating—you know, the headache from the time jump."

"Why me? I never trained. I'm a caveman compared to the agents in 2060."

"One word. *Blood*. The rarest on Earth, remember?"

My damn Rh-null blood again.

"If you're wondering, a bull cock, bubble butt, handsome face, and ripped body will also help immeasurably on this mission." He grinned, groping his crotch. "It's already helping. Ready?"

"I should get some clothes."

"Absolutely not!" He gave me a lecherous smile that contrasted oddly with his angelic face. "Leave your swimsuit here. You'll need it when you return. Otherwise, Leo will wonder where it went."

"Home for dinner, right?"

Ty stretched his petite but muscular frame. His erection was very evident in his tight jeans. "Right after we save the world."

ACKNOWLEDGMENTS

A number of years ago, while surfing the internet I ran across a series of six striking watercolors painted in 2003 by a well-known German artist, Rinaldo Hopf. They were titled, rather generically, "Blue Car 1" through "Blue Car 6." I'd seen them before and liked them, but on that particular occasion it struck me that three of the six—close ups showing unusual, interesting expressions on the face of a young, blond-haired man—might be better than the sum of the parts if framed separately but hung as a group. I bought them, although only one was from the original series; the other two were repainted in noticeably darker colors. They still hang in my bedroom.

Sometime later, by sheer coincidence, I stumbled upon the paintings' blue car in a video clip. It was a distinctive Forties or Fifties sedan driven by Lance in Good Times Coming. The images in the watercolors were drawn from the film, and the man in them was Lance.

That chance discovery stoked my curiosity, and I delved into Lance's mostly sad history. Of course, one can't read about him without running across Leo Ford. The two men will be closely linked forever because of their famous scenes in Leo & Lance and Blonds Do It Best that propelled them into gay porn stardom. They remain two of the biggest gay porn icons of the Eighties (and perhaps of all time).

I found Lance's story bittersweet and eventually hit upon the idea of a book that would bring him to life and be something of a homage to his films and gay porn of the pre-AIDS Eighties. I can't pinpoint exactly when I started penning Lance & Leo, but I believe it was sometime in 2012. A rough first draft was finished by early 2013. After that I worked on it periodically, put it aside, returned again and again, and finally decided to seek a publisher.

Needless to say of an effort that spanned eight years, the book underwent a number of changes. I want to single out two immensely talented men to thank for their suggestions and guidance; I can say with certainty their input made this a much better book. I met Jerry Wheeler in Denver and asked him to read the manuscript before I sought a publisher. His keen insight helped improve it significantly. And Steve Berman showed once again that he is one of the best at editing fiction. His sage plot and character suggestions were spot-on.

I owe a debt of gratitude to both of them.

THE ERA &
THE PERFORMERS

While a few survived, a great number of the performers working in gay adult entertainment during the early and mid-Eighties contracted AIDS and died over the next decade. Reliable biographical information on these men is sketchy for a number of reasons; many performed under stage names and, in the internet age, statements are all too often repeated as fact despite being incorrect or spurious. The history of the actors and the era remains surprisingly thin.

The historical information mentioned in the book is, I believe, largely accurate; the intentional deviations are noted below. Whatever personality I've attributed to the actors is entirely fictional.

The Era. After a fledging start in the Seventies, the gay adult entertainment industry exploded in the Eighties. From the handful of producers of gay porn in California and New York in the late Seventies, seemingly overnight the industry expanded dramatically.

The legal environment slowly liberalized as a result of court cases, although progress varied by state. Progress was uneven though; as late as 1988 President Reagan and Attorney General Ed Meese ordered a crackdown on porn producers, reportedly including William Higgins.

As legal changes made it less risky to produce porn, new technology—in particular, the advent of the VCR—transformed it forever. Films that could only be shown in a handful of dingy adult theaters suddenly could be watched at home instead—indeed, even rented from a neighborhood video store. Higgins had the idea of selling *The Boys of Venice* on VCR, and it became a resounding success. In a 2018 interview he described the first day he collected orders for the film as the best day he ever had in the porn business (he'd waited several days before visiting the maildrop to get comfortable it was not being watched by the police). Higgins tagged the Eighties as the "big profit days" in the gay adult entertainment industry.

The production side changed as well; rather than the expensive process of shooting on film and then developing and processing it (coupled with the challenge of finding someone willing to risk legal problems by developing it), filming could be done much cheaper on video. *The Other Side of Aspen II*, starring Kurt Marshall, was reportedly Falcon's first production shot entirely in video.

Lance (David Alan Reis). Born on November 25, 1962 (though reports differ as to whether he was born in Santa Barbara, Arizona or Oklahoma). He died of AIDS-related complex (ARC) on May 26, 1991 in Santa Clara, California. At least one writer claims he was gay-for-pay. He was purportedly raised in foster homes, had an IV-drug problem, and was arrested several times. In a 1991 interview, William Higgins tagged him with the "baddest of the bad boys" line, recalling a time when Reis called him from jail, crying. Higgins bailed him out only to have him say, "Fuck you," and walk out. Because of his looks and his chemistry with Ford, he had an outsized impact on the gay porn industry; some lists describe him (along with Ford) as among the top ten or fifteen greatest gay porn actors.

Leo Ford (Leo John Hilgeford). Born on July 5, 1957; died on July 17, 1991. Leo was born in Dayton, Ohio and reportedly attended college for a short spell in Boston, moved to Miami where he opened a business, then crossed the country to San Diego before spending four months in India, studying yoga and meditation; he was apparently celibate for a spell. His first movie was J. Brian's *Flashbacks*, where he appeared with Jamie Wingo, his lover at the time. He performed at Follies in New York, had a long-term relationship with the drag icon Divine, ran a tourist business in Hawaii, and had a mail order business selling his own work. It is not clear if he contacted AIDS, although Craig Markle, his lover at the time of his fatal 1991 motorcycle accident, died of the disease in 1993. Leo volunteered for AIDS charities in Los Angeles and San Francisco and a gay erotic video humanitarian award was named after him. He was cremated in Los Angeles and his ashes sent to San Francisco, where reportedly they were scattered near the Golden Gate Bridge after a wake at Josie's Bar. He remains one of the more recognizable gay porn stars of the era.

The motorcycle awarded at the end of *Class Reunion* was in fact won by Leo Ford (Lance won it in the book to create an alternative reason that Leo survived into the 21st Century). Leo was riding the motorcycle with Markle when they were struck by a truck making illegal turn onto Sunset Boulevard. He suffered massive head injuries and died two days later; Markle suffered only minor injuries. Ironically, Leo played a victim of a motorcycle accident in 1982 in *Games*, starring with Al Parker.

William Higgins. Born on December 19, 1942; died on December 21, 2019. Higgins directed and produced a staggering number of films (reportedly over 3,000) over a career extending more than forty years. He founded the Catalina studio, filming Kip Noll in several of his early films (including *The Boys of Venice* and *The Class of '84*), introducing Jeremy Scott and directing a number of pictures staring Leo Ford, including *Leo & Lance* (the only time he worked with Lance). He relocated to Prague in the early

Ninetles after his house was raided in 1988 and he became disgruntled with the legal environment in the U.S. He continued to direct and produce up until his sudden death from a heart attack.

Kurt Marshall (James Allen Rideout, Jr.). Born on November 13, 1965; died on October 10, 1988 (ARC). Kurt was born in Waterville, Maine, one of fifteen children. In high school he lettered in swimming and track, and afterward attended San Francisco State University. He performed in only four films, in 1984 and 1985. He apparently was nicknamed "Bambi" by some of the Falcon performers and had a reputation of being high maintenance on the set, possibly because of cocaine use. He was diagnosed with AIDS in 1986, came out to his family shortly afterward and entered a drug rehabilitation program. He moved to San Diego briefly before working in construction in Los Angeles, where he died a month before his twenty-third birthday. The official cause of death was listed as kidney failure due to substance abuse. Despite appearing in only four films, his impact was outsized, being listed by some commentators as among the top and most influential gay porn stars. His 1986 interview in *Stallion*–the only one he ever gave—paints a picture of an intelligent man who understood full well what he was getting into when he agreed to film porn. He is quoted as saying, "I think to be gay is to be blessed. We have so much freedom, so many choices. This isn't our moment to party or to think we're going to stay young forever…maybe it's our time to find someone to be safe with…to be happy with."

Ty Cashe. Very little information exists on Ty. He was apparently nineteen when he made his porn debut in 1985 in *Blonds Do It Best*. He performed in only one other film, also for Richard Morgan, 1987's *Pump*, where he was paired with Brad Stone. He may have been credited as Ty Castle in later compilations. His memorable scenes are a favorite of the publisher.

Jamie Wingo. Born in 1961, Jamie was Leo Ford's lover for three years in the early Eighties. He reportedly grew up near Atlanta and worked for a gay advertising agency there before transferring to San Francisco, where he met Leo Ford. He was active in gay porn industry from 1979 (perhaps earlier) until 1985. Leo made his porn debut with Jamie in J. Brian's Flashbacks in 1981, when they were lovers. Apparently the couple broke up not long afterwards (unlike what is portrayed in the book). Jamie reportedly worked for many years as an escort.

Kip Noll (Thomas Earl Hagen?). Born on August 7, 1957, died on May 21, 2001 (*perhaps*). Described as a "lean-muscled, shaggy-haired, free-spirited surfer type," he reportedly died of a heart attack while married and living in Salt Lake, although that account has been questioned. He also filmed under the names Joe Holt and Kip Knoll. He performed in New York at the Eros Theater in 1980, the Follies Theater in 1981, and with Lance at the Follies Theater in 1984. He was first filmed by Higgins in silent loops in 1977, did *The Boys of Venice* for Higgins in 1979 and filmed *Roommates* in 1980. His last acting role was in 1983, in a film he produced. He was popular enough—and the Noll name was marketable enough—that a series of other actors were cast as his supposed brothers and relatives.

Jeremy Scott (Troy Andrew Meyers). Born on October 7, 1961, died on May 28, 1994 (ARC). He reportedly worked for Higgins for three years before filming. He performed for over ten years, from 1979 until the early Nineties, appearing in almost forty films. His trademark curls were the result of a perm; he got the idea from an April 1979 pilgrimage to James Dean's birthplace in Indiana when Ian Ayres, his lover at the time, permed his hair and died it blond (apparently at Jeremy's suggestion).

Buster / Bill Baker (Jeffrey Wayne Cole). Born on August 23 (most sites say 1956, but it appears 1958 is correct), died on May 10, 1991 (ARC). He was born in Virginia, graduated from high school in Albuquerque and spent three years in the Marines. His film career, including The Big Surprise in 1980 and Buster Goes to Laguna in 1982, spanned the late Seventies to 1985. His look changed dramatically over that time, from a bushy-haired blond twink to a handsome brown-haired man. Higgins cast him in 1983's *Sailor in the Wild* (Leo Ford was also in the film) and his final film was 1985's *Night Flight* for Falcon, starring Kurt Marshall. In 1986, after retiring from porn, he ran unsuccessfully for a city council seat in West Hollywood, only reluctantly conceding that, "Maybe some of [his films] were X-rated."

Tim Kramer (Douglas Murrel Cooper). Born in 1958, died on April 15, 1992 (ARC). Kramer was from West Virginia and performed in nineteen films between 1981 and 1987, three of them with Leo Ford. He directed and acted in 1982's Pegasus.

Erik Stryker (Michael Skrzpypcak) Born in 1954, died on February 19, 1988 (ARC). He also performed as Mike Kelly, Noel Kemp and Mike Saunders. He was born in Erie, Pennsylvania, served in the Air Force and then worked in construction in Phoenix before moving to L.A. His lover died of AIDS in 1984 and he was diagnosed as HIV+ after that. He was active in AIDS organizations until his death.

Cory Jacobson. Also performed as Guy Cory. His career spanned 1983 to 1988. In addition to *California Student Bodies*, he appeared in 1988's *Black Force*, which also starred Jeremy Scott.

Rob Montessa. He filmed *Leo & Lance* and *California Student Bodies* in 1983 and three other films in 1984. He also performed as Gavin Burke and Rusty Tanner.

Aaron Gage. He also performed as Aron Gage and Eric Gage. His film career started in 1982 and among others he appeared in *Leo & Lance, California Student Bodies* and *Class Reunion*.

Tim Richards. He performed in six films for William Higgins between 1982 and 1985, including *Leo & Lance* and *Class Reunion*.

Rock Hudson. Born on November 17, 1925, died on October 2, 1985 (ARC). I cannot add anything to what has been written elsewhere. The character of Dmitri is wholly fictional.

ABOUT THE AUTHOR

Colton Aalto is the pen name of an author who lives in a century-old brick warehouse in the LoDo section of downtown Denver with his husband and a Samoan-sized cat who doesn't understand how good he has it. The same can be said about Colton and his husband.

Colton grew up in Colorado, but after graduating from the University of Colorado he was lured east by a graduate school scholarship and the prospect of experiencing a different part of the country. He spent a decade on the East Coast, learning about trains, Italian food, and humidity, among other things. He collected a masters and a law degree from Ivy League universities along the way and had a brief criminal justice career. He returned to Colorado when the appeal of snow skiing and Colorado's sunny skies proved too great to resist. He has authored a well-regarded legal treatise and practices law, except on powder ski days and bluebird cycling days.

Colton and his husband have bicycled on six continents, pedaling up passes in the Alps, hiking into Machu Picchu, riding elephants in Thailand, enduring triple digit temperatures while biking in Death Valley, and sleeping on the sands of the Sahara (admittedly in a lavish tent). He does his best writing in his head while showering, bicycling, skiing, or listening to a symphony, but he seldom remembers the captivating images or witty dialogue long enough to get to a keyboard—and when he does, the words on the computer screen are never quite as entertaining as they were in his head.

He has authored several short stories published in gay-themed anthologies and Christmas collections and has written flash fiction included in several of Queer Sci Fi's annual anthologies. *Lance & Leo* is his first published fiction novel. A number of other novels reside on his computer, waiting to be finished.

www.ingramcontent.com/pod-product-compliance
Lightning Source LLC
Chambersburg PA
CBHW020757250626
47155CB00003B/1115